HAVEN

HAVEN

HAVEN

John Hansen

Contents

ISBN: 979-8-9890304-0-8

First Printing, 2023

I

THE RAPTURE

"Matthew 24
40 Then two men will be in the field: one will be taken and the other left."

The old fishing boat 'Diversion' carried Henry Bibber and his grandson Billy. They had spent the entire morning fishing for mackerel and had a basket brimming with fish to show for it. Each line and hook bore the evidence of their success in capturing the elusive schooling fish within the majestic Casco Bay. The Bay itself was tranquil, its surface as smooth as glass, undisturbed by even the faintest ripple or breeze. The ocean, a deep blue expanse, stretched out beneath a cloudless sky. It provided a much-needed escape from a world ravaged by the virus that had claimed countless lives and an escalating famine. Meanwhile, Russia, Iran, and Turkey were embroiled in a war against Israel, with Russia already in control of Ukraine and China having fully occupied Taiwan. These tumultuous events seemed like a prophetic superstorm. For Henry, this fishing trip offered respite from it all—no radio blaring, just the solace of peace and quiet.

Henry's grandson gleefully played with the fish in a bucket on the bow of the boat. The vessel was anchored, and its motor was turned off. The melodic calls of seabirds reverberated across the bay, providing the perfect soundtrack. The magnificent Herring Gulls gracefully soared above and around the old wooden fishing boat, which had once served as a lobster boat in the sixties. With great care and affection, Henry had restored the classic vessel, using it for fishing trips like the one they were currently enjoying. A beach towel had been spread out on the front cabin for Billy to play on, while Henry made sure the young boy wore his puffy orange life jacket—because safety was paramount for any fisherman. Laughter filled the pristine Maine air as the two cherished every moment of their time together. Henry was reluctant to leave; the joy of the present overshadowed any desire to return home. However, lunchtime was drawing near, and a few more fish would make his wife happier, as she particularly enjoyed mackerel. Soon, it would be time to head back, secure the old boat, and call it a day. Suddenly, Billy popped his head through the open window and whispered, "I'm thirsty, Grandpa... Can you give me a juice box?" Without looking, Henry reached down and grabbed a grape juice box, extending it through the window. To his surprise, there was no response. Alarmed, Henry glanced out the window as quickly as possible, only to find a jumble of clothing, a life jacket, and Billy's baseball cap piled on top of the cabin.

"Henry yelled in a panic, 'Billy, Billy... Billy! Where are you?'" Henry's voice echoed across the bay. "Billy, please answer me." He was speechless, and his face started to turn white.

Billy was gone! There was no splash, no yell—nothing!

Then the sounds of explosions from the nearest highway, miles across the bay, could be heard. Driverless cars and trucks were smashing into each other. The sounds carried across the once-quiet ocean, demonstrating how sound travels on water. Flashes of fire and smoke filled the air over the heavily-used highway—it was utter chaos! Tears streamed down the old man's face; sadness, fear, and the loss of his only grandson consumed Henry's thoughts.

How many times had Henry laughed at the idea that Jesus would take his children home? How many times had his daughter told him about the prophecies in the Bible passing at an alarming rate and the imminent rapture, but he never listened? He thought it was a big joke and expressed it every time he saw the bumper sticker that said, "In case of Rapture, this car will be driverless."

Right then, a 747, flying a hundred feet above the boat, zoomed by at over five hundred miles per hour! The roar of the jet engines filled the air as the speeding plane passed overhead. The wind from the aircraft snatched Henry's hat right off his head! Faces peered out from the windows as the jet raced by with tremendous momentum. In less than two seconds, the back of the plane came into view. The red and green lights continued to blink. The plane crashed into Shelter Island, causing a fiery explosion that illuminated the blue sky! Henry collapsed on the deck of his boat, trembling, curling up in a fetal position, and crying. Then he rolled onto his back and gazed up at the heavens. In a whisper, Henry said, "I'm so sorry, Jesus. Take me as well." And that's exactly what Jesus did—it was Henry's time.

The event was too overwhelming for him, and his heart stopped, causing him to die right there on the deck of his boat called 'Diversion,' his blue eyes still gazing up at the sky.

Meanwhile, Mary had been feeding the pigeons while sitting on a bench in Chelmsford, Massachusetts. At ninety-one, she thought she had witnessed everything, but the sight of people disappearing, planes plummeting from the sky, and a train speeding through the town, mowing down cars, was beyond comprehension. Despite the chaos unfolding around her, she tried to maintain her daily routine as if nothing had happened.

Sitting on the park bench where she had sat every day since her husband passed away over twenty years ago, Mary looked around in a dazed state, surrounded by immense agony. As she glanced to her right, she saw a red eighteen-wheeler tanker, filled with gasoline, careening down Chelmsford Street at a speed of fifty miles per hour, with no one at the wheel! The truck crossed Main Street and crashed into the renovated old building known as 'The Fort.' The impact caused the truck to explode inside the structure, with flames shooting up into the air. Tragically, Mary was too close to the scene and was instantly killed, suffering burns from head to toe.

In Boston, people were walking around in a state of shock and bewilderment at what had occurred. They were crying, wailing, and screaming out loud while the sounds of cars crashing and exploding filled the air, creating balls of flames. Buildings were engulfed in fire, with flames shooting into the sky. Men's hearts were failing as they witnessed the terrifying sights and sounds. The last remaining planes desperately sought a runway at Logan Airport to ensure a safe landing.

The Boston Strong community was stunned by the devastation, and rightfully so. Christians had played a crucial role in powering the city's machinery and technology, and now they were suddenly gone. The question arose: who would step in to fill their places? Complete confusion reigned in the streets and the air. Children were separated from their pregnant mothers in an instant, finding themselves in the presence of Jesus. The Fourth of July parade, in its final loop, was interrupted by the rapture, leaving piles of scattered clothing as a haunting reminder of the countless people who had vanished. The remaining people were overwhelmed with anger, fear, and anguish.

In Jacksonville, Florida, situated on the Saint Johns River, boats were entering the famous river without any drivers at their helm. Military planes flew aimlessly, pilotless, crashing into the city one after another. While it is unclear how many men in the military were Christian before they were called to Christ's side, the impact on the militaries in the once-great United States of America was devastating. All six branches of service—the Army, Navy, Air Force, Coast Guard, Marine Corps, and Space Force—along with military forces worldwide were affected. An estimated one billion born-again Christians on Earth had vanished, reducing the global population from almost eight billion to approximately seven billion.

The number of people who accepted Jesus as their savior during this time was unimaginable. Many individuals came to the realization that their Christian friends and family had been right all along. These newfound Christians had a lot to learn in a short span of time. Most of them had little to no knowledge of God's word, the Bible, which is often referred to as the double-edged Sword of God. It had never been an integral part of their lives. Additionally, they had no idea of the magnitude of the forthcoming challenges, which would surpass anyone's wildest imagination.

While some people may have previously listened to Christians conversing among themselves, often for mere amusement, the situation had now taken a dramatic turn. The tables had turned, and no one was laughing anymore. These new believers would come to be known as the "Tribulation Saints." They faced seven years of tumultuous and demonic times ahead, and some would even become martyrs for their faith in Jesus.

As for who would be able to survive the tribulation, only God knows the answer to that question.

2

LISA AND TIM BROWN

1 Thessalonians 5:2

2 For you yourselves know perfectly that the day of the Lord so comes as a thief in the night.

The siblings navigated their way through the enchanting, dense woods of Northern Maine. Lisa remained shocked after witnessing the most extraordinary event she or anyone in the world had experienced since the resurrection of Jesus Christ over 2000 years ago. She trudged through the thick woods, her breath strained, her blonde curly hair in disarray.

"So... we were in our backyard, enjoying a barbecue with the church members. Dad was tending to the grill, and Tim was in the pool flirting with the Pastor Frank's daughter, who's just seventeen!"

Tim retorted, "I wasn't flirting with the Pastor's daughter, and she'll be turning eighteen next month! That's only a one-year age difference!"

"She's my age Tim."

"So you're admitting that you were too young to date Shawn LeClair?" Tim questioned.

"My brother was talking to the Pastor's daughter in the pool, that's all."

Tim responded, pushing some branches out of the way. "Much better!"

"The aroma of Dad's food filled the air. He took another steak off the grill and added it to the plate already filled with cheeseburgers and hot dogs. We had potato salad, green bean casserole, and Greek salad. I'm starving right now Tim!"

"Can you please stop talking about food!"

"That's when the Pastor's daughter and you came out of the pool. I bet you remember that part, right Tim."

"You're so annoying. Too bad Shawn wasn't there, right?"

"Yeah, really. Then he would be here with us. Mom was chatting with the ladies, and suddenly they all disappeared. It was like a pile of clothing was left where everyone had been standing! I watched the plates and their napkins fall to the ground. Everyone just vanished, and we were the only two left," Lisa continued.

"Sis, please stop retelling me this story. I was there, I saw it."

"I really need to vent! That's when that pickup went through our house at, like, a hundred miles an hour!"

"I don't want to talk about the truck again! I'm the one who grabbed Dad's emergency backpacks. Dad knew something was going to happen sooner or later!"

"Those backpacks had been there for over a year! God told Dad about the rapture — wow!"

"Thank God we have instructions to come out here, Sis!"

"Out here in the middle of nowhere, in the sticks!"

"I beg you to stop talking for ten minutes, no, five minutes, just five minutes of silence!"

"But..."

"Quiet, please, five minutes."

"Tim?"

"Four and a half minutes, you can do it!"

Lisa sat on a fallen tree and cried, "I miss Mom and Dad. We've been running for two days now. I'm so tired, my body is really sore. The dirt bike and sleeping in a tent last night... I was freezing cold all night!

Why did Mom and Dad leave us instructions to go to a cave? Do you think we're going to live in a dirty cave? Are we like cavemen now?"

"I don't know much right now, but I do know that Mom and Dad wouldn't send us to a cave if it weren't for our own good. We'll see what's going on when we get there."

A few more miles passed by, and both were still in disbelief. The hardest part of the trip was wading through a waist-deep stream. The water was bitterly cold, and their hiking boots were soaking wet. Tim had stashed the bike in the woods in case they would ever need it again. He had covered it with a camouflage tarp and placed a pile of brush and pine tree branches on top.

Tim had a tent in his backpack, and they huddled together the night before. She was cold and scared all night. But for Tim, it was almost like a camping trip, except his dad wasn't there, and that was truly devastating. The two were always together. His frightened sister was next to him, trembling as she clung to him. He was protecting her. She had spent her life on her cell phone, and now it was gone. They had destroyed their phones so they couldn't be tracked. It was better to be safe than sorry. She had no idea where her friends were. She used to be the leader of the cheerleader squad. He had dark hair and was a good-looking young man, standing at six foot two. They were both physically attractive, but that didn't matter anymore. Good looks don't help when you're walking through the woods. They had to grow up quickly if they were to survive the next seven years!

They finally reached a cave in the lush green woods of Maine. The cave was situated partway up a magnificent mountain that pierced the sky. The mountain wilderness was adorned with pine trees. As they walked, the two of them gathered and consumed berries, a vital resource for their survival. It seemed like berries might be their primary source of food for the foreseeable future. Following the stream, they arrived at a beaver pond.

Tim carried a handheld GPS device intended for camping, but it was rendered useless due to the blackout. However, he knew that the GPS would come in handy later on. For now, he relied on a map and the knowledge his dad had imparted to him. The map contained landmarks that his dad had marked, guiding their way up the immense mountain.

They were aware that the new world order would target anyone who refused to accept the mark of the antichrist, though that might take some time to come into effect. Wars continued to rage across the globe, with Russia and China displaying increasingly aggressive behavior. Russia, Iran, and Turkey were launching attacks on Israel, yet Israel was putting up a formidable defense against these three nations.

Tim was tired, and he said, "I will lift up mine eyes unto the hills, from whence cometh my help. My help cometh from the Lord, which made heaven and earth. He will not suffer thy foot to be moved: he that keepeth thee will not slumber."

That was the first time she found the sound of God's Word comforting and remembered, saying it with a mix of pride, sadness, and a hint of shame. "That's Psalms 121, one of Mom's favorites!"

"She could quote the whole Bible by heart!"

"Think about that... she was so awesome!"

"She's still awesome, praising Jesus in heaven. We'll see her before you know it. We just need to get through this tribulation!"

Lisa sarcastically replied, "Oh yeah, seven years will fly by!"

"I think we're here at the place."

"Are you sure?"

Tim held a small brown leather manual in his hand and pointed to a page. He said, "It says here the door is a boulder... that's weird."

Lisa's face tightened, "A boulder? Like a big rock?"

"I'm trying to keep my mouth shut, but yes, a boulder is a big rock. I think this is it!"

They both began pushing on the boulder and to their surprise, it moved and opened like a door. It rested on hidden steel wheels and emitted a rolling noise. Tim and Lisa exchanged disbelieving glances before stepping into the opening of the cave. Ahead of them was a short, dark, damp, and dreary hallway. They closed the boulder behind them, and Tim retrieved a penlight, shining it on the inside of the boulder.

The massive rock had been cut in half, with the interior chipped away. They proceeded down the corridor toward the next door, which was crafted from oak. Tim hesitantly knocked on the door, but there was no response. Lisa looked at him and exclaimed, "I guess no one is home. This is so cool!"

"Are you kidding me? This is crazy!" Tim replied, still amazed.

Tim opened the heavy wooden door, revealing a large shelter crafted from pine wood. The walls, ceiling, and floors were all made of wood, creating a cozy atmosphere. As they entered, the scent of clean pine wood shavings filled the air, reminiscent of a well-maintained hamster cage.

Lisa found a light switch next to the door and flicked it on, flooding the space with bright illumination. The lights revealed something far beyond their wildest dreams. Both of their mouths dropped open, and they stood there in awe. Then, in perfect unison, they exclaimed, "Oh my gosh!"

Lisa pointed to the right, saying, "There must be twenty bunk beds here!"

"Sis, this place is about the size of a basketball court," Tim remarked, amazed.

He gestured to the left, adding, "Look at the freezers, sinks, and those cabinets are massive!"

"They're more like walk-in closets. And the freezers are huge too!" Lisa replied.

"Well, at least we'll have couches to relax on. It would be nice to watch a game, but I don't see a TV," Tim observed.

"I see a place to lay down!" Lisa exclaimed.

3

WHY ME?

"Titus 2:13

13 looking for the blessed hope and glorious appearing of our great God and Savior Jesus Christ,"

Thirty-six-year-old retired Marine Special Operations Teams (MSOT) commander and youth leader Greg Oliver, all six foot five and two hundred and forty pounds of him, collapsed on the perfectly manicured green grass at Bowdoin College field in Brunswick, Maine, a few days after that dreadful July day. He rolled over onto his back and stared into the sky in disbelief, his hazel eyes gazing at the smoke-filled skies caused by fires. The whole world was still in utter disarray, reminiscent of his tour in Afghanistan a few years before.

He wondered how he missed the metaphorical "bus" to be with Jesus Christ. Just two days ago, precisely at one thirty-two, all the born-again Christians had been raptured to be with Jesus. The aftermath of what was left behind in the world was worse than any book or movie could ever portray, with the cities throughout the planet suffering the most.

He kept repeating, "You forgot me!" over and over again.

He closed his eyes and opened them again to a sky with no airplanes, as all were grounded, and martial law was in effect. Youth Pastor Greg looked across the green field at the clothing that still lay in little piles across the soccer field. The children had been playing a soccer game when the rapture hit. There was still a seven-months-pregnant soccer mom there, walking back and forth, trying to fathom what had happened to her two children. Rubbing her loose stomach skin, she said, "They were here and then they weren't. They were here and then they weren't. I don't understand. Where's my baby? I want my baby back! Give me all my babies!"

Greg, too, was trying to comprehend what had happened and why he was still on Earth. After all, he was the Youth Pastor at the Church of God. He had received an education at a Bible college in the United States before he went into the military, and his knowledge of the Bible was good. He knew what was to come; there was no excuse. Shortly after the rapture, a seven-year period known to Christians as the Great Tribulation would take place. He was a tribulation saint; that's what they were referred to by the Christians who were now with Jesus. Prophetically, the Antichrist was going to make a peace agreement between Israel and her enemies.

Finally, Greg knew that knowing the Word of God and Jesus as his Savior were completely different things. Only a personal relationship with Jesus Christ would bring them to heaven. How many times had he heard that message preached? Pastor Greg himself had shared that message with the youth group in the church. It was unfortunate that he hadn't truly believed it at the time. He had witnessed so much death in Afghanistan, Pakistan, Syria, and several other countries, including Colombia, a topic he was not allowed to discuss with anyone.

With tears streaming down his face, Greg angrily yelled at God, "I saw so many people killed—my friends, the enemy, children dying... Where were You then? I've taken the lives of so many people! And it doesn't matter, does it?"

Greg was so upset that he gritted his teeth, but his anger was mostly directed at himself. He let out a loud yell and confessed, "I was just playing Church! I had other priorities that took precedence over You, every single time! I often wondered if You were even real! Honestly, I didn't believe in You! But I guess I believe in You now! The joke's on me!"

A few years ago, while Greg was in Afghanistan, his best friend Will was tragically shot in the head and died in Greg's arms. Greg had been struggling with that painful memory, especially considering that Will was a devout Christian. Now, in the midst of the tribulation, Greg found himself preoccupied with other thoughts rather than dwelling on his loss. Will was in heaven, and Greg was not.

Greg recalled how he had felt disconnected from the Church and its people. He couldn't relate to them, and they couldn't understand the wars and battles he had been through. He had witnessed so much, but he had never confided in anyone. He often wondered how, if there was a God, his life had turned out the way it had. He believed that only his fellow soldiers who had experienced war could truly comprehend his struggles and the life he had lived. Once again, filled with anguish, he cried out to the Lord, "I was angry with You! I was furious! Will died in my arms!"

So many people died in front of me! How could You let that happen?"

So many thoughts were running through Greg's head, but clarity entered his mind, and he knew what he needed to do. It was time to get right with his Maker! He sat up, wiped the tears off his reddened face, and then knelt down to pray the sinner's prayer in the middle of that green field, something he should have done a long time ago.

"Jesus, I'm so sorry for the things I have said and done against You. The sins; the many sins, take them from me, wash me clean, and be my Lord. I will never yell at You again. I acted like a fool, please forgive me. I would ask You... what should I do next? Direct me, use me, fill me with Your presence. In Jesus' name, I pray. Amen."

Then he stood up, feeling the Holy Spirit surging through his body. He had never felt like this before; it was like an electrical charge that started at his toes and went to his head. Finally, he had a perspective on the situation. Finally, he had direction from the Holy Spirit!

Finally, he knew what God wanted from him!

Pastor Greg possessed an impressive fitness level, clearly evident in his well-toned physique. Every movement he made showcased his strength, with his muscles flexing in perfect synchrony. He had honed his skills through rigorous training as a member of the Marine Special Ops Team, making him the ideal comrade to have by one's side on the battlefield. However, the upcoming seven years held a different calling for him. He could no longer employ his lethal abilities; instead, he needed to find new ways to utilize his skills.

Apart from his military background, Pastor Greg harbored a deep passion for basketball. There was a time when he even contemplated pursuing a professional career in Brazil prior to his military service. This held particular significance because his father hailed from North Brazil, while his American mother had met him during a mission trip many years ago. Afterward, the two settled in Maine, where Greg, their only child, was born. Tragically, his parents were raptured in Florida, rendering any attempts to contact them futile, as they were undoubtedly rejoicing in the heavenly presence of Christ.

The Brazilian and American mixture made the women ooh and ah. Greg was a very handsome man, and he had taken advantage of his looks on more than one occasion. He said out loud, "All that sin is a thing of the past for me, God. I'm free!"

He was a soldier of the living God, and this was the most important tour of duty he would ever undertake! With God directing his path, he ran to his new tan Jeep, which he had just bought in April. Tears of joy were still running down his face as he drove to the Church of God in Brunswick, the place where he had spent so much time before. Greg opened the door.

There wasn't a soul in the Church; it was completely empty. Even with the presence of the Holy Spirit that dwelled inside Greg, he still felt very much alone. He made his way to Pastor Frank's office and opened the door. On the Pastor's big oak desk, his well-read Bible was open. Greg pulled out the old chair, which held all of Pastor Frank's clothing. The Bible was open to Revelation 3:10. "Pastor Frank must have been preparing tomorrow's sermon," Greg thought.

"Because you have kept my word about patient endurance, I will keep you from the hour of trial that is coming on the whole world, to try those who dwell on the earth."

Pastor Greg looked at Pastor Frank's bookshelf and noticed all the books that Pastor Frank had read, including a King James Bible from 1809. It was a big book and hard to miss. Greg remembered how Pastor Frank had repeatedly urged him to check it out someday. The Holy Spirit-driven youth pastor felt compelled to take a closer look at the old Bible.

As he reached for the Bible, he felt its weight in his hands. The pages were thicker than those of modern Bibles, and a musty odor emanated from them. As Greg opened the Bible, he noticed a corner of an envelope sticking out. His curiosity piqued, he carefully pulled out the envelope and was astonished to find his own name on it.

"Greg Oliver"

4

THE YOUTH GROUP

"Revelation 3:10

10 Because you have kept My command to persevere, I also will keep you from the hour of trial which shall come upon the whole world, to test those who dwell on the earth."

Greg was completely baffled by the presence of an envelope with his name on it inside the old Bible. With a mixture of curiosity and awe, he opened the envelope and began to read the contents.

"Dear Greg,

I'm so sorry that you are still here. It seems like you missed the boat, brother. Yes, I was aware of what was happening in your spiritual life. But Greg, there's no time to feel sorry for yourself because God is in control of everything. It's time to make up for lost time. God needs you right now! Do you remember my favorite verse in the Bible?

'Romans 8:28

And we know that all things work together for good to those who love God, to those who are the called according to His purpose.'

Greg, you have been called according to His purpose. Alex, Liz, and Brandon should arrive at the Church, if they're not already with you now. We ask that you teach the teens about God, the Bible, and what's going to happen in the next seven years. I can only imagine how witnessing the rapture has impacted you.

It has happened right before your eyes that you have now accepted Jesus Christ as your Lord and Savior. This is your chance to demonstrate your leadership abilities to God. May God bless you.

With much love,

Pastor Frank"

Pastor Greg had no time to dwell on the guilt he felt; things were about to take a dangerous turn. The front doors swung open and then slammed shut. It was Alex, Liz, and Brandon, and they were terrified! Gunshots echoed outside! Greg cautiously poked his head out of the office door and signaled the kids to come in by waving his hand, silently mouthing, "I'm in here!"

The kids were amazed to find Greg there and hurried into the office, with Greg swiftly closing the door behind them. A raging mob of people stormed into the church, filled with confusion and anger. They were going from house to house, desperately seeking answers as to why their loved ones had vanished. Unaware of the concept of the rapture, they directed their fury at the church, even though they couldn't comprehend the reason.

The church was very old and had served as a hiding place for slaves during the early 1800s. It was part of the Underground Railroad, providing refuge and aiding their journey to freedom in the North. Beneath the floor, there lay a concealed tunnel where the slaves slept and ate. Pastor Greg was aware of this and opened the trap door, guiding the three kids into the dark tunnel. Inside, everyone remained still and silent while the mob outside clamored for justice. As they made their way to the Church of God, the office door suddenly swung open, banging against the wall, and a few men entered.

One of the men cast a hateful gaze upon the Christian books, shaking the bookcase until all the books fell to the floor. They stomped on the books while cursing God. Dust fell upon Greg and the three kids below. Greg imagined the anguish the slaves must have felt when they, too, were once hunted, just as the Youth Group was being hunted at that very moment.

Liz, only sixteen, could be seen through the dimness under the Church floor, her big blue eyes welling up with tears. In the span of just two days, the young girl had already endured so much, and now, faced with an angry mob in the Church, it became overwhelming. She began to tremble, tears streaming down her face. Alex gently covered her mouth with his hand and whispered, "Liz, please compose yourself." Finally, the men exited the office and joined the furious crowd that still lingered in the main part of the church. They walked out through the grand front doors, which slammed shut loudly. The enraged mob departed, seeking answers elsewhere.

As the four of them climbed up and made their way through the old hiding place, which hadn't been used in over a hundred and fifty years, Alex couldn't help but ask the pressing question, "What are you doing here, Pastor Greg?"

Pastor Greg said, "I came to the Church to see if anyone else was still here."

Liz spoke up, her voice filled with confusion and concern, "But you're our Youth Pastor, so why are you still here? Aren't you supposed to be with Jesus?"

Pastor Greg, feeling ashamed and embarrassed, replied in a low voice, "He knew me, but it seems like I... well, I didn't truly know Jesus. I knew His word, but I was as lost as all of you were."

Brandon chimed in, "I think we can all agree that they were right about the rapture."

Liz cried out, her voice trembling, "We witnessed people vanish on Main Street, right next to Brandon's house!"

Brandon, a seventeen-year-old African American with a gentle disposition, quietly added, "Yeah, they were there one moment, and then they just vanished!"

Alex, an eighteen-year-old nerdy-looking kid known for his exceptional intelligence, like his brilliant engineer parents who worked for

NASA, sadly stated the undeniable truth, "All of our moms and dads were raptured, just like the rest of the church, and it really stinks!"

Responding quickly to the kids' remarks, Greg said, "Alex is right. They are with Jesus now. Has anyone here not yet accepted Jesus Christ as their Lord and Savior? Now is the time. We should have done this long before the rapture, but it's not too late. Let's all gather at the cross and pray." The youth group joined together, praying the sinner's prayer and shedding tears as they repeated the same prayer Pastor Greg had said in the field just hours before.

"Brandon asked Pastor Greg, 'Where's your backpack?'

'Backpack, what backpack?' Pastor Greg replied.

Liz happily chimed in, 'Yeah, we all had backpacks that our parents prepared for us, you know, in case of an emergency... like the rapture or something.'

'I don't have a backpack, and what instructions?' Brandon questioned.

Alex logically interjected, 'I need to point out that if the church members took care of us, and we are all here at the same time, then the obvious conclusion is that they knew you would be here too.'

Liz added, 'We all have instructions from our parents. That's why we are here, to meet you. It's a God appointment in a way.'

Brandon, a skinny kid with a tight military-style haircut, looked at his instructions and said, 'It says here that an extra backpack is in the hole beneath the church. It must be in the tunnel we were just in. It was too dark, so we didn't see it.'

Greg asked, 'What else do the instructions say?'

Alex slowly responded, 'We are supposed to go to a GPS coordinate, that's a Global Positioning Satellite, Pastor Greg.'

'I know what it means! I'm a retired Marine! I was actually in special forces... Marine Raiders! We don't have internet, so that won't work! The satellites are out, shut down or something?' Greg exclaimed."

Alex said, "Pastor Greg, this GPS is from my parents. Most unquestionably, it works." He held the most up-to-date technology in his hand.

Curious, Greg wondered aloud, "I wonder what other kind of surprises your parents have for us?"

Unbeknownst to the kids, Greg had experienced a great deal of carnage during his time in the service. They also had no knowledge of his training in the art of war, making him truly dangerous. However, he was now saved by the blood of Jesus Christ and knew that he was not meant to kill, although he might have to harm a few individuals in order to ensure the safety of the children.

Greg returned to the office and opened the trapdoor, finding his backpack in the darkness. To his surprise, the backpack turned out to be an extremely heavy military duffle bag. As he unzipped it, the first item he saw was the faithful Beretta M9. Underneath, there were military clothing, socks, and boots tied to the handle of the duffle bag.

Pulling out a shirt that read "Master Sergeant Greg Oliver," Greg looked at Alex with confidence and remarked, "These clothes are legit. They must have come from your parents... very cool."

Realizing the need for transparency, Pastor Greg decided to confess his past to the kids. He spoke with conviction, "Now I see why God has brought us together. I am here to keep you safe. We will make it through these seven years, not because of me, but because of Jesus."

Liz looked at Greg and asked, "So you're dangerous and stuff?"

Brandon added, "Yeah, master sergeants lead teams into battle, so that's definitely dangerous!"

Alex chimed in, "We knew you were in the military, but in Special Forces. Why didn't you tell us?"

Greg responded, "I didn't tell you because how would it sound if I said, 'Oh, by the way, I was a Master Sergeant'? I didn't want to talk about it. Pastor Frank also advised me to keep it to myself."

Greg changed into his camouflage military uniform and took out his instructions. The whole situation felt surreal to him, considering all the missions he had been on in Iraq, Iran, and Colombia. And now, he was heading to the mountains in Northern Maine. Shaking his head, he focused on the instructions, and his military training kicked in. He was now in military mode.

"It says here that we are supposed to go to the mountains in northern Maine, which is more than three hundred kilometers away. That's almost a four-hour drive. We need to leave now! I have my Jeep parked out back, fully fueled. We also need to destroy our cell phones, tablets, and any laptops, so we won't be tracked. I'll use the phone in Pastor Frank's office," Greg explained.

Once in the office, Greg called Sarah Green, a close friend whom he had grown up with in the same neighborhood. Sarah had also served in the military, though she hadn't seen active combat. She was trained and could be a valuable asset for Greg's new mission. Plus, Greg trusted her completely. They had briefly dated as teenagers for two weeks before deciding they were better off as friends.

As Greg dialed her number, he thought to himself, "She's a doctor and has combat training. She's exactly who we need."

The phone rang Sarah's landline until finally, she answered. "Greg, you're here! I thought for sure you would be with the rest," Sarah said with relief.

Sarah was taken aback by Greg's presence and exclaimed, "What are you still doing here?"

Greg chuckled and replied, "Seems like that's the question of the day. Let's just say I didn't make the cut. So, you know what has happened then?"

Sarah nodded, her voice filled with peace, "Yes, all the Christians have been taken by Jesus. I just accepted Jesus as my Lord and Savior. I've never felt more at peace, even in this craziness."

Greg felt relieved that he didn't have to explain the circumstances to Sarah, but he was concerned for her safety. "If you want to live, I can pick you up at your house and take you with us. We have a plan and a place to hide. The next seven years are going to be hell on earth."

Sarah laughed, her voice laced with amusement, "If I want to live? Sounds like a line from a bad movie! Who's 'we,' and where are we going if I come with you?"

"Listen, Sarah, you are in danger, and you need to come with us... please. We need you," Greg earnestly pleaded.

Knowing Greg well and sensing the truth in his words, Sarah made up her mind. She had heard about the rapture from her Christian father, who had disappeared, leading her to accept Jesus quickly. She responded, "Okay, come pick me up at my place. I'll be ready in an hour."

"Good. Pack as if you're going on a mission: Beretta M9 ammo, clothing, water, and some snacks. I need you to listen carefully. It's imperative that you don't tell a soul that you're leaving or who you're going with," Greg instructed.

"Absolutely," Sarah agreed, determination evident in her voice.

5

WORLD WATCH

Matthew 24:33

"33 So you also, when you see all these things, know that it is near—at the doors!"

Joe Smith, the director of World Watch, kept looking at the numerous holographic computer screens throughout the floor in a hidden building near Langley. He was yelling at the images of different unknown entities, "Someone tell me what I'm looking at!"

Bewildered, Alice said, "They look like UFOs?"

Director Smith responded, "Then why isn't it on our radar? Something of that size should be detected by World Watch Radar!"

More than a hundred people gazed at the images on the screens, including a furious director of operations.

A voice near Director Smith said, "Sir, check this out."

"Yeah, Maria."

"Look at that screen right there!"

"That's CMN, Maria. Turn up the volume on screen five."

The volume was increased, and all the crew members looked on in amazement. The newscaster spoke in a baritone voice, "If you just tuned in, we have been informed that millions upon millions of people have allegedly been abducted by aliens. Spaceships are hovering over cities worldwide. Many congress members and governors have also been taken. This is one reporter who, for the first time in my life, is speechless. Back to you, Susan."

Director Smith shouted over the newscast, "SPEECHLESS! Abducted by aliens? Abducted my butt! Those are holograms! Maria, can you determine the source of the holograms?"

One of the crew members said, "It seems they are not holograms, sir! If they are, the technology is far superior to anything we've got!"

The director, visibly furious, exclaimed, "This is impossible! An unidentified flying object is hovering over the White House! I refuse to believe it!"

An uncomfortable pause filled the vast open floor as the director turned and stated, "I'll be in my office! I want to get to the bottom of what's going on!"

"Director, sir."

"Go ahead, Jimmy, but make it fast. I need to make some phone calls."

"It's the ships, they're gone."

"GONE! Where the heck did they go?

Maria quietly said as everyone stopped talking, "They took off so fast. I have no idea where they went."

The staff all stared at their screens, and Maria reluctantly added, "They just disappeared. It's so strange."

They had all seen the footage from NASA when they released records of numerous UFO sightings. It had even made the news with interviews featuring military personnel sharing their experiences with these extraordinary crafts performing unearthly maneuvers. They could hover one moment and reach the speed of light in less than a second, completely silent! There were rumors that some world leaders had even communicated with these aliens. The truth couldn't be concealed any longer. Christians were claiming they were fallen angels, demons. The grand deception was in full swing!

Director Joe Smith declared, "Everyone, this is a level ten alert!" Then he stormed into his office and slammed the door shut!

Maria looked at Jimmy and asked, "Do you think I can call my family?"

"Maria, you better do that in the bathroom. And Maria?"

"Yes, sir."

"Call my house too."

Maria and the entire crew appeared deeply concerned, reflecting the gravity of the situation. Despite their extensive training, nothing could have equipped them for the astonishing phenomenon unfolding before their eyes on the live screens. It was the most monumental event in human history, unfolding right in front of them.

Moreover, with the increasing number of people vanishing, paranoia spread rapidly across the world. The Russians, Turkey, Iran, and other countries found themselves at war with Israel, questioning whether the United States had formed an alliance with the aliens. Confusion gripped everyone.

6

THE PRINCE OF DARKNESS

"1 John 2:18

18 Little children, it is the last time: and as ye have heard that antichrist shall come, even now are there many antichrists; whereby we know that it is the last time."

Among the bureaucrats, one man stood out like no other in the United Nations. This man's name was Lorenzo Calvo. He was able to settle everyone down and had a charismatic way about him that everyone liked. He was tall, dark, and handsome, and spoke everyone's language fluently. He had a hypnotic way of talking and had a great plan to unite all of humanity. It was time for the prophetic event to be implemented, known as Daniel's seventieth week peace deal.

He addressed the assembly, speaking all their languages at once. No translator was needed this time; it was a miracle! "The world is coming together in a great way!"

The world leaders looked at him in disbelief as he spoke in all their languages simultaneously. He would disappear and reappear in different locations throughout the room, never missing a beat as he spoke. He gazed at the assembly of people from all four corners of the earth and spoke as if he knew all of them personally. "My brothers and sisters, we need to come together today. This will be a day that history will never forget. This will be a day when the world will be as one! Together, we can lead our world to a wondrous place. I believe that these aliens are here to help us, and in fact, I know they are because I'm one of them! People, the world needs to go green, and we shall show you the way. The war needs to stop, and I have a solution."

All the people in the U.N. looked at Lorenzo Calvo in awe as everything he said made perfect sense. He appeared to be much more intelligent compared to the other leaders, and he seemed to be performing miracles right in front of them.

They were all hopeful that he would help them solve the world's problems. He was seen as the answer they had been longing for. Countries like Russia, Turkey, and Iran, who desperately wanted the war to stop, saw him as the "do-it-all" person who could bring about the desired change.

Lorenzo Calvo directed his attention towards Israel and confidently stated, "Israel will finally achieve peace and security with its neighbors because your neighbors will become your brothers. Peace and security will prevail in all our nations because we are now united. We will stand together in this endeavor."

He continued, "I know for a fact that the people who have gone missing, taken to the many ships, have been brought there for reconditioning, to understand the importance of this historic hour. Addressing climate change is of utmost urgency. The climate issue surpasses any other problem in the world. We possess technology far more advanced than yours, and we can completely eliminate greenhouse gases. Our power grids, cities, cars, trucks, and trains can be powered by a tiny piece of gemstone like this. It has the capability to fuel anything!"

He then took out a tiny green gemstone from his pocket and showed it to the leaders, capturing their attention. Whispers spread among them until one brave individual stood up and voiced what everyone was thinking. "Lorenzo, you will be our leader. We need you!" The room erupted in agreement, with all the leaders roaring in unison, "Yes, you will lead us together."

Calvo, with humility, responded, "I humbly accept your invitation, but only if you are all with me one hundred percent." The entire United Nations expressed their unwavering support for Mr. Calvo. He was seen as the ultimate problem solver, the man with all the answers.

Under Calvo's leadership, the healthcare systems worldwide would undergo transformation, and shelters would be established for the homeless. The key to success was unity; they had devised a plan involving special ink tattoos that would serve multiple purposes. These tattoos would not only track location and health status but also modify DNA to fight against viruses, facilitate buying and selling, and much more.

A global currency would be introduced, ensuring that purchases could only be made through this unified monetary system. Without the designated mark, known as the Lifeline, no one would be able to engage in commercial transactions. Unbeknownst to them, they were unknowingly giving their allegiance to the antichrist. Their lack of knowledge regarding God's word was their greatest vulnerability.

As the plan unfolded, it became apparent that some individuals had accepted Jesus Christ as their Savior and refused to take the mark. These faithful individuals would become an obstacle for Calvo, the fly in the ointment, as he sought to bring the entire world on board with his vision.

"I'm saying that at this time we need to all be together! Who's with me!"

The U.N. was buzzing with excitement! Everyone embraced and applauded everything he said, pledging their support for him.

In his office behind a large oak desk, Director Smith of World Watch was on the phone with one of the only two individuals on the planet he trusted: Congressman Ed McGwire. The other trusted person was his top aide, Maria Silva. Ed McGwire had initiated World Watch five years ago, and Director Joe Smith answered solely to him. Joe's frustration was evident as he tried to contain his anger while asking, "Ed, what is happening?"

Ed, with his deep scratchy voice likely from his daily cigarette habit, was an older, out-of-shape man with a bald head who had been in office for far too long. He spoke deliberately and slowly, "Joe, you won't be in charge anymore. The UN is sending a team to your office, and you will comply with them. I still need you to assist and quarterback this situation, but the new owners of World Watch will be the UN."

Joe exclaimed, "I won't be in charge anymore? What do you mean? I've led this black ops for five years, and now I'll be sidelined to people I've never even met. This is unacceptable, Ed! You can't let them do this!"

Ed's voice dropped to almost a whisper, "There's nothing I can do, Joe. The leader of the UN himself informed me that he wants his team in place. Why? I don't know. Everything is undoubtedly chaotic, but it seems like the UN has a plan."

Joe demanded, "What is happening? Do you have any idea?"

"All I can tell you is that millions of people have just disappeared. A lot of Congress is gone, and President Clark and the V.P. too. We all need to come together for the greater good of the world. The world needs to unite, and I think the UN can help us do that. The world will never be the same, Joe. It's the only way! Can I count on you?"

"Yes, I'm with you all the way, you know that. One more question."

"I really have to go, make it quick!"

"You know if the UFO thing is a scam? Where did everyone go?"

"I don't know. No one knows yet, but we need to focus on the present. You have your orders. I have to go. I'll let you know when I find out about this alien thing."

The director pondered the resources he had at his disposal. He had computers that could perform trillions of calculations per second, voice recognition technology, and the ability to hack into any camera on the internet or elsewhere. He possessed technology that even the President of the United States didn't know existed. He could infiltrate a Russian satellite without Russia detecting the hack.

Using a satellite, he could peer through the window of a house and, with a person's laptop or cellphone in the room, listen to conversations and observe the individuals speaking. Smith knew that his office would soon be inundated with unfamiliar and untrusted people. However, he had confidence in Maria Silva, who had been working with him long before World Watch. He believed that with her, he could maintain some control in the office. She was his most capable agent in every aspect—technology, tracking, guidance—and she could easily neutralize any problematic individuals. In comparison, her peers seemed primitive. Deep down, he acknowledged that she was even more intelligent than Joe.

He peeped his head out of his office door and signaled her to come in, and she dropped what she was doing, and he closed the door.

7

THE CAVE

"Psalms 18

1   I will love You, O Lord, my strength.

2   The Lord is my rock and my fortress and my deliverer;
My God, my strength, in whom I will trust;
My shield and the horn of my salvation, my stronghold.

3   I will call upon the Lord, who is worthy to be praised;
So shall I be saved from my enemies."

The room was vast, with tall ceilings. Along the right wall stood a row of thirty bunk beds, each one meticulously covered in plastic to ward off dust. Crafted from wood, the bunk beds extended into the spacious room, their headboards firmly attached to the wall. Seven of the bunks bore engraved names, while the others remained nameless. Two shelves adorned each headboard, equipped with crossbars to prevent items from falling. These shelves served as storage for neatly folded clothing, carefully enclosed in airtight plastic bags. Adjacent to the bunks were small cabinets, containing New King James Bibles and a few other books. Some of these books delved into the concept of the rapture, while others explored the events expected during the great tribulation. The occupants of the room wished they could turn back time and listen to Pastor Frank's sermons about the astonishing events that unfolded before their very eyes, allowing them to accept Jesus before the great disappearance occurred.

Tim, nearly nineteen years old, was a star athlete on his high school football team, with a promising future ahead. Strong and physically fit, he excelled in sports, poised to secure a basketball scholarship at Yale. Tim and Youth Pastor Greg often engaged in spirited discussions about sports, but the dream of playing ball at Yale had been shattered.

Father and son shared a love for hunting and fishing, as well as a penchant for watching survival shows on television. They found joy in observing the art of outdoor living—constructing shelters, starting fires without modern tools, and surviving off the land. They would chuckle whenever a survivalist on the show made a critical mistake. Little did Tim know that he would have to put into practice all that he had absorbed from those shows, alongside his father, in order to ensure their survival in the years to come. Tim fervently hoped that he would not commit any critical errors during those challenging times.

He spotted his name on the top bunk, and just below it was Lisa's assigned bed. Both of them hurriedly uncovered their mattresses, tossing aside the protective plastic, and leapt onto their cozy beds. Tim rested his head on the pillow and gazed at the photos of his family hanging by his bedside. He was taken aback to see a picture of his mom, dad, and little sister.

Meanwhile, Lisa turned her attention to the small mirror her mom had hung next to her bed. She beheld the reflection of a weary girl—her once soft blond hair was disheveled, and her lovely face, which had captured the attention of many guys at school, was now smudged with dirt. She had been one of the most popular girls in school. Her hair was soiled from the arduous two-day journey to reach the sanctuary. Despite the grime, her light brown eyes still gleamed in the mirror, and no amount of dirt could conceal the beauty of her sorrowful gaze. Inside that charming teenager resided a desolate girl, as her mommy, daddy, and four-year-old sister Emily were no longer with her. Like Tim, she also possessed the same family photo.

Whispering so that only God could hear, her eyes welling up with tears, she said, "I miss my family, God. Please help me get through this."

She softly continued, "Mom and dad were right. The Pastor was right. The entire Church was right, and now they're in heaven while we're here, in a cave."

Tim turned over in his bed and lowered his head to look at his sister in her bunk. He spoke, "Yeah, Sis, they were right." With a burst of enthusiasm, he hopped out of his bunk and exclaimed, "Look what they've made for us! This is more than a cave—this is a haven, a fortress, a refuge. We're safe here! Let's call this place the Haven!"

'It couldn't have been just Mom and Dad who built this; it was the people in the Church, plus obviously some other Christians. I mean, look at this place! Haven, great name!'

'Well, at least we know what they were doing on Saturdays!'

'There are thirty bunk beds here. We are the first to arrive at the Haven.'

Tim said, 'Did you see there's only seven names?'

'The six names are all from the youth group at the church, but I don't know anyone named Sarah in the church.'

'Did you see that my buddy Greg's name was on one of the bunks?'

'Youth Pastor Greg?'

'Yeah, our youth pastor!'

Lisa said, 'I remember overhearing Mom and Dad talking about him and his lack of zest for God at all. They wanted another youth pastor at one time now that I think of it.'

'He was our youth pastor. He knew the whole Bible. How could he not be in heaven with the others? He was like my hero; he saw action in Iraq and a few other places that he couldn't tell me.'

Lisa asked, 'How did the people who made this know that we weren't into the whole Jesus thing anyway? We went to church. I even sang in the church and read verses from the Bible.'

"Lisa, we were more than obvious—remember when we rolled our eyes at Pastor Frank while he would preach on the rapture? We laughed when he would preach about Jesus too."

"We missed church a lot!"

"Too much partying, Sis!"

"It annoys me so much! The pastor said many times how church doesn't save us, Jesus does. Let's face it, He was last on our list."

Lisa started to cry and kicked her legs in her bunk bed. "Why didn't we listen to them?"

"Looking back at it, I don't know. It sounded so far-fetched, everyone would just disappear into thin air. Who would have ever dreamed it was real, like so much worse than Pastor Frank said it would be? We're lucky that we lived through it."

The Lisa who didn't care about Jesus before would have never said this. "Luck had nothing to do with it. That was God!"

Tim spoke quickly, "Thank God we finally accepted Jesus before we left our house!"

Lisa smiled at Tim. "Maybe it was the truck going through our house without a driver that got to me. How about you?"

Tim jokingly said, "I guess for me, it was the pastor's daughter disappearing in front of me!"

"That's too funny! I bet that was a surprise!"

The two laughed, and their laughter echoed throughout the Haven!

Tim quoted another verse with a confidence like never before: "Romans 8:31. What then shall we say to these things? If God is for us, who can be against us? No one, Lisa."

"I feel different, not scared anymore. What's the worst thing that can happen? They kill us, and we go to heaven. Don't get me wrong, because I want us to make it until Jesus comes! I'm not frightened now."

"I have to go pee."

"I have to go too, let's race!"

8

JOE AND MARIA

"1 John 3:2-3

2 Beloved, now we are children of God; and it has not yet been revealed what we shall be, but we know that when He is revealed, we shall be like Him, for we shall see Him as He is. 3 And everyone who has this hope in Him purifies himself, just as He is pure."

Maria Silva walked into Joe's office. Her family were immigrants from Mexico, and she had olive-colored skin and spoke with a slight Mexican accent. Standing at five foot three with big brown eyes, she was thirty-four years old, unmarried, and dedicated to her job. She was extremely loyal to Director Joe Smith.

Joe tried to portray a man in control, but inside he felt uncontrollable. Nonetheless, he spoke to Maria as if he had full command of the situation. "Please, have a seat, Maria."

"Thank you, sir. So, what's on your mind?"

Joe took out a bottle of old whiskey that he had stashed in the bottom drawer of his desk. "How about a drink? I don't know about you, but I could sure use one."

"Yes, sir, please."

He poured two glasses half full and pushed her glass toward her. "I would make a toast, but I can't think of a good reason why." He leaned

back in his old chair. "Maria, we've been working together for quite
some time, and I trust you completely."

"As do I, sir."

"I'll get straight to the point. Soon, this office will be overrun by
strangers. They will be taking over World Watch. I want—no, I need to
know why all these people disappeared. I believe the office will be used
for other things, although I have no idea what exactly. I need you and
me to work together, and to be blunt... keep it between us."

"Absolutely, sir. You can count on me. Sir, if I may speak about the
missing people, I believe I know what happened to them. While you
were in here, I followed up on some leads."

"And?"

"The more I looked, the more I found out. Most, if not all, of
the people were Christians. In fact, every single one of them was a
Christian. I believe that the rapture happened, sir."

"Rapture; what the hell is that!"

"You've never heard of the rapture?"

"That's some kind of religious thing — right?"

"According to some of the sites I looked at," Maria continued, "it
says that the Christians would be caught up in the air with Jesus Christ
in less than a blink of an eye. That sure sounds like what happened
to me, sir."

"I need more than a fairy tale, Maria! I need cold hard facts! Get me
some more information, anything other than this. Maybe it was a UFO
or Russia, even China. I need solid proof of what happened. I can't
deal with that religious crap. I've already heard enough of that before.
If the Christians are gone, then hallelujah! So annoying, thank God
they're gone!"

Maria Silva stood up and placed her drink down. "I won't let you
down, sir. You can count on me, sir."

Maria didn't say it to Joe, but all her family members were raptured.
She knew what had occurred, and she needed to accept Jesus before
it's too late! Things were going to move faster in the cities! The great
tribulation was falling upon the world like a terrestrial rainstorm.

The door to the main office opened! Men dressed in black suits with "UN" emblazoned on their right sleeves walked confidently into World Watch. One of them spoke out loud as Maria and Joe walked out of the office. He had a deep, loud voice, and he was very bossy.

"My name is Antonio Rossi. I've been sent by the UN to take charge here. You will all be reporting to me. Where is Director Joe Smith?"

"Yes, that would be me. Welcome to World Watch."

"We are aware of our location. I require an office, and my team will need desks. We are in control, and if any information from this office is leaked, there will be severe consequences." He raised his voice a little to ensure everyone heard him, "Absolutely nothing is to be leaked from this office — is that clear?"

The entire office responded in unison, "Yes, sir!"

Joe retreated to his office, which he still occupied. He received a text on his phone from Congressman Ed McGwire, "Take a look at this video directly from the U.N. It features a man named Lorenzo Calvo, who claims to be one of these aliens. I must admit, I'm skeptical and unsure of what to make of it."

Joe smiled in utter disbelief and shook his head as he read the message aloud, "What on earth is this?" He played the video on his phone and leaned back, listening to Lorenzo Calvo addressing the United Nations in English. Interestingly, regardless of the language anyone spoke, they could understand the video—whether it was Mandarin Chinese, Hindi, Spanish, French, Arabic, or Russian. Joe was captivated by it all.

He pondered to himself, "The Christians are being educated to comprehend the significance of this moment in history. It makes perfect sense, and they will return, aligning themselves with the rest of us—perfectly."

2 Thessalonians 2:9

"9Even him, whose coming is according to the working of Satan, with all power and signs and lying wonders,"

That is precisely what Lorenzo Calvo was doing in front of the United Nations, and most of the world leaders were completely buying into the lie. Lorenzo had the ability to vanish and reappear at will, while spreading false claims about his desire for peace. In reality, this dragon had no intention of seeking peace; he craved lawlessness. His true motives were deception and murder!

It was only a matter of time before he deceived the majority of the world. While some individuals would embrace Christ, the majority would be swayed by Calvo. Unfortunately, people disregarded the word of God, leaving them defenseless against this wolf in sheep's clothing. Calvo would exploit climate change and illnesses to manipulate the masses.

9

THE TRIP

"Psalm 91 4 - 5
4 He shall cover you with His feathers, And under His wings you shall
take refuge;
His truth shall be your shield and and armor.
5 You shall not be afraid of the terror by night,
Nor of the arrow that flies by day,"

Greg felt like God was directing him to pick up Sarah Green. Greg
came out of the bathroom to Alex right in-front of him, he hoped he
didn't hear him talking to Doctor Sarah. Greg was annoyed and said,
"What do you want?"

"My laptop, do you have any idea what I have on this thing, or what
I can do with it?"

"It's a laptop and it needs to be destroyed, end of discussion!"

The leader in him Came out," he said, "It's too much to explain right
now. All our electronics can be tracked. If you want to live, we need to
destroy your laptop. Your parents, being heavily invested in end-time
prophecies, must have known we were nearing the rapture and probably arranged a hiding place for us."

Alex looked at him proudly and responded, "Pastor Greg, no one,

I mean no one, can track my laptop. It's impenetrable. I can hack into anything. We need it."

He gazed out the window and added, "Remember the massive power outage in Washington DC last month, Pastor Greg? That was me! Wasn't the President pissed off!"

"You know, I actually believe you," Pastor Greg replied. "Bring it, but let's not disclose it to the others just yet. We'll inform them later."

Pastor Greg packed the youths into his Jeep and led a heartfelt prayer, with the kids joining in. "God, help us reach the place You have prepared for us safely. Surround us with Your angels for protection. We thank You for Your mercy, love, and power. In Jesus' name—Amen."

The Jeep sped off towards the mountains in Northern Maine, making sure to pick up the doctor along the way. The scene in Midcoast Maine resembled a war zone. Smoking houses and leveled apartment buildings showed the aftermath of destruction. It was a harrowing sight, but the presence of the Holy Spirit within them provided strength to cope with the horror.

Greg hurried to Sarah Green's house, and Liz whispered with a slightly elevated tone, "Why are we stopping here? Does the doctor live here? We could be caught, you know."

Greg asked, "How did you know we were picking up a doctor?"

Alex pointed and replied, "It's right here in the instructions."

Sarah emerged from the side door and quickly made her way to the jeep. "Guys, this is Doctor Sarah Green. Brandon, get in the back."

They all greeted her, saying, "It's nice to meet you, Doctor Sarah."

Soon, they were speeding down the highway. Greg was driving fast, but the police were preoccupied with searching for their own families. Amid the deafening noise of the oversized tires, Alex yelled, "Pastor Greg!"

"What is it?" Greg responded.

"You know we need to abandon your Jeep before we reach this place, right?"

"How do you know that?"

"It's clearly stated in the instructions. We have to get rid of the Jeep and continue on foot."

"Get rid of my Jeep?" Greg exclaimed, surprised.

"Sorry, Pastor Greg!"

Brandon exclaimed, "Another jetliner went down on the highway, it's burning!"

Liz, with fear in her small voice, screamed into Pastor Greg's ear, "The instructions say not to stop for anything or anyone!"

Pastor Greg skillfully maneuvered through the wreckage of the plane. Amongst the scattered bodies, one person appeared to be very alive. Pastor Greg shouted, "We must follow the instructions! The only time we'll stop next is to get rid of my Jeep—no matter what obstacles lie ahead! Help will come, and I need to ensure your safety!"

Alex, from the back, interjected, "Shouldn't we take the back roads?"

"Alex, find us a safer route!"

He reached into his backpack and pulled out a laptop that was anything but ordinary. Little Liz glanced at it and complained, "Hey, why does he have a laptop? I had to destroy mine! That's not fair, Pastor Greg!"

"I understand, Liz. But his laptop cannot be traced. His parents acquired it, and they had access to technology we've never seen before. Take a look at his laptop."

Alex proudly declared, "They were prepared for situations like this! It's unbelievable that they're gone."

Pastor Greg yelled back, "You will see them again, Alex! Stay focused and find us an alternate route to our destination. Collect yourself!"

"Yes Sir, Pastor Greg!"

The pastor and the others continued without stopping until they reached their destination. For many miles, silence hung heavy in the air. Unable to bear the quiet any longer, Pastor Greg broke into song, and the rest joined in:

"Oh Lord, my God

When I, in awesome wonder

Consider all the worlds Thy hands have made

I see the stars, I hear the rolling thunder
Thy power throughout the universe displayed
Then sings my soul, my Savior God to Thee
How great Thou art, how great Thou art
Then sings my soul, my Savior God to Thee
How great Thou art, how great Thou art
And when I think that God, His Son not sparing
Sent Him to die, I scarce can take it in
That on the cross, my burden gladly bearing
He bled and died to take away my sin
Then sings my soul, my Savior God to Thee
How great Thou art, how great Thou art
Then sings my soul, my Savior God to Thee
How great Thou art, how great Thou art
When Christ shall come, with shout of acclamation
And take me home, what joy shall fill my heart
Then I shall bow, in humble adoration
And then proclaim, my God, how great Thou art
Then sings my soul, my Savior God to Thee
How great Thou art, how great Thou art
Then sings my soul, my Savior God to Thee
How great Thou art, how great Thou art
How great Thou art, how great Thou art"

10

THE INSPECTION

"Psalms 142
I cried out to You, O Lord:
I said, "You are my refuge,
My portion in the land of the living.
6 Attend to my cry,
For I am brought very low;
Deliver me from my persecutors,
For they are stronger than I."

"Lisa yelled, 'This feels more like two locker rooms together, than a bathroom!

'I'm still peeing, give me a sec!'

'Really? But you're a guy.'

'So what?'

'Everyone knows guys pee faster than girls!'

'I really had to go, and I feel better now. Look, we've got soap and sinks. This place is huge too! There are washing machines and dryers, just like at the Laundromat. I need to shower, wash my hair, and change my clothes right now! I've never been this dirty.'

'Sis, I agree, but don't you want to explore this place first?'

'Then shower, eat, and sleep.'

'Let's go back to the door and start from there.'

'Why?'

'Because it'll be like a tour.'

'That actually makes sense Tim. I'm going to close my eyes.'

'Lord... I have a weirdo sister.'

'He knows."

Tim led Lisa back to the front door with her eyes closed, and she exclaimed, "This is exciting!"

"Sure, Lisa."

Once the two reached the front door, she opened her eyes and remarked, "Looks the same, like a cave with a house in it."

"No, it's the Haven!"

They walked to the left side of the Haven and spotted a massive box freezer, resembling something you would find in a restaurant, except it appeared to be hand-built and welded on-site. Three other sizable box freezers were also present. Tim opened the side door of the largest freezer and, although it was functional, it was empty. The other three smaller freezers were likewise devoid of contents. Additionally, there were four large sinks and numerous cabinets above and below, filled with dishes, pots, and pans.

Tim pulled down a lever above one of the sinks, and water started flowing. "It still amazes me that we have running water. This looks like something you'd find in a restaurant kitchen!"

"It's definitely more kitchen than twenty people would need."

Tim pushed the lever back up, then pulled it down again, exclaiming, "We have hot water!"

"YES! A HOT SHOWER!"

To the right of the sinks were five large electric stoves and ovens. Against the wall, to the right of the stoves, were five huge separate closets that reached a height of twelve feet and spanned at least five feet in width, protruding seven feet from the wall. Lisa approached the first closet, which had an enormous door, and pulled it open. Tim joined her to see what lay inside. "Unbelievable!"

The closet was filled with shelves upon shelves, stacked from top to bottom with covered plastic totes. Each tote was labeled, and the largest one was filled to the brim with rice. It was enough rice to last for a very long time!

The second closet was similar to the first, packed with totes just as before. Tote after tote contained different kinds of beans—white beans, black beans, brown beans, every imaginable variety. Lisa wasn't thrilled, as she had developed a dislike for beans during a mission trip in Brazil. For two weeks at an orphanage, all they had to eat was rice and beans. She sighed, saying, "Oh, beans—well, that's just great."

Tim stated a fact that they both knew, "Rice and beans are better than nothing, and you, my dear sister, learned how to make rice and beans in Brazil. There's no drive-thru out here in the middle of nowhere."

She smiled and responded, "Oh yeah, so I can teach you how to make beans too."

Tim opened the next closet door slowly, both filled with excitement and anticipation. Closet three was stocked with canned goods of every kind, featuring a wide range of vegetables. The first shelf held hundreds of large cans of tomatoes. The second shelf contained canned soups, while the remaining shelves were filled with items like corn and other vegetables.

Tim said, "We have a lot of bunk beds, so that would mean that more than likely more people will be here, right? All this food, but it's still not enough for seven years."

"Yeah, really."

Both of them were exhausted. The truth was, they had been arguing constantly at home, but that was all in the past now. Tim glanced at Lisa, growing weary of her attitude. She was familiar with that look, but this time she had to pay heed to what he was conveying with it. They both needed to assess the situation calmly and rationally. "I'm sorry. I tend to get like this, and I don't even know why."

Lisa then said, "We're going to be here for a long time. This food won't last for over a year, especially if more people are coming. We're going to need additional means to obtain food."

For the first time in a while, Lisa sounded like Tim's mom, instructing, "Tim, there are two more closets, and there's a whole back wall that we haven't explored. We don't even know how the water and electricity work."

The two opened closet number four. Lisa exclaimed, "Wow, check this out!" There were numerous shelves stocked with supplies: shampoo, conditioner, soap, combs, and other hair products. They also found bleach, floor cleaners, insect repellents, LED light bulbs, first aid kits—everything one could possibly need for an extended stay, but still not enough for seven years!

The two approached the final closet, and that's when they truly grasped the magnitude of their situation. Lisa locked eyes with Tim as they both placed their hands on the colossal doorknob. With determination, Lisa uttered, "Let's do this."

The two opened the door, revealing the closet's interior. The inside was full of guns, rifles, compound bows and arrows, night vision goggles, and things the two didn't even know existed in the fifth closet.

Tim said, "Cool!"

On the other hand, Lisa was frightened and said, "Not so cool! That's like going to war stuff! I've seen enough." she tried to push the door shut, but it was so heavy that Tim had to help her. As Tim assisted her in closing the door, he remarked, "Let's keep going. There's a lot more to explore. We can't stop at just one closet. Besides, I can go hunting and bring back deer and other game with these guns. We have freezers for a reason."

She fearfully looked at him and said, "Looks like we're going to war or something!"

"I'm sure that some of that stuff is just in case. Thou shalt not kill... right."

Between the closets and the back wall were five enormous couches arranged in a big U facing the wall with a rug in the middle that made a living room setting. There was a nice oversized recliner with a keyboard in the front middle part. Tim sat in the chair, and with the keyboard on his lap, he pressed on.

Along the wall, nine holographic monitors appeared! The highest technology in the world, and these two were looking at it! World Watch technology wasn't even close to what they saw.

Lisa laughed and said, "I guess we'll have entertainment!"

"I bet this is to keep an eye on the news and stuff. Alex will know about this stuff sis."

"His name was on one of the bunk beds."

Tim pressed a few buttons and tuned in to the national news. A journalist in a boat near the New England Aquarium appeared on the screen while the camera crew captured the horrifying scene behind him. "As you can see, most of Boston is engulfed in flames! This historic city is ablaze! Despite the efforts of firefighters, the fires continue to rage on," he reported.

Then the news stories would flash to the next:

A massive tsunami hitting New York

Earthquakes in California

Tornadoes wreaking havoc in Canada

The list of catastrophes seemed never-ending. It was complete pandemonium. The anchorwoman began discussing the numerous missing people and the speculation that aliens abducted them. She stated, "We have footage of the spacecrafts before they departed from Florida, New York, and California." She continued describing the hundreds of spaceships hovering over cities worldwide. Images of the spaceships were displayed on holographic screens in front of the two siblings and the entire world watching. It was a horrifying sight.

Tim asked Lisa, "Do you remember how I did a science project on Holograms in the sixth grade?"

"Yeah, you got a hundred on it."

"That was years ago, and technology has improved a lot since then. I bet those ships are holograms, just like these monitors."

"Makes sense, everybody now thinks that their loved ones are in those spaceships. I think the church talked about that scenario."

"Look Tim another story."

The newscaster spoke, "The west-coast was hit by a massive tsunami! The destruction was immense! This just in, China, many people have taken ill again with a new virus, and this could take the lives of much of the world population."

Lisa pleaded with Tim, "Please, shut it off!" She started to tear up again. Tim, too, felt his eyes welling up, and he quickly turned off the television and set the remote down.

"Wow Sis, It's not just The United States, it's the whole World."

The two walked towards the back wall where the bathroom was located and opened the door. The bathrooms were divided in half on the left side of the wall. Lisa commented, "We've been through a lot, but I'm going to take a hot shower now.—God is so good!"

"All this inside a cave—amazing."

"Tim, do you hear that?"

"Yeah it sounds like water splashing or something."

The two opened a door adjacent to the restroom, revealing a spacious room with a continuous four to five feet wide waterfall. The water cascaded endlessly, with pipes diverting and collecting the water. It was distributed throughout the cave. There was a stainless steel wheel with spinning paddles during the falling water. The wheel had a stainless steel pole in the centre, leading into a box. Emerging from the box were small PVC pipes branching out in various organized directions. The door on the box warned, 'DANGER HIGH VOLTAGE.'

Tim opened the door carefully, "This is how we have power Sis. So simple, as long as the water keeps running, we're good! It's called hydroelectric power. I studied about that!"

Other, bigger pipes were catching water and sending it into a large heater. That's how the Haven was heated. The pipes distributed hot water throughout and under the floor. That kept the Haven at a steady seventy degrees. Also, that was where they got hot water for bathing, washing clothing, dishes, etc.There was also a blower that took fresh air in through a hole in the wall and sent it thought-out the caves, so they wouldn't have a musty odor.

Wires funnelled into the PVC pipes and branched out into the caves. Lisa yelled over the water falling in the room because it was so loud, "This is way cool!"

Tim said, "This is our power line, it heats, it does, everything--astounding!"

The two stepped out of the waterfall room and entered the living area. They discovered a colossal open doorway towards the right on the back wall. The room was pitch black. Tim located the switch with an attached timer and flicked it. The lights on the high ceiling illuminated so brightly that they stung their eyes. As the room came into view, they realized it was an expansive space, equivalent to two football fields in size. There were no wooden walls; instead, it resembled a cave with a massive door at the far end. The floor was covered in nutrient-rich soil, perfect for cultivating a garden. Adjacent to the left stood a large wooden shed housing shovels, rakes, and all the necessary tools for an underground vegetable garden. They found plastic bags brimming with seeds on one of the shelves inside the shed. Additionally, PVC pipes were installed on the ceiling, presumably for watering the garden.

"Lisa this is too much to even take-in! We'll have a garden, and grow our own vegetables." "They really thought of everything. We have all we need to survive is in a cave. Those lights are bright as the sun!"

"I am blown away, and we've only touched the surface, and that big doorway over there?"

Lisa laughed, "I can get a tan in here! I'm beat and hungry, let's open the door later? I don't even think I could walk all the way to that door right now. We can take showers and eat something, go to sleep and try to figure out what we should do next."

"Yeah, we'll shower, eat, and sleep. I saw some spam in one of the closets. We have a lot to do tomorrow, like starting a garden for one."

"I can't wait to take a shower and change these clothes!"

That's precisely what they did. Once the two settled into their new beds, the lights automatically began to dim at 7:30 P.M. due to a timer.

Tim switched on his reading light and perused through some books. He stumbled upon a dark leather notebook among them and recognized his mom's handwriting. Tim started to read,

"My dearest Tim,

If you are reading this, then you were not raptured with us. I want you to know how much I love you! Take care of your little sister. You are a survivor, and you need to be strong. I need you to be the man God intended you to be because the next seven years will be the most challenging years you'll ever have to go through. I would imagine you have taken Jesus into your life by now. I want you to pray and go to sleep. You two must be so tired, Honey. Sleep in the peace that only Jesus can give you. We will be back in seven years.

Love, Mom."

He knew his mom couldn't hear him, but he whispered the words anyway. "Mom, both of us accepted Jesus into our hearts on the way here. We'll see you in seven years." Tim turned off the light and offered a brief prayer, feeling too weary to say much more. "Father, thank you for revealing Yourself to my sister and me. Please keep us safe. I'm so exhausted, God, and I wish I had the energy to say more to You. In Jesus' name, amen... and thank you once again."

Tim and Lisa were so sleepy after the last two days, and they slept like never before—so soundly.

11

RIDE OF A LIFETIME

"Proverbs 3:5-6

Trust in the LORD with all your heart, And lean not on your own under-standing; In all your ways acknowledge Him, And He shall direct your paths."

They gazed at the breathtaking landscape and then turned their attention to Greg, enduring what felt like the longest journey of their lives. They all realized they had missed the opportunity to board the plane to be with Jesus, for He was their gateway to heaven. The tribulation was unprecedented, surpassing any hardships humanity had witnessed since the days of Noah and the Great Flood. None of them could fathom that a refuge awaited them. Only Greg possessed a deep understanding of the Word of God, making him the sole individual with some insight into what lay ahead. He thought while driving about the parties he went to in New York, where no one knew him. He thought of the sinful lifestyle that he was part of. He would shake his head in complete disgust as he tried to keep the tan Jeep on the road! He went to school to become a pastor, just like his dad. Then, he joined the military and was soon in special forces; he was built for combat. He never really believed in God. He thought he had fooled the church and Pastor Frank, but the only one he fooled was himself. Greg needed the money that the church paid, and he liked kids. He wasn't the first pastor that made that charade.

They were only a few miles away from the place to dispose of the Jeep and go in by foot. By now, they were in the middle of the mountain range and had been going up and down hills and mountains for a while.

"We are here Pastor Greg!"

"I see that, Liz!"

Brandon looked over the massive cliff with a small stream on the bottom and said, "I think that's where you need to take care of business, like your Jeep. I'm so sorry, Pastor Greg; I know you love this Jeep."

Greg pulled the Jeep over to the side of the road. "I know, Brandon. Does everyone have everything? Liz, Brandon, Alex, Sarah, we need to get out. We'll push the Jeep over that cliff."

Everyone looked into the Jeep and said, "Yep, Pastor Greg, we have everything."

He pulled the Jeep around and pointed the front end at the cliff. He put the Jeep in neutral, and Greg said sadly, "I'll do it guys."

Alex hastily said, "We might need that Jeep Pastor Greg someday! I think that we should stash it somewhere. Take the license plate off and stuff."

Greg loved that idea and said quickly, "We need to scrape off the serial numbers."

Sarah said, "We would definitely need to wipe down the fingerprints. We need a place to stash this thing."

They all surveyed their surroundings, and Greg noticed an animal trail leading into the woods. It was narrow, but the Jeep seemed capable of traversing it.

He skillfully reversed the Jeep into the animal trail and maneuvered through thick brush. The kids then concealed the nearly new Jeep with additional brush and sticks, making it incredibly difficult to spot. Perhaps the Jeep would remain there, gradually succumbing to the elements, but they knew its location if they ever needed it.

Greg, Sarah Green, and the children strapped on their backpacks and ventured into the woods on the other side of the street, making their way toward a colossal mountain. It took them nearly two hours to reach the steep ascent. Greg said, "Watch your step so no one turns an ankle or worse. This is a great thing that the path is like this."

Liz was breathless but could say, "Why would that be Pastor Greg?"

Alex added, "That's a great question Liz!"

Sarah said, "Let the kids catch their breath Greg, and me too."

He stopped and said, "First of all no one will be able to track us if we keep stepping on the flat rocks. Second of all, you see all these pine trees, they stop people from seeing us. We are stealth."

Brandon said, "Who would be able to see us? There's no one around here, this is the sticks."

Still breathing hard, Sarah said, "Sweetie, he's talking about satellites... they can see us from the sky if we didn't have trees covering. That's what Greg is talking about."

Greg was feeling great, to the point where he could even contemplate climbing the mountain if desired. His words were filled with knowledge and confidence as he addressed the group. "Considering today's advanced technology, a hummingbird could easily be mistaken for a military drone, and that's just the beginning. Such an innocent bird could carry a camera feed monitored by individuals on the other side of the world. We may have some safety for a few months, perhaps a year, but they will make every effort to track down and eliminate all Christians. The longer we wait, the more difficult it will become. I have so much to teach all of you, but rest assured, we will be alright. Just another hundred yards, and we'll reach our destination. Let's go, everyone!"

Alex said, "I know a lot about what they can do with satellites. The hummingbird drones, I've played with them, and they look like a real hummingbird. I'm worried about the battery in my laptop, how can I charge it if it goes dead? I have a little solar powered charger. I can't believe that I forgot that!"

Brandon slapped Alex's back and said, "I have this incredible feeling that God will supply all are needs."

Liz said, "Isn't that a verse in the Bible Pastor Greg?"

"Yeah, it's uh—Philippians four nineteen."

They arrived at the specified coordinates and halted their journey. The group gazed around with a mix of confusion and curiosity. Greg's eyes settled on a cluster of boulders, and he remarked, "According to my directions, one of these boulders is a door." Intrigued, everyone began exerting strength to push the large rocks and boulders. When Pastor Greg applied considerable force to one specific boulder, it shifted slightly, leaving them all amazed, except for Greg. He calmly stated, "I've encountered something similar before, back in Afghanistan."

They walked unknowingly into the hall, and Pastor Greg opened the door to see Lisa and Tim working in the kitchen. They were utterly speechless! Alex and Liz pushed the boulder door shut. There was a lock, but it wasn't needed at this point.

Tim yelled across the cave, "Pastor Greg how come you're still here?"

Greg was coming to Tim to hug him and said, "I guess I didn't make the cut like you guys!"

Tim took a step back and yelled out, "We decided to call it, the Haven! I can't wait to give you the tour! Oh, and again what are you still doing here on the planet earth?"

Pastor Greg deflected the question and yelled out with an echo while everyone ran in, "Are you joking me, this is so awesome!"

Liz playfully tackled Lisa, and their close bond formed through their shared experiences in church. They were not just best friends; they had become sisters in Christ, united by their faith. God had an effective plan in store for them and the entire group.

As Alex surveyed their surroundings, his eyes landed on the advanced technology present in the cave. He was instinctively drawn to it, recognizing the familiar touch of his parents. The organization and pristine appearance of the technology hinted at their involvement. Alex possessed a deeper understanding of its capabilities compared to the others. He could access satellites discreetly, surpassing the limitations of World Watch. The technology was remarkably advanced, granting him unparalleled capabilities.

He envisioned tiny pea-sized cameras scattered across the vast expanse of the mountain, and to his surprise, his imagination turned out to be accurate. Alex knew of a hummingbird drone, which could be perched on a tree branch or hovering outside. The drone had a long-lasting battery that could sustain it for at least seven years, if not more. Alex's gaze shifted to the numerous bunk beds far behind him while sitting comfortably in the recliner.

The thought of using his resources to locate other Christians and bring them to the cave crossed his mind. He pondered the possibility that fellow believers might be living within an hour or two of their location and they could be rescued. Some individuals had turned to Christ following the rapture, and this cave could serve as an underground railroad of sorts, reminiscent of the Underground Railroad beneath churches in history.

Alex swiftly took command of the keyboard, and in seconds, the holographic screens came to life, displaying various images on each one. He uncovered the hidden UN video on the web and played it on one of the screens, amplifying the volume. Alex's conviction grew stronger as Lorenzo Calvo delivered his speech to the world leaders. He recognized that Calvo was the antichrist, a realization that became evident to anyone with the Holy Spirit dwelling within them.

Alex yelled, "Guys, you need to see what's happening at the UN! Pastor Greg, come on over here; check this guy out!"

Liz, Lisa, Sarah, and Brandon remained in the garden room while Tim and Greg explored the weapons, their thoughts centered on tomorrow morning's hunt. Upon hearing Alex's urgent call, they swiftly closed the door and hurried over. Alex replayed the video, saying, "Pastor Greg, you have to see this!" Greg approached, his eyes fixed on the screen, witnessing the antichrist captivating the world leaders. They all observed Lorenzo Calvo delivering his speech, disappearing and reappearing before the astonished leaders.

Greg gathered everyone around, arranging them on sofas and an oversized, old chair. He had Alex pause the video, which was nearing its end. Drawing upon his knowledge of the gospel, Greg spoke, "My brothers and sisters, that is the antichrist. He has a counterpart on Earth, a demonic figure resembling the opposite of John the Baptist. And as for Lorenzo Calvo, he possesses a demonic spirit. Many will receive and follow him, embracing his mark. They will be required to receive a special tattoo infused with advanced technology, granting them the ability to buy and sell. However, this mark not only affects them physically but also corrupts their DNA. Those who bear it will be unable to inherit the Kingdom of God. We still have some time before he begins seeking out Christians. There will be tribulation saints, like us, and perhaps this is our divine calling."

Brandon said, "This is a ministry! A calling from Jesus! A wonderful thing!"

Lisa said, "We need a nickname."

Tim said, "How about the people?"

Liz said, "The rock dudes!"

Lisa said, "The cave dwellers. I like tropical fish and a lot of them live in caves."

Alex said, "I like it!"

Liz said, "You like it cause Lisa said it. The rock dudes is a great name!"

Tim said, "You're the pastor, what do you think?"

"The Holy Spirit dwells in us and we live in a cave. I like it!"

Tim said, "The cave dwellers from the Haven, that's good Sis!"

"I have my moments."

"Alright, my fellow cave dwellers, where was I? Ah, yes. We must ensure these freezers are stocked with venison, wild turkey, fish from the nearby lake—anything and everything to sustain us through this bleak winter. Alex, you will be our source of information, keeping us informed about the happenings in the world and around this mountain. Additionally, Alex, if you come across any sincere Christians nearby, we will extend an invitation to join us here. I trust you can handle that task?"

Alex answered Pastor Greg like he was in the military because they were warriors for Christ, and they all knew it, "Yes sir, I can do that!"

Pastor Greg spoke again, and no one interrupted him, "Tim tell me quickly about this place."

Tim exclaimed, "We have hydroelectric power and bathrooms that resemble a school locker room. The best part is, through that hallway, there's a tremendous space for a garden. We just need to plant the seeds stored in a large shed. I suppose we could call it the garden room. However, there's a massive locked door at the back of the garden room, and we haven't been able to locate the key."

"We need an enormous garden, in this Haven, you guys need to focus on that. We need to get that door open too."

They shook their heads simultaneously and said, "Yes, sir, Pastor Greg."

Finally, Greg acted like a leader, a shepherd, and directed his flock appropriately as a pastor should.

12

THE DAVIS COUPLE

Lamentations 3:22-23

"22 Through the LORD's mercies we are not consumed, Because His compassions fail not.

23 They are new every morning;

Great is Your faithfulness."

It was late September, and the leaves were starting to change colors. Mr. and Mrs. Davis, an elderly couple, had just risen from their knees after accepting Jesus Christ as their Lord and Savior—a decision they should have made years ago. Like many others, they had attempted to earn their way into heaven through good works. They had donated money to charities, volunteered at a soup kitchen in New York City, and faithfully attended church on Christmas and Easter. However, they had evidently never come across these verses in the Bible.

Ephesians 2:8-9

8 For by grace you have been saved through faith, and that not of yourselves; it is the gift of God, 9 not of works, lest anyone should boast.

They were at their beautiful cottage in the Maine mountains, enjoying the fruits of a lifetime of working in the Big Apple. In their mid-fifties, Elijah and Ruth Davis were an African American couple who exuded health and vitality. They had a harmonious relationship and had been happily married for thirty years. Alex recognized that Elijah and Ruth were the ideal candidates for the Haven. Their garden was a sight to behold, brimming with an abundance of vibrant flowers, although they also cultivated some vegetables.

Alex had been watching them off and on for months. He could look right through their patio window with the many satellites at his disposal. He saw them in their living room, both reading the Bible. Alex saw them on their knees, crying out to Jesus at times. Alex had all nine screens going simultaneously; he didn't miss anything.

The Davis's home was approximately twenty miles away. Alex speculated that they might have stocked up on supplies, which would be beneficial. However, he understood that the Davis family would eventually be targeted for elimination. At present, Lorenzo Calvo had not yet initiated a search for Christians in the remote woods of Maine, nor had he divulged his plans to the urban populace. Many people in the cities, desperate for sustenance and guidance, succumbed to accepting the tattoo—the mark of the beast—on their right hand. Lorenzo Calvo's new world order offered a semblance of leadership in a time of starvation and need.

A few people saw what Calvo was; they had become tribulation saints and were silently being whisked off to detention centers, soon to be killed off, and hardly anyone knew. The internet was sanctioned, and anyone who spoke about Jesus Christ was investigated. The Bible was considered hate speech! Alex was everywhere and nowhere on the internet. Things were terrible and would get worse and worse.

Alex had organized a rescue mission for Greg and Tim on their second successful hunting day. The presence of a satellite proved invaluable as Alex guided them using walkie-talkies to locate the deer. Their equipment was of military-grade quality, ensuring their conversations remained encrypted and incomprehensible to anyone eavesdropping. Although their current situation didn't pose a significant threat, they were aware that eventually, they would be pursued, much like the deer they hunted daily.

Pastor Greg and Tim, "Guys, you two need to check this couple out!"

Alex had the Davis house displayed on one of the screens. On another screen, Mr. Davis could be seen chopping wood, while through the kitchen window, Mrs. Davis was observed going through an empty refrigerator.

With pride, Alex leaned back and said, "These are the Davis family, newly born-again Christians. I believe they would be an ideal addition to the Haven. They are diligent workers, and more importantly, we need them as much as they need us. Take a look at the screen on the right."

"Those are pictures of their garden back in August. They have green thumbs, and that's something that none of us seem to have."

Tim said, "The garden room isn't living up to its name."

Greg said, "The garden is pretty pitiful."

Tim smiled and said, "Your being too nice Pastor."

Alex said, "You see why we need them more than they need us."

Greg said, "We need each other. You don't think that the UN military won't catch up to them? Of course they will, eventually."

Alex said, "I've been praying and feel as if God wants them here. They wake up at six every morning. They're from the big apple and while they were vacationing here the rapture hit."

Greg said, "They probably have no idea what's coming."

Alex said, "They're first names are Elijah and Ruth, yes my friends you need to go get them and convince them that we have a safe place."

Greg said, "What are do they have for rations?"

"Those two are getting hungry. Their food is gone, and they've eaten their vegetables."

Greg said, "We could bring them something to eat, that might help."

Tim said, "They might think it's a trick."

They all agreed with that assessment. Being a born-again Christian had become increasingly dangerous, with people growing more paranoid and the dangers intensifying.

"I have the rescue plans on this tablet that was here, don't worry it can't be tracked. Maybe take a few pictures of us, and the Haven?"

Pastor Greg looked at Alex, then glanced at Tim and closed his eyes as he leaned back on the couch. "Father, we pray for the Davis family and ask for Your mighty grace and protection to guide us in reaching out to them. We sense that You, God, are leading us to discover new companions in this cave. Lord, we ask for Your help and safety. Amen."

In Jesus Holy name, amen."

Tim asked Alex, "What's the plan?"

"The Davis family live to the west of us. It looks like it's actually a pretty easy smash and grab."

Pastor Greg laughed, "A smash and grab!"

Lisa emerged unexpectedly, vaulting over the back of the sofa and gracefully settling into a yoga seated position. Before her newfound faith in Jesus, she had been an avid yoga practitioner. "What are you all up to?" she inquired curiously.

Alex, still gleaming, said, "You see that house and people on all the monitors? You see that guy chopping wood on monitor two? You see the woman sitting at the kitchen table praying in monitor three? Meet the Davis's. We're going to get them."

Tim said, "If they'll come."

Lisa laughed, leaped up, tackled Alex on the recliner, and said, "You, my nerdy brother in Christ, are so cool! When do we go get them?"

Alex always liked Lisa just like every other guy in their school did, but he needed to put that aside, "I have a plan, but it's for Pastor Greg and Tim. It's twenty miles away and you just can't walk down the road, you need to go through the woods, sleep a night, it's a two-day trip."

Greg said, "And it's not summer anymore."

Tim said abruptly, "How far away is your Jeep pastor Greg?"

"I guess it's a mile or two away, almost a two-hour walk?"

"You told me that it has a quarter tank of gas in the Jeep. Alex, obviously they have a car or something right?"

Alex clicked on monitor five, and Greg said, "Check out the size of that land yacht! An old Lincoln Continental! I bet that bad boy has some gas!"

Lisa listened, jumped off the couch, sat next to Alex, and said, "I'm going! Oh yeah, I'm going! I've been stuck in this cave for mouths and I'm going! Tim can keep on hunting 'cause I'm going!"

Then she looked at Pastor Greg sweetly and said as cutely as possible, like a puppy, "See how honest my face looks? I know you do Pastor Greg! I can talk them into coming to the Haven! I know I can! I'm going on a field trip! I'm going on a field trip!"

Alex said, "Logically you and her would be much more trustworthy than two guys they don't know, and you should be able to do it in a day."

Lisa said, "Pastor Greg you still need to improve on your people skills, and I can teach you."

"My people skills are fine."

Tim, Alex, and Lisa had a good laugh at that one!

Greg recognized the plan's merit, particularly the importance of fully stocking the freezer before the arrival of winter. He agreed, affirming, "Indeed, it's a solid plan... let's proceed with it."

Lisa jumped across the floor, hugged Pastor Greg, and said, "You're my favorite pastor!" "I'm the only pastor."

13

THE DAVIS HOUSE

Galatians 5:1

"Stand fast therefore in the liberty by which Christ has made us free, and do not be entangled again with a yoke of bondage."

The following day Greg and Lisa were out before daybreak. They made their way to the Jeep, and this time Greg had a camouflage tarp so he could hide the Jeep better on the return trip; he found the tarp in the garden room. It was time to start bringing people to the Haven. Simply, it was their calling from God; we all have one.

About two hours later, they uncovered the Jeep covered with branches. They both jumped in, and Greg looked at Lisa and said, "I didn't even pray before we left. I don't know why God chose me to lead this group. I'm so under-qualified."

"Moses was under-qualified. He stuttered and didn't speak well in front of a crowd. He even lost his temper at times, yet God still used him. God uses you because you are humble."

"Thank you, Lisa! You're so much nicer as a Christian—amazing!"

"I was always nice; you just never really talked to me before." She paused, feeling convicted, and said, "Okay, I wasn't always nice before. God is changing me! I've never been this happy! I had everything back in Brunswick, and I was miserable. Now, living in a cave, I've never been more upbeat!"

"That's the Holy Spirit that lives in you, God has made you into a sweet young woman, you remind me of your mom. We should pray."

"Please let me pray this time. Lord, watch over us during this trip and keep us safe. Help us persuade them to come to the place you have provided for us to live, the Haven. I pray in the name of Jesus—Amen!"

Greg turned the key, and the Jeep roared to life. They maneuvered through the woods on an animal trail, and suddenly as if emerging from the bat cave in Batman, they found themselves on the road leading to Davis's house. Leaves and small branches rustled and flew off the Jeep as they sped along. Lisa reached for the encrypted walkie-talkie tucked in her flannel jacket pocket because she heard Alex and playfully said, "Hi, who's speaking?"

"It's me, I'm watching over you guys and the road looks clear from where you are to the Davis house—God's speed guys!"

"I don't know anyone named me. I'm sorry you must have the wrong number."

"It's me, Alex. I don't have the wrong number; this is a walkie-talkie."

"Alex—name sounds familiar, wait one second please. Pastor Greg, have you ever heard of an Alex?"

"Let me have the walkie-talkie Lisa! Like she said, we don't know any Alex!"

"Okay, I guess I called the wrong number, I'm so sorry. The road is clear for someone else in a tan Jeep."

She keyed in the walkie-talkie and playfully remarked, "We're in a tan Jeep, aren't we, Pastor Greg? You're our eyes and ears, and I think I'll keep you all to myself."

She made Alex's face turn red, which she had been doing a lot lately. They were constantly joking around. It was clear that Lisa was very fond of Alex, and that was helping Alex's self-esteem.

In less than an hour, they were pulling into a beautiful cottage. They both got out and walked to the door. Greg had his bible in his right hand.

Lisa knocked on the door while Greg stood beside her in a military stance. Lisa said, "Would you chill Pastor Greg!"

Elijah answered the door but opened it only a few inches; he looked worried, and his big voice said, "Good morning, can I help you?"

"Hi! my name is Lisa, and this wonderful man is Pastor Greg."

Pastor Greg said, "We believe that God has sent us here to help you. Do you and your wife have a minute or two?"

Lisa said, "I thought that I was going to do the talking pastor!"

"Let them in dear! Jesus sent a pastor to us—praise God!"

He invited them to sit down in their beautiful living room. Pastor Greg said, "I just need to be as honest as I can. We, you, and your wife are Christians. We missed the rapture, but you already know that don't you?"

Both shook their heads up and down at the same time in shame.

"You both come from New York City, and you can't go back there. The antichrist system, including the mark of the beast is already hitting the cities first, not to mention that New York is half destroyed. We've been watching you through a satellite system and some extremely advanced technology. How do I explain this to both of you without sounding crazy?"

Lisa butted in and said, "We live in a house inside a cave! We have electricity. We have bunk beds. We have food. There's seven of us."

Pastor Greg said, "Only if you want. We can help you. We can offer you shelter. Your lives here in this beautiful cottage are limited. Soon the UN military will target all Christians. It will be a choice between taking the mark or facing death. God has provided a way out for you both, if you choose. We have nearly seven years before Christ returns. I must be honest, I don't know if we'll even survive, but we have a chance if we hide in a cave. It will be incredibly challenging. I urge you and your husband to consider it."

"Wait, wait, I have pictures of the Haven. Pastor Greg forgot about that. Check it out!"

"Dear they have a kitchen!"

"You guys have electricity?"

Lisa said, "We do, and hot showers, washers and dryers. See right there."

Greg said, "Show them the garden room."

"I don't think we should, pretty sad looking. Alex said that you guys are out of food. I have cooked food in my backpack in the Jeep, you guys hungry?"

Ruth spoke almost before Lisa got done, "We're starving, dear!"

Lisa ran out to the Jeep and grabbed enough food for the four of them and ran back. They checked the garden room, "Dear, where's the garden?"

Greg said, "We aren't really gardeners."

Lisa said, "We all stink at the garden thing! We saw the pictures of your garden last summer."

"How'd you do that dear?"

"We have our ways. I'm just kidding. The Haven has internet, and we can connect into the atmosphere."

"She means we have some of the best technology in the Haven and we're able to go through the satellites without being traced."

They made their way to the kitchen table, sat down, and got to know each other. It was more than just food; it was the fellowship that Elijah and Ruth Davis needed, as well as Greg and Lisa.

With a mouth full of food, Lisa said, "I don't think we could grow a field of weeds."

"She has a point. We have everything we need. A huge garden area!"

"Don't forget the shed with shovels and stuff."

Elijah laughed, saying, "You guys definitely stink at gardening!"

Lisa laughed, "Agreed!"

"I was in the military; we didn't grow gardens."

Lisa looked at Ruth and said, "I love your place, it's beautiful here!"

Ruth said, "Yes we love it here. We bought this cottage twenty years ago. It's so peaceful, I mean compared to New York City." She leaned back in her chair and said, "It's going to be hard to just leave this place isn't it dear."

Greg said, "Do you two have children?"

"Dear, I don't think that Elijah wants to talk about that today."

Elijah sighed, "Maybe someday we'll get into that, but not today."

"Oh, I'm sorry."

Elijah said, "We love this place. I'm going to really miss it here. Pastor Greg, let me get this straight... you guys have electricity in a cave with a house in it, and a garden room?"

With a big smile, Lisa said, "And you two have green thumbs!"

Pastor Greg finally joked, "They don't look green to me!"

Elijah laughed, "No they're actually brown."

Lisa corrected and said, "I'm seeing green, must be a supernatural gift from Jesus or something."

Elijah laughed, "This Haven, I have to see it; what about you, Ruth?"

Ruth smiled at her husband and said, "A garden room in a cave, I'm ready to go yesterday!" Lisa said, "Maybe in seven years you guys can come back here! God is good, and maybe He'll watch over this place."

Greg looked out the window, "I noticed that you have a 1970 Lincoln Continental in great condition."

"Yes, I love that old car, it's a moving living room. How did you know that it was 1970?"

"I have a thing for older cars. How much gas is in that bad boy anyway?"

"It has about three quarters of a tank, about enough to start it."

Now they were all laughing!

Greg looked at him straightly and said, "We need all the gas we can take, or we'll be walking half the way back to the Haven."

Lisa said logically, "A jeep would definitely be better driving off road than your moving living room."

"Isn't she sweet Ruth!"

"She's adorable, Honey."

"Maybe we can adopt you!"

Greg laughed, "She's free if you want her!"

"Hey, Pastor Greg that's not nice! I'm very expensive!"

They finished eating, and Ruth and Elijah packed their suitcases with clothing. Ruth also grabbed some seeds, not just vegetables, but flowers. She looked at Lisa and said with a smile, "Flowers make everything look beautiful, dear, even a cave."

Lisa smiled and said, "I can't wait to see what you guys grow!"

They got into a Jeep with a full tank of gas and five gallons in a can for Tim's motorcycle. Then they went down the road headed to the Haven.

14

MARIA'S ESCAPE FROM WORLD WATCH

Matthew 6:33
"But seek first the kingdom of God and His righteousness, and all these things shall be added to you."

Maria was at work when she swiftly slipped out of the back door and hurried to her SUV. She drove as fast as she could to her apartment, parked, and sprinted up twelve stairs. Despite her petite frame of five foot four and a hundred and twenty pounds of muscle, she was not even out of breath. She unlocked the door and sank onto her couch. But suddenly, she collapsed onto the carpeted floor, curling up into a ball and sobbing uncontrollably, knowing that her family was no longer with her. Many years ago, a renowned pastor visited their city and preached, leading her entire family to accept Jesus Christ as their Savior. As the youngest of her three siblings, Maria could barely recall the details, but she vividly remembered the profound transformation that had taken place in their household.

Her dad stopped drinking, and they all went to church twice a week. Maria thought it was boring and wanted nothing to do with it, but still had to go.

Those were some of her childhood memories. She got her green card and went into the army. She was an overachiever and a jack of all trades. Later, she ended up on the World Watch, a dream come true for her! She was young, strong, intelligent, and up-to-date on the newest tech. She quickly got up and grabbed her laptop, which looked a lot like Alex's, completely stealthy but a newer model.

She had already accepted Jesus, and she knew that she needed to make a break for it and find a haven. Thoughts of New England, mountains, or perhaps Montana crossed her mind as she considered the options. She started exploring the possibilities in Maine. Believing in God and His guidance, she understood no coincidences regarding His children. Anyone who believes otherwise would be greatly mistaken.

She spotted four people getting into a Jeep in a mountain range in Maine and hit the follow button before heading to the kitchen. After making herself a sandwich, she sat and watched as the tan Jeep slowly descended the road. The vehicle had suitcases in the back and a bright orange gas can. Curiosity piqued, she zoomed in on the license plate Greg had reattached for the trip and decided to run a check on it.

As she inspected the license plate, she couldn't help but think, "Commander Gregory Oliver, a Marine Special Operations Team Leader—very impressive." Her curiosity grew as she noticed what appeared to be a bible resting on the Jeep dashboard.

The Jeep stopped, let out three people near a mountain, and they entered the woods. Maria did not doubt that she was the only one watching them. A God lead Holy Spirit appointment was needed, and she knew that!

"A young white woman and two older African Americans? I wonder where this Jeep is going...." She watched a split screen, and both things played out before her.

The Jeep backed into the woods, and within twenty minutes, Greg Oliver ran out briefly before reentering the woods near the exact location where the other three individuals had entered.

The satellite camera stayed on the best it could, with the trees hanging over and around them.

They made their way up the mountain.

"They must be living up there!"

She talked with God as if He was in the living room with her because He was. "Lord, help me to know what to do!"

Another twenty minutes and they disappeared completely. She marked their GPS location.

Maria Silva had her bug-out gear and was always ready. That included a false driver's license, passports, weapons, cash, a one-man tent, a sleeping bag, rations and clothing.

At precisely six in the evening, Maria Silva, with a duffle bag, baseball hat and fake glasses on, left her apartment by the stairs because there weren't any cameras. Two blocks from her apartment, in a parking garage, she had a 2010 Toyota Prius... 50 MPG! The gas tank was complete, and she left Virginia and headed north towards the beautiful Maine mountains. Her mission was to park her car next to Greg's Jeep. She knew how often she'd have to stop for gas, only in the Latino neighborhoods. She conveniently forgot English and would only speak Spanish until her Prius was side by side, hidden with Greg's Jeep.

Without God's help and that handy little laptop, she would've never made it. She mapped out a trip to Maine while missing all the police roadblocks. Martial law was still in effect. Any unpassable roads she avoided. She sneaked into her little car. She had jeans, a pink hooded sweatshirt, white sneakers, and a baseball hat; no one looked at her twice; she was just another freaked-out soccer mom making her way north—completely harmless. The truth was that she was trained in combat, kind of like Greg. She was World Watch's assassin, and when they needed the best, they called her! She was very dangerous!

The whole trip was uneventful. She arrived fifteen hours later in Maine. She was at the exact coordinance where Greg parked his Jeep. She ran in to make sure that she wouldn't get stuck. All the tire tracks for Greg's Jeep were gone; he had whipped the trail clean. She never would've found his Jeep if she wasn't trained in the military. The tarp was big enough for her Toyota Prius to slide in next to the Jeep, then cover them both. She removed her tire tracks, grabbed her duffle bag, and headed to the location. This whole thing was a faith trip; before she was a Christian, she would've never done anything like this, but she was the perfect addition to the Haven. Greg, Alex, and her together would be priceless! She didn't know that, but God sure did. She grabbed her Bible and put it in her right hand. She was hoping that Greg or someone would see her.

Alex didn't miss a thing, "Pastor Greg! Who's this lady heading towards the path that goes to the Haven?"

"I have no idea. Did she come by car?"

"I didn't see a car, but no one is getting near this mountain without me seeing! Let me go back a little, she parked her car near your Jeep. "

"Alex, I have absolutely no idea who she is, but that's a bible in her hand?"

Lisa jumped onto the couch and said, "Bible in her hand? Someone new? Totally awesome! The more people the better! We have a lot of bunks beds, five couches and a nice chair that a certain someone is always sitting in!"

The Davis couple were sound asleep, the walk up the mountain and the overwhelming tour of the Haven was a little more than they could handle.

Pastor Greg asked, "Tim is right near there hunting, call him on his walkie-talkie. Let him know what's going on! She maybe someone new for the Haven that God sent?"

"Hey there's a lady heading to your location. She looks harmless, try not to freak her out."

He stood between her and the rest of the trail with his gun pointed down, a bad idea because she already had Greg's facial recognition engraved in her memory. Tim was not Greg, and she didn't know if he was a threat. She wasn't going to take a chance. She acted like she was scared; she closed the distance between the two. Tim never knew what hit him. Tim was disarmed and flat on his back in less than twenty seconds with a hunting knife at his neck. The whole thing was being watched through the watchful eyes of a hummingbird drone.

"I'm going to ask you some questions! Do you understand me?

Tim was taken entirely off guard and said, "Yes, I definitely under-stand you."

"I'm looking for a Commander Gregory Oliver, a Marine Special Operations Team Leader! Do you know him?"

The walkie-talkie had stuck out of Tim's shirt pocket.

She recognized the walkie-talkie was military grade. She grabbed it and spoke confidently, "I'm looking for Commander Gregory Oliver, a Marine Special Operations Team Leader— comprendo!"

"That would be me, and who do I have the pleasure of speaking with?'

Maria spoke with her Mexican accent, "My name is Marie Silva. I was a sergeant in the army. I need to speak with you face to face... sir."

Greg smiled at her toughness, "We can arrange that. Can you let Tim back up, try not to kill him as he stands. I see that you have a bible; you born again?"

"I am as of yesterday, sir."

Greg laughed, "You know that Thou shalt not kill is a commandment in the Bible... right? Try not to kill the guy that's hunting down your next meal."

"Yes, I do sir, I guess I acted on reflexes. I imagine that you of all people understand. I'm new at this Christian thing."

"As we all are, Maria.

Tim, can you hear me?"

"Yes, Pastor Greg."

"Bring her up to the Haven."

"But Pastor Greg, how can we trust her?"

"Well, your still alive for one, and I feel like God is speaking to me. She's been sent here by Jesus and part of the plan."

Then the two of them made their way to the Haven. Tim was quiet on the walk. Honestly, he was utterly shocked at what had just happened. He thought that a soccer mom was walking towards him. She was lethal; balancing Christian ethics and the will to live would be hard for her. Tim happened to be in her way. Oh, she would've found the Haven, but again, only a handful of people could find that cave, and most of them lived in or fought in the middle east.

15

WORLD WATCH AND ANGRY JOE

"Ephesians 6:12

For we do not wrestle against flesh and blood, but against principalities, against powers, against the rulers of the darkness of this age, against spiritual hosts of wickedness in the heavenly places."

Director Joe Smith was in his office, growing increasingly concerned. He had already tried calling Maria Silva five times, but there was no answer. Joe had left three messages for her, as Maria was known for her impeccable attendance, never being late or absent. This unusual situation worried him, and he didn't want to escalate the issue unnecessarily, especially considering Maria's status as his top officer. Meanwhile, the UN personnel were present in the main room at World Watch.

Joe Smith, known for his impatience, hastily grabbed his briefcase and stormed out of the office, shouting, "I'll be back shortly!" Unbeknownst to him, the UN personnel in the main room were oblivious to his departure, as they had their concerns. Joe's presence was inconsequential as far as they were concerned.

He quickly drove to Maria's apartment and, utilizing a unique key, unlocked the door. Upon entering, he noticed that the apartment appeared well-maintained. A couple of inexpensive paintings adorned the walls, and there was a table with a vase of plastic flowers. However, there was no note or indication of her departure, except for her absence. In fact, it was the first time Joe had set foot inside her apartment. He stormed out and planned to track her phone once he returned to the office.

Joe returned to World Watch and said, "Jimmy, I need you in my office ASAP!"

Jimmy jumped up quickly.

"Jimmy, close the door. I've called Maria multiple times, but there's been no response. I went to her apartment, but there was no sign of her. I don't know if she decided to leave or not. She had been mentioning something about religious matters lately. It seems like she genuinely believes in it!"

"She mentioned some of the junk to me too, sir."

Joe was visibly upset about what was happening with Maria; she was a great agent, the best, and highly loyal.

"Oh, and Jimmy, this stays in house."

"Yes Sir! Copy that!"

Jimmy, one of his top agents, swiftly obtained Maria's location within ten minutes. Joe Smith, well-connected and resourceful, wasted no time reaching out to a friend in the FBI, requesting assistance retrieving Maria. He promptly shared Maria's location, along with the most recent photograph he possessed of her.

It took three FBI agents to locate the bus in the customs queue. They swiftly approached it, declaring, "This is the FBI! Put your hands up!" After inspecting the photograph, they realized that Maria wasn't among the passengers, but her phone was discovered onboard. One of the agents asked, "Has anyone received a new phone today?"

Maria had wiped her phone clean and handed it to a little girl and her mother boarding a bus bound for Mexico. The girl excitedly held up the phone, but they discovered it had been wholly erased upon inspection. The likelihood of ever reencountering Maria seemed grim, and Joe was well aware of this reality. As one of his most proficient agents, Maria possessed intelligence and a dangerous edge. Joe was confident she wouldn't have fled to Mexico, yet he had already dispatched individuals to investigate her family's residence, which unsurprisingly turned out to be vacant.

Maria was lying in her new bunk, supporting her head with two pillows while her laptop rested in front of her. She was gazing at Joe Smith's face through the laptop's camera. Comparing her laptop to his, they were vastly different. Maria possessed a laptop given to her by her close friend, Loren, who had experienced action in Venezuela. Loren had access to some of the world's finest technology.

She sent Joe a text on his phone.

"Sir, I'm sorry that I had to leave like that."

"Where are you? You need to get back here. These UN guys aren't messing around! I'm going to have to tell them that you're gone!"

Always maintaining her polite demeanor, Maria said, "Sir, you know I can't come back. I felt that I owed you one final gesture before disappearing indefinitely. Both of us understand that I could be anywhere on this planet right now. I might even be at your own residence without your knowledge. I simply wanted to express that my belief in the rapture was indeed correct. Joe, I implore you to accept Jesus Christ as your Savior before it's too late... I beg of you!"

Joe's face turned red with anger, "I'M NOT ACCEPTING ANYONE FOR MY SAVIOR! YOU

GET YOUR BUTT BACK TO THIS OFFICE, OR I WILL MAKE IT MY MISSION IN LIFE

TO FIND YOU, AND YOU WILL SIT IN A VERY SMALL AND COLD JAIL CELL FOR A LONG TIME! YOU HEAR ME!?"

"Good luck on that Joe. I'll be praying for you. Don't go near Lorenzo Calvo, he's the antichrist; don't accept him as your Savior since you don't need one. God bless you Joe and be careful. I'll stay in touch, letting you know how I'm doing; right now, dinner is ready. Bye Joe."

Joe was furious as he stormed out of his office, gripping his phone tightly. He couldn't care less about the presence of the UN agents; his anger consumed him. He shouted in frustration, "Maria Silva has deserted her post! She just sent me a text declaring that she's done! I need to know her location immediately! And all of you, listen up! This is my territory! I don't care who sent you here! I am in charge, this is my domain, understood?"

Even the UN agents took a step back while Joe took back the reins of his office with anger!

One UN personnel took Joe's phone and attempted to trace a location, but their efforts proved unsuccessful. Another agent joined in the search, and soon a circle of agents gathered around Director Smith's cell phone. Despite their efforts, locating Maria seemed impossible. The technology available to them paled compared to what Maria and Alex possessed, along with the capabilities of Haven's advanced computer system.

Joe walked back into his office with his phone, which still had Maria's text messages, slid it onto his desk, and smiled. He knew Maria better than anyone, not in a friend way, but in an agent way. He realized that she was gone. He smiled, "She'll probably text me once a week, and I won't be able to do anything—unbelievable! Even when she betrays me, she's loyal."

All the places on the earth and the chances of World Watch finding Maria Silva in a cave with a house in it would be impossible. They were safe at the Haven, thanks to Jesus.

Maria lay in her bunk, watched a famous soap opera from Mexico, and leaned back to relax finally. She was entirely at peace with her decision. God's peace.

16

NIGHT EVERYONE

"Psalms 91:11

For He shall give His angels charge over you, To keep you in all your ways."

The lights in Haven were set on a timer, automatically dimming according to a schedule. Each morning at six o'clock, the lights would initiate with a click, gradually brightening to mimic the sun's gentle ascent from the east. By eight o'clock in the morning, the lights would be fully illuminated. This specially designed lighting system aimed to replicate the natural sunlight, helping to mitigate any potential issues with depression among the residents who spent much of their time in the underground Haven. Additionally, the provision of vitamin D proved beneficial in this regard.

At seven o'clock in the evening, triggered by another click, the lights began to dim gradually, and by nine, the area was nearly enveloped in darkness. It remained possible for individuals to navigate their way to the kitchen or bathroom, albeit with limited visibility. However, reading or engaging in activities without a small light became challenging in the almost complete darkness. While there were a few scattered LED lights reminiscent of a Christmas tree throughout the Haven, they provided minimal illumination.

The darkness would go for everyone except Alex and Maria, who had the two laptops. There were probably only ten laptops like theirs; no logos were on them. They all drifted off into a deep sleep.

Greg was beaten and out like a light. He thought he was done on the battlefield, having witnessed Will's death in his arms, but the trauma wouldn't go away! Night after night, he was plagued by nightmares. Each time he woke up drenched in sweat, he would pray fervently, asking God to take away these haunting dreams. Sometimes, God answered his prayers, and the nightmares disappeared, but other times, they persisted. It seemed that perhaps God wanted Greg to heal gradually through a process. Only God knew the purpose behind it all. Sometimes, God miraculously heals a broken heart instantly, while other times, He allows us to work through it ourselves.

Greg contemplated talking to Sarah about his nightmares, but then he considered Maria. She had also experienced the horrors of battle, not to the same extent, but enough to empathize with him. Greg knew he needed to find a way to purge these haunting memories; otherwise, how could he effectively lead his people? He understood that he, like everyone else, was not perfect; only Jesus was perfect.

Tim was fast asleep in the top bunk next to Greg. He dreamt of playing basketball in high school when suddenly, the dream shifted to the deer he had shot recently. Although Tim enjoyed hunting, he despised the act of killing. Then his dream took another turn, and he found himself lying on his back with Maria on top of him and a hunting knife pressed against his neck. Dreams are peculiar, and occasionally, God communicates with us through them, but that wasn't the case for Tim or Greg.

In the bunk below Tim's, Lisa dreamed about the Jeep ride she had recently. The wind was in her hair. Her right leg was bent like her sneaker was hanging out the window; she felt so alive! Then she was next to Alex on the couch. She had never dreamed about Alex before. She liked him. In the blink of an eye, she was at her family's house in Brunswick. Her mom was lovingly looking at her. Her dad and sister disappeared in front of her. Then Pastor Frank waved at Lisa before he vanished with a smile. It was a horrible dream. She was looking at the barbecued food but was unable to touch it. Her dad tried to grab her, and he vanished in her arms.

Liz lay on the bottom bunk, immersed in a vivid dream. She found herself within the confines of a church, deep beneath the ground in a dimly lit tunnel. The memory of her fear washed over her, causing her body to tremble like a shivering infant. She struggled to utter a word in her dream as a group of enraged individuals searched for her, their presence known to her friends. There seemed to be no escape, only a desperate need to find a hiding place. Restless, she tossed and turned in her bunk, the intensity of her dream suffocating her, making it difficult even to breathe.

Meanwhile, in Brandon's dream, he found himself preaching passionately on a bustling street, only mercilessly attacked by evil angels. Desperately seeking respite, he stumbled upon a concealed back door at the far end of a mysterious garden within a cavern. To his horror, the moment he opened the door, he was confronted by grotesque creatures lurking within. Despite his desperate attempt to flee, his legs remained paralyzed, refusing to respond to his commands.

Sarah was dreaming about a hospital full of people—the aftermath of the rapture. The hospital was packed with individuals shouting her name, but she could not assist anyone. Her fingers refused to cooperate, and her arms remained immobile. She couldn't offer aid to anyone, not even herself.

Ruth and Elijah were both having horrible nightmares too. They had both worked in the North Tower of the World Trade Center complex in Lower Manhattan. The first terrorist impact was the American Airlines Flight 11 at 8:46 am slammed into the one hundred-and-ten-story building. They were on the fiftieth floor, and in their dreams, they were always running down the stairs holding each other's hands. She shouted, "Elijah, tell me we'll be alright!" He would shout, "Just keep running, Ruth; we gotta get out of here! We'll be okay if we keep running!" It was a horrendous event, not something that one shakes off, even nineteen years later.

Maria's dream involved a heated, fiery argument with Joe, with both yelling back and forth at each other. The altercation escalated, and they fought physically in Joe's office. Suddenly, agents from the UN stormed in and forcibly removed Maria from the office, dragging her to a cramped holding cell. The cell was so tiny that she couldn't even lie down comfortably. Amid her confinement, she began to see the faces of the people she had eliminated, their expressions flashing and smiling at her.

Alex had a dream where all the electronics around him were engulfed in flames, and he felt powerless to extinguish the fire. He pondered how he could safeguard the group in this dangerous situation. Desperate for help, he called out to Jesus, but the fire raced, filling the Haven with thick smoke.

They all woke up at once. Maria yelled, and Liz screamed; others were shaking in fear and sweating profusely.

Then, in an instant, two battle angels materialized before them! Resembling Roman soldiers, they stood at an impressive height of at least nine feet each. Clad in leather sandals that laced up to their knees, their muscular legs emanated strength and power.

Their muscles were coming out of their partially buttoned-up short sleeve white shirts, and they had massive biceps that their loose shirts couldn't cover. They had short beards, and both had brown hair with an old battle helmet.

One spoke deeply while all nine listened, "God has sent us here to give you all something."

He had nine little vials in his colossal hand, each with oil. All nine took one vial of each sweet-smelling oil and jumped out of their beds.

Then the other angel said, "Open them and pour it on your heads."

They all did that. They all felt a surge go through their bodies at the same time! It was a remarkable feeling as non of them had experienced before! God anointed them through these angels! No one feared these angels!

The angels both had a very masculine voice, and one said, "Jesus said to give you this word!

The other angel spoke.

"Jesus said, Peace I leave with you, My peace I give to you; not as the world gives do I give to you. Let not your heart be troubled, neither let it be afraid."

Then the other angel said, "God has sent us here to tell you that there are battle angels watching over you! God will confuse the enemy! Know that God has sent us and others just like us to you to give this message. Your bad dreams have come to a stop in the mighty name of Jesus Christ!"

One of the angels took a few steps toward Pastor Greg and reached under his mattress. There, they discovered a small tear with a key hidden inside. Handing the key to Greg, the angel said, "You will need this key for the back door, Pastor Greg. This Haven is a sanctuary for God's workers to find nourishment and rest. Some of God's servants will be sent back into the world to spread the gospel of the Lord, while others will remain within these sacred walls." Then, the angel turned to Brandon and proclaimed, "Jesus chooses you to preach throughout the earth! Be prepared, for God's servants will seek you out!"

Brandon was speechless, and tears ran down his face. Greg put his arm around Brandon's shoulders.

The other angel said, "God, through His many servants, has prepared this place for all of you. You are among the fortunate few who have been blessed with such safety. As the world's situation worsens, people will seek refuge, seeking solace within God's fortress. Jesus is the foundation of our salvation... May God bless you all."

In a flash, two swords appeared in their right hands and shields in their left hands. The shields were red with a gold cross on them. Then they vanished in less than a blink of an eye!

The lights started with a low click as it was morning. The nine of them were standing in a line, each with a small empty vial in their hands. Lisa said, "Did that just really happen? That was so cool!"

Tim shouted, "That was way better than cool!"

Alex said, "I don't think that there's a word to describe how awesome that was!"

Elijah said, "I had no fear of them, intuitively I knew they were from God. What a life-changing experience!"

Pastor Greg, with a key in his hand, looked at Maria, then at the rest of the other cave dwellers,

"Apparently we have a key! Let's go check out the back-door shall we!"

They hurriedly approached the back door, with Pastor Greg leading the way. They moved with determination and a sense of purpose. Tim and Lisa talked calmly about the remarkable encounter with the two angels. Maria followed closely behind Greg, her expression solemn. In the past five years, she had shed tears only once, and now a solitary tear streamed down her face.

Once they got to the gigantic hardwood door, so big someone could drive a small car through if it was open. Greg took the key, put it in the keyhole, and slowly turned. He pulled the oversized handle, and the door creaked open; the lights clicked on, and what was before they was mind-blowing.

The inside of this new cavern was a half a mile square with a ceiling that was thirty feet tall! The lights were on a timer there, too; they activated them when Pastor Greg opened the door.

To the right were massive piles of lumber, boxes, and boxes of nails and screws.

There were sinks, and pipes, boxes of wires. Looked like a hardware superstore had been put in the Haven.

Tim said, "I don't think they were done yet; they must've planned on building small houses in here or something. I think that the rapture took them by surprise too."

Greg said, *"Matthew 24:36 -But of that day and hour no one knows, not even the angels of heaven, but My Father only."*

A basketball court was there with a hoop at each end. The court wasn't beautiful, but a place to play ball.

Sarah surveyed the hospital equipment, now covered with plastic, and it dawned on her why God had led her to the Haven. Countless bags filled with supplies such as oatmeal, sugar, and flour. Rows upon rows of mattresses, bundled up and encased in plastic, along with pillows and blankets, caught her attention in just a glance. The sheer quantity of plastic containers that needed to be opened and labeled seemed overwhelming. Yet, they contained everything necessary to sustain themselves for seven years in the cave. To the left, ample space could accommodate a small village. As a married couple, Elijah and Ruth required a modest area with enough room for a full-size bed, allowing them a semblance of privacy. As Pastor Greg looked around in astonishment, he exclaimed, "Brandon, your father was a carpenter, correct?"

"Yeah, he was and before you ask me if he taught me anything, yes he did."

Little did Pastor Greg know, but Brandon was a carpenter and a skilled one with a passion for building. Building things together had been a cherished activity between Brandon and his father. Their collaborative efforts resulted in remarkable projects, such as an impressive tree house in Brandon's previous backyard. The tree house wasn't just a simple structure—it was a fully-fledged house nestled within the branches of a tree.

Pastor Greg said, "Let's eat breakfast and have a meeting. I have many coming our way in the next seven years.

17

LORENZO CALVO WAS UP EARLY

"II THESSALONIANS 2

1 Now, brethren, concerning the coming of our Lord Jesus Christ and our gathering together to Him, we ask you, 2 not to be soon shaken in mind or troubled, either by spirit or by word or by letter, as if from us, as though the day of Christ had come. 3 Let no one deceive you by any means; for that Day will not come unless the falling away comes first, and the man of sin is revealed, the son of perdition, 4 who opposes and exalts himself above all that is called God or that is worshiped, so that he sits as God in the temple of God, showing himself that he is God."

With a nasty grin on his face, a manifestation of pure evil rose from his bed. He was fully aware that he held the world within his grasp. The hubris and conceit radiated unmistakably to any discerning believer in Christ, but to the majority of people in the world, he appeared as a charismatic leader. Preparing for interviews on morning shows and various social media platforms, he knew that the world was desperate for anyone to guide them, and he cunningly positioned himself as their savior. The inhabitants of Earth were hungry, having endured weeks of hunger. The sensation of hunger is peculiar; a starving individual would resort to nearly anything for sustenance. Mister Lorenzo Calvo understood this as one of the numerous vulnerabilities he would exploit to gain followers worldwide.

His servants obediently opened the door, granting entry to the reporters who arrived at his colossal mansion. Lorenzo Calvo harbored no semblance of patience for humanity. He despised everything God had created and was repulsed by the notion that humans were made in God's image. Deep within the dungeon-like confines of his residence, Lorenzo Calvo held captive a hundred Christians and Jewish individuals. The area had been meticulously soundproofed, boasting an expansive room with jail cells. Positioned before a gold throne was a chilling setup—a guillotine accompanied by a bucket. Through the aid of demonic soldiers, Lorenzo Calvo orchestrated a sinister ritual: one person at a time would be brought forth for beheading. At the same time, some sang hymns even in their final moments. Certain captives renounced their faith in Christ, accepting the mark of the man of perdition for the illusion of freedom. Yet, the cost they paid was immeasurably high— eternal salvation in Christ forfeited. This gruesome spectacle served as Lorenzo Calvo's twisted form of entertainment. Contrary to what one might assume, he hated the notion of a One World Order. He reveled in lawlessness and detested any form of order.

He spoke calmly, his voice carrying an air of authority. "To the people of the world, I am Lorenzo Calvo. The war between Russia, Turkey, and Iran has ceased, and Israel has refrained from retaliation. The United Nations, in collaboration with me, has devised a plan to provide sustenance for all. Trucks have been dispatched to cities, towns, and suburbs worldwide to distribute food and water. The UN has assumed control and appointed me as the leader during these challenging times. Each truck in your area will have a team present, offering a small tattoo for the back of your right hand if you haven't received one already. This tattoo serves as mandatory identification, known as the Lifeline. It utilizes the finest ink technology, enabling access to medical assistance and free online services, ensuring greater organization. I am here to assist every one of you. Together, we will overcome this dark chapter in history and emerge stronger. Place your trust in me. I represent a distant planet known as Luciferia. My brothers and sisters and I brought humanity to this planet two hundred thousand years ago, and we are profoundly disappointed in your failure to care for the Earth responsibly. We are actively addressing the environmental issues even as I speak. Remember, the only gods that exist are yourselves. I shall guide you. I am your deity, and we are all divine beings. United, we will resolve world hunger and restore our environment to its former glory!"

It was as if almost everyone was in a trance, including the world leaders, while they watched him.

Lorenzo Calvo waved his hand in a big half-circle, and a transparent map appeared.

"This is the map of the world as of now."

He gestured with a wave of his hand once more, asserting, "The one hundred and ninety-five former countries shall now be restructured into ten distinct sections. As you can observe, North America will encompass what was previously Mexico and Canada. Central America will form a unified entity, as will South America and so forth. This division brings ease and logic to our organization, for organization is paramount. Together, we are constructing a new world that shall surpass any prior achievements. Allow me to introduce my esteemed associate, Mr. Higgins. He possesses comprehensive knowledge and can provide you with any necessary information. Thank you."

Then, like the crooked serpent he embodied, the Antichrist slipped away through the back door and went to his dungeon. There, he indulged in breakfast while reveling in the sight of people being mercilessly killed. Timothy Higgins, a figure of sinister nature, stepped forward, his small stature belying his entirely malevolent essence. "Greetings, I am Timothy Higgins, a thoroughly demonic presence, and I shall be assisting Lorenzo Calvo during this period of transition. It feels as though we have initiated a reset, allowing us to commence anew. The construction of the new temple on the temple mount in Jerusalem is already underway. I understand your concerns, but rest assured that your departed loved ones have been transported to the planet of Luciferia.

They are being gently educated to participate in this new world order. They are receiving nourishment and garments, and the connection between our worlds will be established soon. We had to undertake drastic measures to capture the attention of the people on this planet before it was too late."

He took a breath and kept the lye going, "We are here to help this world that has partially been destroyed. We have technology well above yours that can power cars and your houses without greenhouse gasses pouring into the atmosphere. We can give electricity to the cities, towns, and the suburbs and again; it's completely green! The weather is completely out of control, but Lorenzo Calvo will fix that."

Following a brief pause, he continued, "My esteemed companions, life as you have known it has undergone a remarkable transformation for the greater good. All of this progress can be attributed to Lorenzo, as it was his visionary concept. To be completely candid, we had lost hope in you. We, too, are devoted followers of his. His power stands unmatched in the vast expanse of the universe!"

Higgins walked out and entered the same door that Calvo had gone through. The demonic staff showed the media to the exit. There were no shouts from the reporters as they were mesmerized by what they had witnessed.

The cave dwellers were watching this while eating their oatmeal. They finished breakfast, and Pastor Greg stood up to speak to everyone.

"Everyone, we must accept that we have no control over Calvo and his associate. Instead, let us redirect our attention towards our true mission from our Lord, Jesus Christ. We have a pressing task at hand—to tidy up the back room, which is currently a mess. I suggest that Brandon and Dr. Sarah take charge and thoroughly examine the contents left to us. Label the boxes, create a comprehensive inventory, and organize to the best of your abilities. I will also be overseeing the progress, for I am as curious as all of you to uncover what's back there!"

He looked at each one of their faces and said, "The angels that visited us last night, that was something special! We've been anointed by God through them, this should help immensely to get through these hard times! The angel visit reminds me of Joel two twenty-eight, how God would pour out His Spirit in the last days!"

"I can only imagine how many people it must have taken to stockpile supplies in that back cave. Undoubtedly, it was a miraculous feat orchestrated by Jesus Himself! Rest assured, more people will soon find their way to this Haven, guided by the Holy Spirit. These are exhilarating times to be alive! We must remain steadfast in our current endeavors. Tim, I encourage you to continue your hunting expeditions, and why not bring Maria along with you? I trust you are well-versed in the art of hunting, Maria?"

Maria looked at Greg with a confident smile, "Oh yeah, I know how to go hunting!"

"That's perfect you two can get together and bring in more game so we'll have plenty of food to get through this winter, wild turkey sounds really good right now. A moose would fill one of the freezers!"

Tim excitedly said, "I've seen a lot of wild turkey Pastor Greg! I also know that there's a moose that visits the beaver pond quite a bit, but I'd need big-time help to get the meat here!"

Greg commented, "A moose is a huge undertaking, and we'll have to take a day and all do that together."

Greg confidently said, "How about some trout or pike at the lake? I would say it's less than a half a mile away. Now is the time to do this before they have troops looking throughout these mountains!"

Alex said, "The lake is exactly a half mile away Pastor Greg."

"Maybe Tim and Maria can go to the lake one of these days and spend sometime there fishing and bring back as many fish as you can possibly catch."

With her little accent, Maria said, "I know how to make a big fish trap. I learned how to make them as a little girl in Mexico. My grandfather was a fisherman."

"Alex, I need you to be watching over everyone who's outside the Haven at all times, to make sure that they are not surprised by the new military. You said that the UN is at the place that you worked at Maria?"

"Yes, Pastor Greg, we're watching them as they watch the world, so we have a pretty good idea of their actions. I know that they must be looking for me right about now." Maria said with a smile."

Pastor Greg laughed, "By the looks of your face you're not to worry about that?"

"Definitely not!"

Their bond had grown incredibly strong, and it was evident to all observers that they were deeply enamored with one another. Though they attempted to conceal their emotions, their affection for each other shone through with utmost clarity. His voice would transform whenever he engaged in conversation with Maria. However, falling in love amidst the tumultuous times of the great tribulation could present its own challenges.

Pastor Greg proceeded, "I am eagerly anticipating the arrival of those whom God shall send to this place! Lisa, Liz, I must commend you both for your exceptional work in the kitchen. Do not hesitate to seek assistance from others when necessary, whether it be in washing dishes or any other tasks you require aid with. In truth, it is a responsibility that should be shared among us all. And Elijah and Ruth, I am excited to see your gardening skills in action."

Elijah said, "Wait until you see that garden room a month from now! We've got everything we need to make it flourish pastor!"

"Now that we can get into cavern in the back, it's humongous! Brandon the Davis's need a little bungalow, a small place to have some privacy. You think you can build them something?"

"I can make a nice little place. There's so much space and lumber back there that I could make a small city of one room cottages."

"I'll be helping you and Sarah—let us pray."

They all held each other's hands as the pastor led them in prayer,

"Father, I humbly express my gratitude to You for bringing us together in this sacred gathering place, a refuge crafted by Your divine hand. I beseech You, Lord, to continuously safeguard us, keeping us secure from all harm. Fill us abundantly with Your Holy Spirit, providing us strength and guidance during these tumultuous times. In the mighty name of Jesus, I rebuke any forces of darkness that may seek to assail us. Lord, grant us the gift of invisibility to the spirit of the Antichrist. In the holiness of Jesus' name, we offer our prayers, and may all present say, 'Amen.'"

"Amen."

18

SIX MONTHS LATER

Revelation 5

8 Now when He had taken the scroll, the four living creatures and the twenty-four elders fell down before the Lamb, each having a harp, and golden bowls full of incense, which are the prayers of the saints. 9 And they sang a new song, saying: *"You are worthy to take the scroll, And to open its seals; For You were slain, And have redeemed us to God by Your blood Out of every tribe and tongue and people and nation,*

10 And have made us kings and priests to our God;

And we shall reign on the earth."

Then I looked, and I heard the voice of many angels around the throne, the living creatures, and the elders; and the number of them was ten thousand times ten thousand, and thousands of thousands, 12 saying with a loud voice:

"Worthy is the Lamb who was slain

To receive power and riches and wisdom,

And strength and honor and glory and blessing!"

13 *And every creature which is in heaven and on the earth and under the earth and such as are in the sea, and all that are in them, I heard saying:*

"Blessing and honor and glory and power

Be to Him who sits on the throne,

And to the Lamb, forever and ever!"

It was January, and the cave dwellers didn't know it, but incredible things were happening in the heavenly realm. Jesus was opening the seals, and the tribulation was worsening. Every time Jesus opened a different scroll, more horrible things would happen to the world and the people who lived in it.

As was their routine for the past six months, the crew gathered around, watching the numerous screens while enjoying their breakfast. Suddenly, Alex leaped to his feet, exclaiming, "Everyone, take a look at monitor nine! There's an enormous space storm that seemingly materialized out of nowhere! Those meteors hurling through space at a staggering speed of forty-four miles per second, and some appear to be quite sizable!"

Then Alex quickly did the math and exclaimed, "That's approximately 158,400.0000051 miles per hour! Meteorites will rain down from the sky horizontally all around the globe! Picture a hailstorm preceding a tornado, but instead of icy pellets, it's fiery rocks bombarding cars, trucks, houses, buildings, and even people! Nothing can halt a blazing rock at that velocity—it would penetrate a skyscraper without hesitation!"

That's what was headed toward the Earth! The crucial question was whether the cave dwellers would be safe in the Haven. Another concern arose regarding the satellites encircling the Earth. Would the meteorites obliterate all of them? If that were to happen, the team would lose the ability to monitor global events. World Watch would also be unable to keep a vigilant eye on the world!

The first meteor storm struck California, decimating a significant portion of the city! Soon after, Las Vegas also faced the impact! The Middle East was not spared either, as these blazing rocks at three thousand degrees pummeled the region. The devastation in Sydney, Australia, was unimaginable and far surpassed anything depicted in movies; the scene was horrific! The wrath of God was being unleashed upon the Earth in an unprecedented manner. As the meteorites relentlessly pummeled the mountains, the ground shook, and dust filled the air, causing great fear and terror among the people in the Haven.

Greg yelled, "Everybody, take each other's hands and let's start praying on our knees! I don't believe that God has put us in this place to be killed by rocks!"

Liz said, "I'm scared Pastor Greg!"

The storm only lasted a few minutes in the mountains, and it didn't damage the Haven other than a little bit of dirt and dust on the floor, which they could sweep up.

God was protecting them; it was apparent. A lot of the world was not so blessed! Millions of people have lost their lives in less than ten minutes. The people in the cave started singing Amazing Grace after the falling rocks stopped.

It was a close call, but they knew they had to persevere if they would survive through all of this. Maria and Tim had filled all the freezers with various types of meat, fish, turkey, and even partridge. They even found some mushrooms that the Davis family used to cultivate. Alex and Lisa diligently monitored the world, searching for outspoken Christians amidst the chaos. Half of the 4,550 satellites in orbit were destroyed, which wasn't as catastrophic as it could have been.

On the other hand, Ruth and Elijah had their own cozy bungalow in the back cavern, skillfully crafted by Brandon. It featured a comfortable double bed and a window at the front. It was a rectangular space with enough room for a couple of chairs near the bed and a small table. The couple was overjoyed to have a semblance of privacy. After being married for a long time, privacy had become an invaluable luxury for them. Ruth had brought along some pictures from their past life, which she proudly displayed on the wall.

She also had some flowers in a cup on the table.

19

THE GARDEN

Isaiah 61:11

"For as the earth brings forth its bud, As the garden causes the things that are sown in it to spring forth, So the Lord GOD will cause righteousness and praise to spring forth before all the nations."

The garden was flourishing beyond expectations! Rows upon rows of vibrant vegetables stretched out, showcasing a variety of cucumbers, tomatoes, peppers, eggplants, string beans, green peas, corn on the cob, beets, and black beans—to name a few. It was a true feast for the eyes. The soft sunlight casts a serene glow over the lush vegetation and blooming flowers. Brandon's craftsmanship extended to the garden, as he had thoughtfully crafted benches for people to sit and admire the beauty around them.

Ruth's touch added a touch of elegance to the garden. She skillfully intertwined the vegetables and flowers, creating a harmonious blend. The air was filled with the delightful scents of begonias, carnations, dahlias, gerbera daisies, pansies, tulips, geraniums, and even lady slippers, a flower deemed illegal to pick. Still, given the circumstances, no one paid it much mind. The aroma that enveloped the garden was simply intoxicating.

Each day, the dedicated group of nine cave dwellers diligently harvested baskets of fresh vegetables and transported them to the kitchen. Tomatoes were carefully canned for future use, while cucumbers, green beans, and beans were lovingly pickled. Thanks to the collective effort and coordination, the Haven was running like a well-oiled machine. They had honed their skills and were fully prepared to welcome more people into their sanctuary.

Lisa and Liz sat on the bench looking at the thriving garden, "Have you checked out the hummingbird drone thingy that Alex and Maria have been messing around with in the back cavern, Lisa?"

"I have, and it's awesome! Did you see the image that camera gives on the monitor!"

"I did, and wow! If the satellites were to ever go out, we have a hummingbird to watch over the place!"

"That's too funny! We have a hummingbird to watch over us! Did you ever think you'd say that?"

"Lisa, there's a lot of things that I never thought I'd say since the rapture!"

"Let's go visit Ruth and Elijah at their little cottages—shall we."

"We shall."

They both got up simultaneously, laughing, and headed towards Davis's abode. They had painted the house white with green trim after Tim and Greg finished it. Ruth even had a flower box underneath the window with pansies, and their little one-room cottage was adorable. Liz and Lisa looked around the massive cavern. Dr. Sarah and Brandon had organized everything and labeled all the boxes. It was quite a fantastic sight considering they were in a cave. Brandon had started another cottage. He had built an emergency room, so if anyone ever got injured or sick, Sarah could easily take care of them. Sarah also had all the medication that anyone would need in case of an emergency, especially antibiotics. The emergency room was walled in, and a big doorway above it logically said, "Emergency Room."

At least once a day, everyone would gather to play basketball and do physical exercise together. They would run circles around the basketball court to stay in shape. Occasionally, they would switch it up and play soccer, a sport at which Greg excelled. Thanks to his hunting and regular exercise, Tim was growing stronger and could now compete with Greg in daily sports activities. In the far back right corner of the cave were weight benches, free weights, and everything necessary to maintain strength and fitness. They understood the importance of staying in shape because they never knew what challenges might arise. Tim's dirt bike was also gleaming and fully fueled, ready for any need that might come upon them.

Liz yelled, "How are you guys doing this morning?"

"We're doing great dear, how are you two?"

Lisa said, "I can't believe how beautiful the garden is, it reminds me of the Garden of Eden. I just hope that there's no tree of knowledge in the middle!"

Elijah responded with a loud laugh that echoed throughout the cavern, "I definitely know there's no tree of knowledge in the middle of that Garden. My knowledge is limited at best!"

Ruth invited them into their tiny house inside a cave, "You guys have a seat; isn't this place just perfect?"

Lisa said, "I would love a seat. Brandon is definitely quite the handyman!"

Liz said, "This little place is incredible, Brandon did such an awesome job!"

A little wooden shelf on the back wall of the small cottage had cucumbers and tomatoes in a basket.

Ruth said, "Would you guys like it if I cut up some tomatoes and cucumbers with a little bit of salt and vinegar? They're nice and fresh!"

Elijah looked out the window, looked back at the ladies, and said, "Fresh? I picked them this morning!"

He looked out and took a deep breath before saying, "Only God could have prepared such a place for us! Amidst all the suffering happening in the world, we are truly blessed to be here. While I can't say how long we will be able to stay, one thing I am certain of is that God is watching over us. We serve an incredible and awe-inspiring God. Why exactly God chose us, we may never fully understand."

"Well dear, I guess we'll just have to wait until the end to find out."

Elijah said, "Yes, we'll meet Jesus one way or another."

Lisa said, "I hope so cause' I need a Jesus hug."

"Dear, I need a Jesus hug too."

"After all these years of marriage, I still can't do a Jesus hug."

Lisa said, "Do you know that a hummingbird can keep us safe?"

Liz laughed, "I bet you'd never think you'd hear that before, did yah?"

"Oh, dear, after we met Lisa we knew that anything was possible."

They all laughed and knew about the drone. There weren't many secrets in the Haven. Meanwhile, Maria and Greg were walking to the shed to work on the way to shoot tranquilizer darts out of two rifles that they had. Greg said, "Thou shalt not kill, but."

And Maria finished his sentence, "Thou can put people to sleep."

They were getting along very well. They were getting along more than well; they were in love!

They both thought the same way because of their military backgrounds, and he was half Brazilian and spoke Portuguese and Spanish. He had a thick Brazilian accent when he spoke to her in Spanish.

He said, "I want you to close your eyes."

"I'm really bad at these games."

"I have a surprise, but only if you close your eyes!"

"Oh Greg, really?"

"Yes really."

He opened the door, and on the back wall, he wrote with different flowers and a staple gun, "I LOVE YOU, MARIA!"

"You know that I'm in love with you too you big goof!"

Greg looked at Maria and said softly and flirty, "I knew that you feel the same way about me. I can see it in your eyes. You forget, I was trained to read body language in special forces."

In a mildly flirty way, Maria Silva said, "Oh yeah, well, what's my body saying right now—Pastor Greg?"

"It's saying, 'Where has this gorgeous man been all my life', right?"

"Maybe it's saying that... a little."

"A lot!"

They both laughed, and Greg got on his knee and looked deep into her big brown eyes, "I've been praying about this so much! I don't know how to say this? I love you so much! I love your laugh! I love your smile! Maria Silva, will you marry me?"

Tears ran down her face as she said, "Yes, I absolutely will!"

It just so happened that Liz and Lisa were watching the whole thing. They were returning from the Davis's, and both yelled in unison, "Pastor Greg and Maria!"

They were unaware of being watched, and Greg wasted no time sharing his idea, "Ladies, I have a plan. I will ordain Elijah as a pastor so he can officiate our wedding. This means we'll need a special bungalow in the back, near Ruth and Elijah's place. I'll talk to Brandon about it as soon as possible!"

Lisa said, "An exceptional bungalow! Wow!

Maria's face was red; both she and Greg laughed!

Lisa looked at Liz and said something to each other like the other two weren't even there, "I had a feeling that those two are falling in love, did you see the way they've been looking at each other?"

"I saw that the two were really close, but I didn't realize that they were that close!"

Greg said, "We are close, but we're not that close so you two relax! We're going to get married like the tribulation is not even happening; because I love her!"

Lisa jumped in the air and shouted, "Can I tell the others?"

Greg looked at Maria to ensure it was okay; she gave him the okay nod, and Pastor Greg said, "Sure, tell the others!"

The two hurried into the cave house to inform everyone about the news. Ruth and Elijah approached the affectionate couple, and with his gentle and calming voice, Elijah spoke, "So, I'm going to be a pastor?" He embraced Greg and Maria tightly, while Ruth joined in the hug and remarked, "Pastor Elijah, that has a nice ring to it, doesn't it, honey?"

Greg said, "You deserve it, brother! You've been studying the Bible so much! I am so proud of you and happy to have you marry Marie and me. Then Greg smiled and jokingly said,

"That's if you want the position or not, I can go grab Timmy, I'm sure he'd take it."

The four of them laughed, not at Tim becoming a pastor, for indeed, he had grown enough in the word of God to become an ordained pastor. The idea was to get married during the great tribulation with the nine of them in a cave.

Then Elijah spoke earnestly, "We have all witnessed the growth of our faith, but let me tell you about Brandon. That young man, I believe he has the entire Bible memorized. You don't see him like Ruth and I do. He constructs things over there, like Dr. Sarah's emergency room, while reciting the Word of God. He always keeps his Bible close by. I have never witnessed someone recite the book of Isaiah from beginning to end without looking. It's truly supernatural, Pastor Greg—straight from God!"

"I've heard him say the whole book of revelation too. Did he get something special from those two angels that we didn't?

Elijah happily smiled as he lightly patted Greg's back and said, "I wish I got a little of his oil from the angels!"

"Me too brother, me too... but I'm happy for him, and you, all of you!"

That night, a blizzard struck the mountain and northern Maine, covering the area with over sixteen feet of snow. The cave was surrounded by snow, making it impossible to open the front door without risking it collapsing into the hallway. The roads around the mountain were also buried under snow, leaving no means of travel. The dwellers knew they had to clear a path and shovel their way out before the snow turned to ice, trapping them inside. However, given the state of the world, their focus was primarily on survival rather than plowing roads. People were trying to endure and make it through the winter. There was very little travel happening, especially in New England. Being confined to such a small space, they began to feel the walls closing in on them. They relied on the Comforter to guide them through until spring. While they had enough food rations to sustain themselves, they longed for the freedom of the outdoors.

20

EARTHQUAKES AND VOLCANOS

Luke 21:11

11 And there will be great earthquakes in various places, and famines and pestilences; and there will be fearful sights and great signs from heaven.

It was morning in the Haven; they were all sitting on the couches and recliner, having breakfast which had become a daily ritual. They were joking around, talking about how they needed a big table. When they least expected it, the mountain began to tremble! The entire world was contorting and convulsing.

Volcanoes exploded worldwide, spewing lava and toxic gases into the atmosphere. The earthquakes were ripping old buildings down, it was a catastrophic event, and the inhabitants of Earth were all feeling the effects.

Greg screamed, "EVERYBODY GO TO THE HALL!

Liz screamed while they were running, "I'M SCARED, PASTOR GREG!

Sarah yelled back, "WE ALL ARE!"

Brandon fell on the floor, and Elijah grabbed his rough hand and pulled him up to his feet; they both ran towards the big wooden front door! Brandon was praying while the two were running.

The dishes drying next to the sink were falling onto the floor. The refrigerators were rocking back and forth, the cabinet doors flinging open and shut, and pots and pans were clanging together, shooting across the room. Even the blankets were falling. The entire room seemed to come alive, resembling a ship caught in a violent storm on the verge of sinking. The noise of the Earth's movements rumbled beneath their feet, blending with the booming sounds echoing through the cavern.

Tim ripped open that door, and everyone jumped in; Elijah shut it! The problem was that they were snowed in, so there was no way that they could open the boulder. If they opened it, all they would see was a wall of snow, and there was a chance that the snow would fall in on them!

Greg said, "We should've shoveled this out!"

The mountain still shook! They only had a 4.3 magnitude earthquake; the rest of the world had 6.5 magnitude and up. The number of people that were perishing was uncountable! The great tribulation was starting to accelerate like a woman in labor, her contractions getting closer and closer. Jesus Christ was opening the seals in the heavenly realm, the King of kings and Lord of lords!

Jesus is not a baby in a manger anymore! He's seen enough sin and violence and heard enough blasphemy!

Then Elijah yelled out loud, "1The Lord is my shepherd; I shall not want. 2 He maketh me to lie down in green pastures: he leadeth me beside the still waters. 3 He restoreth my soul: he leadeth me in the paths of righteousness for his name's sake. 4 Yea, though I walk through the valley of the shadow of death, I will fear no evil: for thou art with me; thy rod and thy staff they comfort me. 5 Thou preparest a table before me in the presence of mine enemies: thou anointest my head with oil; my cup runneth over. 6 Surely goodness and mercy shall follow me all the days of my life: and I will dwell in the house of the Lord for ever."

Liz said, "I needed to hear that right now."

Finally, the earthquake subsided. The cave dwellers cautiously opened the large door and stepped back into the house area of the cave. They were greeted by dust, broken dishes, and scattered blankets and pillows on the floor. The sofas had shifted from their original positions and sprawled across the Haven's deck. As they ventured into the garden area of the cavern, they found that nothing had been disturbed there. The garden remained stunning, just as it was every day, except for a few larger tomatoes that had fallen onto the soil.

They continued and went into the third part of the cavern, and a couple of small rocks had fallen from the ceiling onto the basketball court, but nothing too serious. It could've been so much worse.

Elijah said, "There's no doubt that God is keeping us safe."

Greg said, "I guess it's time to clean up this place and resume our lives. Why don't all of you sweep everything off, wash the bedding in the washing machines, and if you come across anything damaged, fix it. Tim and I will grab some shovels and dig our way out of this place. Did you say there's sixteen feet of snow out there?"

Alex said, "It all depends on the wind, there might not be that much, or there could be more, honestly I don't know what's on the other side of that boulder."

Greg and Tim made their way to the hallway with two shovels; they pulled open the massive boulder. In front of them was a giant wall of snow shaped like a big rock. Both of them looked at the amount of snow and were trying to figure out where they would put it.

Tim said, "I bet you if we got the wheelbarrows, we could wheel this and dump it down into the waterfall. It's going to take a while but at least it will work, not unless you have any other ideas, pastor?"

"Actually, that's a great idea Tim. It's going turn into ice as soon as things start to melt and freeze again. We need to do this. No procrastinating next time. This is only way in and out."

"There's definitely no back-doors."

"Nope, no emergency exits."

"I wonder where the water goes pastor?"

"What from the waterfall? We don't even know where it comes from."

"A complete enigma."

"Tim that's a perfect word to describe that waterfall—enigma."

They grabbed the wheelbarrows and spent hours shuttling back and forth from the doorway to the waterfall, dumping the snow into the hole where the water flowed, and watching it disappear. It was a tedious task, and they were exhausted by the end. The amount of snow they moved was unimaginable! They cleared an area in front of the boulder, knowing that no one was around for miles and miles. Essentially, they created a small yard surrounded by pine trees, providing security and cover.

That was the first time they had seen the outside world in weeks! They stepped out of the cave, with the other dwellers following closely behind. Elijah exclaimed, "It's so beautiful out here! Look at the sunshine. It's a good thing you've done!"

Sarah said, "We could've have been stuck here until April!"

Liz said, "May!"

Lisa said, "Forever!"

Tim looked at his sister and said, "We could've been stuck forever? Summer is coming someday."

"I'm talking about the earthquake. You really need to keep up."

"Keep up! What are you talking about?!"

Greg said, "Children, please chill."

Then another tremor hit, and the cave dwellers tightly held on to each other. Tim instinctively grabbed hold of his sister, realizing the importance of staying together in such moments. It was a terrifying experience when the Earth moved beneath their feet, leaving them feeling completely out of control. However, the team understood they needed to rely entirely on God, for no human power could save them. Jesus was their only hope, and they acknowledged this truth constantly within the cave. As they stood there, gazing at the rugged Maine mountainscape, they were reminded that God had created all of it—the heavens and the Earth. They returned to the safety of the Haven, taking their seats and fixing their eyes on the monitors that displayed the destruction unfolding in the world. Maria rested her head on Greg's shoulder, sighing, while Lisa, seated next to Alex, did the same.

Greg quietly said, "Brandon, how long do you think it would take to build a cottage next to Ruth and Elijah's place if I helped you?"

"Oh, with the two of us; probably three days, maybe less."

Greg looked at Maria, then at the group, and said, "Today is Monday, so probably Thursday it would be completely done. How about we have a wedding on Saturday?"

Maria hugged Greg, and Lisa and Liz jumped up in the air; both yelled out loud, "Yes!"

Sarah said, "We'll need some tables and chairs."

Brandon replied, "There's a ton of white plastic chairs in the very far back wall."

Ruth added, "I was wondering why those chairs are stacked together. Maybe the basketball court could be a church. Pastor Greg needs a pulpit."

Elijah let out a knowing laugh, "God is omnipotent, all knowing, what a detailed God we serve!"

Ruth said, "I have so many flowers in the garden!"

Maria jumped up and said, "I have to text Joe!"

Ruth said, "Who's Joe dear?"

Alex said, "He's her old boss, she's driving him batty!"

Lisa said, "Why?"

Liz said, "That's not nice."

Greg needed to explain, "Joe is the director of World Watch. She believes that if she engages his attention, he will be less focused on hunting down Christians who have no place to hide."

Alex said, "She's getting very good at bugging him. He's been marked, there's no hope. He's so evil now, at least that's what Maria said."

Elijah said, "All these people want this tattoo on themselves with this Lifeline mark to hell... unbelievable."

Lisa said, "I hope she doesn't invite him to the wedding."

21

WORLD WATCH WAS A MESS

2 Timothy 3:1-
Ever learning, and never able to come to the knowledge of the truth."
World Watch was in complete disarray, with computers strewn across the floor, most of the ceiling collapsed, LED lights shattered, windows broken, and all the electronics ruined! It would take at least two weeks to clean up and restore the operation to its previous working state. The earthquake registered at 6.5 on the Richter scale. The only salvaged items were the desks and chairs. They had large plastic trash barrels in which they collected the damaged electronics before disposing them in a trash compactor. *1 This know also, that in the last days perilous times shall come.*

2 For men shall be lovers of their selves, covetous, boasters, proud, blasphemers, disobedient to parents, unthankful, unholy,

3 Without natural affection, trucebreakers, false accusers, incontinent, fierce, despisers of those that are good,

4 Traitors, heady, high-minded, lovers of pleasures more than lovers of God;

5 Having a form of godliness, but denying the power thereof: from such turn away.

6 For of this sort are they which creep into houses, and lead captive silly women laden with sins, led away with divers lusts,

They had already removed all their information and stored it properly, anticipating the arrival of new electronics. While it was good news that they would be receiving new technology, the downside was that it would take at least two weeks to resume watching the world through World Watch. Currently, World Watch is out of commission.

It wasn't just the earthquakes, but the famine around the world was never this bad before; not in the history of mankind had there ever been this kind of starvation! The Global Elite was eating just fine; it was the little people who didn't have much, to begin with, that nothing, starving to death! The middle-class population was a thing of the past. The worldwide communist regime was being run by the evillest man ever! It didn't work out like the far-left Marxists thought it would. If only Karl Marx knew what his theory would usher in, he might have rethought his ideas. The problem with Marxism is the corrupt nature of man. It was a perfect avenue to lead in the man of perdition.

With the frequent earthquakes, the infrastructure suffered significant damage, rendering many roads impassable. Bridges worldwide had collapsed, including iconic ones like the Golden Gate Bridge, now resting at the bottom of the ocean. The transportation of essential supplies such as food and fuel became exceedingly challenging, if not impossible. The railway system was in ruins, compounding the crisis. As a result, not only were people facing the dire prospect of starvation, but they were also enduring the extreme cold in their homes and apartments. The number of families living on the streets was staggering, leading to the proliferation of tent cities as people sought to survive day by day in any way possible. The situation was far worse than anything experienced before the rapture, making comparisons obsolete.

People were freezing to death while they slept at night.

The Antichrist, the notorious Lorenzo Calvo, and his accomplice, the sinister Timothy Higgins, reveled in their malicious pursuits. They surpassed the likes of Adolf Hitler and Joseph Stalin in their cruelty and spite. The suffering and demise of humanity brought them immense pleasure. Currently residing in Italy, they eagerly awaited the day they would establish their presence in the new temple in Jerusalem. There, Calvo envisioned himself seated upon a great golden throne, brazenly blaspheming the name of God. As the evening descended, they indulged in a feast of the finest cuisine and the most exquisite alcohol known to man. Amidst their repulsive revelry, they would raise their glasses and toast to the abhorrent concepts of starvation and death, relishing in the prospect of agonizing and protracted suffering.

Not only had the majority of the population succumbed to receiving the mark on their right hands, a process made accessible due to their prior experience with a pandemic, but they had also undergone conditioning through various measures. Regular temperature checks on their foreheads or the back of their hands had become routine before gaining access to any location. Their compliance had been primed, and they were willing to follow any orders obediently. Through the mark, they had all become interconnected with the AI system. The Antichrist, lacking the omnipotence of God, relied on technology to surveil the populace. This unholy form of transhumanism represented a dark and dangerous path. Though the ancient dragon could never attain true omnipotence, connecting everyone to the advanced AI system gave him a considerable advantage in monitoring their whereabouts and thoughts. After receiving the mark of the beast, individuals became vessels for demonic spirits, the opposite of the Holy Spirit. Concern for loved ones and their whereabouts faded as they became enslaved to the central mainframe, listening to the deceitful voice of the greatest liar in the universe and complying with his desires. The world had reached new depths of hatred toward Christians and Jews, surpassing any previous manifestation of hatred.

Many volcanoes spew toxic gases into the atmosphere that land in the ocean and the freshwater ponds and lakes, turning them blood red. The fish were dying and a staggering rate. In Northern Maine, because of the way the jet stream was going across the United States, it wasn't bothering the group and the area around them. The lakes, ponds, and streams were still clean for fishing in the spring. It was God protecting these people for some reason, but why them? Director Joe Smith was beside himself, enraged at the situation at World Watch. Maria texted him, "Hi Joe, did you guys make it through the earthquake okay? I just wanted you to know that I'm doing fine and getting married!"

She was looking at his face through the camera on his phone. Maria was on her laptop.

She was battling her fleshly desires of revenge and the constraints of God's law. Director Smith had reprimanded her countless times, which started taking a toll on her. It reminded her of the biblical story of Paul grappling with the temptations of the flesh and the demands of the law. A few nights ago, Maria read about it in her bunk and contemplated the sins Paul was struggling against. She had delved into the passage because she longed to kiss Greg passionately, but she understood the potential consequences. She was determined to save their first kiss for their wedding day.

"Romans 7

13 Has then what is good become death to me? Certainly not! But sin, that it might appear sin was producing death in me through what is good, so that sin through the commandment might become exceedingly sinful. 14 For we know that the law is spiritual, but I am carnal, sold under sin. 15 For what I am doing, I do not understand. For what I will do, that I do not practice; but what I hate, that I do. 16 If, then, I do what I will not do, I agree with the law that it is good. 17 But now, it is no longer I who do it, but sin that dwells in me. 18 For I know that in me (that is, in my flesh) nothing good dwells; for to will is present with me, but how to perform what is good I do not find. 19 For the good that I will to do, I do not do; but the evil I will not to do, that I practice. 20 Now if I do what I will not do, it is no longer I who do it, but sin that dwells in me.

21 I find then a law, that evil is present with me, the one who wills to do good. 22 For I delight in the law of God according to the inward man. 23 But I see another law in my members, warring against the law of my mind, and bringing me into captivity to the law of sin which is in my members. 24 O wretched man that I am! Who will deliver me from this body of death? 25 I thank God—through Jesus Christ our Lord!"

Joe screamed as his fingertips texted back,

"I DON'T KNOW WHERE YOU'RE HIDING BUT I WILL GET YOU!"

"Oh, Joe, you really need to stop drinking so much coffee and relax."

Then Joe started swearing at her, completely unhinged, almost punching his thumbs through the phone.

She was trying to be composed, but she was getting angry. She texted, "You really should be nicer to me. You need to cool down!"

Then Maria typed quickly on her keyboard! The fire alarm went off, and the water sprinkler system spewed water all over the already demolished office!

She observed Director Smith's angry outburst, witnessing him scream and hurl his phone against the wall, causing the feed on the device to cease abruptly! The phone shattered into countless fragments. Overwhelmed with guilt, she turned to God and uttered, "I deeply apologize, Lord. Please forgive me in the name of Jesus."

She heard Jesus say, "You are saving your brothers and sisters, don't stop."

Joe found another cell phone in his desk drawer and turned it on to see another text from Maria. It read, "I'm deeply sorry for my actions, Joe. That was not the Christian thing to do... God bless you."

Despite being soaking wet, Joe couldn't help but smile. He recognized her loyalty and acknowledged her intelligence. She was once undoubtedly his best agent, and that meant a lot.

2 2

KNOCK KNOCK

REVELATION 14

"1Then I looked, and behold, a Lamb standing on Mount Zion, and with Him one hundred and forty-four thousand, having His Father's name written on their foreheads. 2And I heard a voice from heaven, like the voice of many waters, and like the voice of loud thunder. And I heard the sound of harpists playing their harps. 3They sang as it were a new song before the throne, before the four living creatures, and the elders; and no one could learn that song except the hundred and forty-four thousand who were redeemed from the earth. 4These are the ones who were not defiled with women, for they are virgins. These are the ones who follow the Lamb wherever He goes. These were redeemed from among men, being first fruits to God and to the Lamb. 5And in their mouth was found no deceit, for they are without fault before the throne of God."

The cave dwellers were on the couch the next day when someone knocked on the door. Greg and

Marie both went and grabbed weapons and pointed the guns at the door. Pastor Greg looked at Alex and mouthed, "What is going on?!

Alex mouthed back, "I don't know!"

Greg approached the door as a knock echoed through the cave again. Greg finally said, "Who are you and what do you want!"

A voice on the other side of the door said, "My name is Isaiah. We are like you: Christians."

"The Lord has sent us here; we pose no threat. I understand that it's difficult to trust anyone in these times, but if you open the door, you will witness the truth. We have received an invitation to the wedding! Oh, and by the way, congratulations to Maria and Pastor Greg. I kindly request that you lower your weapons, for 'thou shalt not kill'—remember?"

Greg looked at Alex and said, "How did we not see this person on the monitors?

"I don't know, and it's these people, more than one! I was watching the whole time and I didn't see anybody coming!"

"So, we have no idea how many people there are on the other side of the door?

Alex looked at Greg, shrugged his shoulders, and said, "Yeah, pretty much!"

Maria yelled to Greg, "Just open the door I got this if things go wrong!" Maria had a gun pointed at the door! "It might be World Watch; Director Smith is trying to find me!"

Greg said, "Thou shalt not kill, sounds familiar."

"It's the sixth commandment, Greg! Everyone knows that!"

A voice came from the other side, "We are not from World Watch, we're your bothers and sisters of our beloved Jesus Christ."

Upon hearing the proclamation that they hailed from our beloved Jesus Christ, Greg recognized that individuals marked as followers of the antichrist would never utter such words. With this realization, he swung the door wide open. Subsequently, thirteen figures clothed in heavy attire, covered in snow, entered the room one by one. They surveyed their surroundings within the cave-dwelling, nodding in approval. Isaiah remarked, "This appears to be the right place, precisely what our Lord and Savior would do, keeping some tribulation saints safe! Jesus is so wonderful!"

Brother Isaiah addressed the cave's inhabitants confidently and humbly, stating, "We represent only a fraction of the 144,000 mentioned in the Book of Revelation, Chapter forteen. We have come to leave behind two individuals and retrieve one. Pastor Greg, you have one of our members among you. Could you kindly inform us which one is Brandon?"

Brandon took a step forward and exclaimed, "I am Brandon. Oh, it's me... I'm part of the 144,000!?" Overwhelmed with emotion, Brandon dropped to his knees, tears streaming down his face as everything suddenly made sense. He expressed his feelings in a language understood only by the 144,000 and God. Isaiah approached him, placing a hand on his head. A mark materialized on Brandon's forehead, displaying the inscription, "YHWH."

Together with the other eleven, they raised their voices in a new song of praise to Jesus. Brandon began to radiate with a brilliance reminiscent of Moses descending from the mountain. In a blink of an eye, the twelve found themselves standing before the very throne of God, harmonizing the celestial melody. Time had ceased and resumed without the gang even realizing they had departed. Isaiah said, "God has informed us that the wedding will take place on Saturday. If it suits you, Pastor Greg, we will depart on Monday. I must admit, this cave is truly remarkable. We ought to take some time to rest, for even God's workers require moments of reprieve. This place is perfect!"

Tim said, "This is nothing, you should see the garden part of this cavern and then after that we have a basketball court!"

Lisa said, "It's so great to see new people, welcome to The Haven! Wow, part of the 144,000, here in a cave, with us, who'd thought that would happen?"

Then Greg and Maria and all the rest of them walked towards the people and shook hands and met each other, giving hugs to the cold people. Greg asked Isaiah while shedding their winter clothing, "How did you guys even get here?"

Isaiah responded with a smile, "We actually came by snowmobile. There's only eleven of us that are from the 144,000, these two behind us are just like you guys, you have a mission, it's just different than ours.

Their names are Jamie and David. Like I said Brandon on the other hand is of the 144,000."

Liz spoke up and asked the question that all the other cave dwellers wanted to ask, "We studied Revelation fourteen, and I thought that the 144,000 were Jewish people

Brandon then said, "I am Jewish."

Alex explained, "Yeah, it's like 10 to 12% of Jewish people have darker skin."

Isaiah requested Greg to accompany him for a conversation and a tour. As they embarked on this endeavor, Greg noticed that all the members of the 144,000 had removed their hats, revealing the divine mark on each of their foreheads, bestowed by God.

Isaiah said, "Oh Pastor Greg before I forget I have something for you. God told me to bring it, it's a Cavaquinho straight from Brazil!"

Lisa said, "It looks like a ukulele?"

Pastor Greg looked at the Cavaquinho with a smile, then at Lisa, and said, "It's kind of like Brazil's version of a ukulele, but it sounds a little different; it's definitely smaller and yes I do know how to play!"

Greg proceeded to strum the small guitar-like instrument. Despite it being slightly out of tune, the sound was delightful. He had acquired his skills as a child in Brazil and continued playing during his time in the armed forces. Greg always kept one attached to his duffel bag or backpack. However, he had ceased playing it due to the painful memories it evoked—thoughts of battles and the loss of people, especially when Will died in Greg's arms. Nevertheless, with God's healing through the angel visit and his anointment, Greg felt prepared to use his musical talent to praise and worship the Lord.

Isaiah loudly said, "David plays a little bit of guitar and we have some tambourines and a few other things! Maybe you guys can have a praise and worship band!"

Greg and Isaiah started slowly walking.

"So, Pastor Greg let me tell you about the two people that will be staying with you guys. The first is named David Wessel. He was a commercial fisherman and lobsterman for a long time. He's 40 years old, a strong guy, and like most commercial fishermen, is a jack of all trades and a master of none. I understand that Brandon is quite the carpenter. I believe that David will fit that missing piece. Dave will be quite handy to have around. If anything breaks, I'm sure he can fix it and he definitely has carpenter skills."

Dave stood at approximately 6'1", weighing around 200 pounds, possessing dark hair, a captivating smile, and an inherently easygoing nature. He was known for his laid-back disposition even before his conversion to Christianity. With his ability to dismantle and reassemble motors within a single day, he would undoubtedly be an invaluable asset to the group in resolving any future challenges they might encounter. Dave's unwaveringly positive attitude meant he never complained about any situation.

Jamie Martin hailed from Forest City, situated on the border of Maine and Canada. At seventeen years old, he stood close to six feet tall and possessed blond hair. While Jamie didn't possess any exceptional talents to aid the team directly, he was a physically strong young man who would greatly assist in various tasks, particularly in supporting Tim, who often ventured out on solitary hunts. As more individuals were en route, it became crucial to keep the freezer stocked. Additionally, Jamie's presence would prove beneficial in aiding David whenever necessary, as both individuals demonstrated intelligence and a willingness to deepen their understanding of Jesus.

Isaiah and Pastor Greg settled on one of the garden benches thoughtfully crafted by Brandon, overseeing the serene view. Turning towards Greg, Isaiah began, "You are aware that the next six and a half years will pose tremendous challenges for you and your team. Despite the difficulties, you have God's presence alongside you on this mission you have embarked upon. It's inevitable that, sooner or later, UN soldiers will comb these woods in search of those who haven't succumbed to the antichrist's influence. While some people have embraced Jesus, most will face persecution and lose their lives due to their unwavering faith. Prior to the rapture, there was a notable decline in the number of individuals turning to Christ, resulting in a significant apostasy.

The lack of biblical knowledge is disheartening. In the coming months, more Christians will seek refuge in these woods, just like your group did. Therefore, you and your youth group must remain vigilant, keeping watch at all times."

Isaiah glanced at the garden, then turned his gaze back to Greg. "I suggest that in April, or when the snow has melted, you establish a monitoring watch that operates twenty-four hours a day, seven days a week. It's during the night when the UN soldiers could potentially approach unnoticed. Although we were able to approach your group without difficulty, we had God on our side. Rest assured, Pastor Greg, God is actively protecting you! Nonetheless, I strongly advise exercising utmost caution in these final years. It is wise to commence constant and fervent prayer."

Greg stared intently into Isaiah's eyes, finding it hard to believe he conversed with one of the 144,000 individuals mentioned in the Bible. He had extensively delved into this topic, studying it in church and during his preparation to become a pastor.

"Isaiah, I don't know if you know this, but we had two angels visit us one night and they anointed us with small vials of oil. They handed us each a tiny vial and we poured it on our heads. It was the most incredible, and liberating experience I've ever had in my life!"

"Yes, the Lord told us about that. He said that He sent two messengers to you."

"Isaiah, did that happen to you too?"

"Yes, indeed, something of that nature, perhaps even more awe-inspiring! Pastor Greg, if only you could witness what I see in the spiritual realm right now. God's angels are scattered throughout these caverns, dancing, and others are ready to engage in battle as we proclaim the gospel to the world. We are divinely protected, but my brother, you and the other cave dwellers aren't entirely impervious. It is crucial to maintain courage while exercising caution. God's love for all of you surpasses comprehension."

Greg was a little teary-eyed and looked up at the lights on the ceiling and back down, "Are there others like us that have a fortress like this?"

"You and your group are unique in having a setup like this, but there are people hiding all across the globe. Some are Christians, while others are not. There are also preppers concealed in their shelters with provisions, but for those without Jesus, their prospects are regrettably grim. There may be individuals hidden underground, but their faith does not align with Christianity. I cannot say for certain if any of them will enter the millennial reign of Christ."

Isaiah looked up as if he heard the voice of God and then continued with a somber tone, "Only let in people who have two sticks in their hands and make a cross when they walk up the path into the Haven!"

"I don't understand why God picked me Isaiah?"

"Join the club brother. I don't understand why He picked me either."

They both stood up, and Greg showed him the second part of the cavern, and they continued talking, enjoying each other's company; it was a great distraction from what was happening in the world.

Isaiah continued telling Greg, "It's the second three in a half years that will be bad!"

Just then, Tim and David walked quickly by, and Tim said, "Pastor Greg, we're going to start building a bungalow for the soon-to-be newlyweds!"

Isaiah lightly grabbed Greg's arms and said, "With those two to-gether and David, they'll be a great team!"

Greg proudly said, "Tim is our hunter-gatherer. That young man has put more meat in the freezer than any one man could. I truly love him and his sister, such blessings."

Isaiah directed Greg's attention to a stockpile of small mattresses. "You see those stacks of mattresses? They need to be converted into bunk beds because in a few years' time, this cave will be filled with people. I estimate there are over a hundred and fifty mattresses over there. God intends for some individuals to survive for the millennial reign. Even as we speak, people are renouncing their faith in Christ and taking the mark. Oh, I almost forgot! Pastor Greg, both you and Maria require these rings. They are a gift from God."

Greg looked at the two beautiful wedding rings, and Greg's eyes got a little misty, "Wow! Thank you so very much!"

"Don't thank me Greg, thank Jesus Christ."

23

THE WEDDING

Ephesians 4:2
"Be completely humble and gentle; be patient, bearing with one another in love [...]"

The wedding ceremony took place in the back of the garden room. Greg stood beside Elijah in the far left corner of the almost rectangular cave. The area was adorned with abundant flowers, and David strummed his guitar. Sarah led Maria by the hand, both wearing beautiful attire. Maria looked charming in her lovely sundress. As Dave began playing the Bridal Chorus on his guitar, all the attendees sat in plastic chairs, facing Greg. They turned their heads to catch a glimpse of Maria as she gracefully approached Greg. Suddenly, everyone rose to their feet, their attention on the bride. Elijah offered Greg a reassuring pat on the back and whispered, "She looks stunning, Greg!"

"Yes, she does!"

Greg then quickly redirected his gaze towards the bride. He found it impossible to look away from her, as she was simply breathtaking. Nothing is more captivating than witnessing a bride walking towards her soon-to-be husband. Tears streamed down Maria's face as if she were floating towards Greg. The guitar continued to strum as Sarah reached her seat. The couple stood side by side, facing Elijah, while all eyes in the cave were fixed upon them. They were on the brink of entering into a covenant, uniting as husband and wife, becoming one.

Pastor Elijah's strong voice echoed throughout the Haven,

"You may all be seated." Elijah cleared his throat and started the proceedings.

"Dearly Beloved, we have gathered here today to witness the sacred union of this man and this woman in holy matrimony. They have come together to be joined as one in this blessed union. If anyone present knows of any reason why they should not be joined together, let them speak now or forever hold their peace."

There was a brief pause, and Pastor Elijah proceeded, "The union between a man and a woman in marriage holds a profound mystery. It is mysterious because, like a parable, it reveals a truth about the relationship between Christ and the church. The hidden divine reality within the metaphor of marriage is that God has ordained an everlasting bond between His Son and the church. Human marriage serves as an earthly representation of this divine design. Just as God intended for Christ and the church to become one body..."

Maria and Pastor Greg held hands while the sounds of sniffles from tears of joy echoed throughout the cave.

"It is not a coincidence that human marriage offers a language to describe the relationship between Christ and the church. Human marriage serves as a reflection, not the original. Just as God created man in His own image, He also fashioned earthly marriage in the likeness of His eternal union with His people. Human marriage is an earthly image that mirrors this divine plan. God intended for Christ and the church to be united as one body, and thus, marriage was designed to embody this truth. In essence, the marriage between a man and a woman symbolizes the sacred bond between Christ and the community of believers."

"Do any of you two have a vow you'd like to say?"

Greg spoke as he gulped air, "Maria, I love you more than you could ever imagine. I'm so pleased that God has brought us together, even in the most difficult times, here in a cave. I promise to be by your side and, as God, be my witness to keep you safe. God made the universe, the Stars, the Moon, and the Earth. God has made you to be my blessing, and I am so very happy to have you!"

"Greg, my love for you exceeds what words can express. I am immensely grateful that God has brought us together, especially in the midst of such challenging circumstances. Despite the storm surrounding us, I find peace within the walls of this fortress where God has united us in holy matrimony. Greg, my love for you knows no bounds!"

Elijah spoke with such authority,

"Do you Greg Robson Oliver take Maria Ana Silva to be your wife, to have and to hold from this day forward, for better or for worse, for richer, for poorer, in sickness and in health, to love and to cherish; from this day forward until death do you part?"

Greg looked into Maria's beautiful eyes and lovingly said, "I do."

"Do you Maria Ana Silva take Greg Robson Oliver to be your husband, to have and to hold from this day forward, for better or for worse, for richer, for poorer, in sickness or in health, to love and to cherish; from this day forward until death do you part?"

Maria looked into Greg's eyes and said, "I do."

"The exchange of rings please. This is a symbol of the covenant between Jesus and His church. The ring reminds the couple that they swore an oath of fidelity and perpetual allegiance to their spouses. Please Pastor Greg place the ring on Maria's finger."

Pastor Greg slid the ring onto Maria's finger as tears rolled down his face.

"Fantastic, and you Maria, place the ring on Greg's finger... thank you."

Elijah took a minute to look at the crowd, then at Greg and Maria, and declared with extraordinary jurisdiction and proclaimed loudly,

"By the power vested in me by Jesus Christ, I declare Gregory Robinson Oliver and Maria Anna.

Silva, husband, and wife. Greg, you may kiss the bride!"

Elijah grinned wide as Maria and Pastor Greg shared their first kiss. It was a passionate kiss, perhaps a bit prolonged, but it was the right length. Regardless, the two of them were married in a cave in Northern Maine during the great tribulation, with twelve members of the 144,000 witnessing the union. Elijah's voice raised in excitement as they turned towards the small gathering,

"Again, Mr. and Mrs. OLIVER!"

That's when Greg saw what Isaiah was talking about earlier; it was a glimpse of the heavenly realm. Angels were dancing behind the people throughout the gigantic cavern! They illuminated the Haven! The praise music for Jesus broke through the barrier that separated this world and heaven!

The emotions overwhelmed Greg, so tears streamed down his face like never before. The profound spiritual presence enveloped everyone, and they all wept tears of joy as they turned and witnessed the supernatural spectacle. For a brief moment, the heavens opened up, revealing a glimpse of the divine. Greg pointed to the angels alongside Maria, both filled with overwhelming joy. It was the most extraordinary wedding gift anyone could ever receive.

Afterward, everyone went to the basketball court in the rear cavern for the wedding reception. Impressive wooden tables, skillfully crafted by Brandon and David, were set up for the occasion. The attendees wore beaming smiles on their faces and laughed in sheer joy, having just witnessed their friends' wedding. On the left side, if they glanced toward Greg's and Maria's bungalow, they would see the adorable cottage ready to embrace the newlyweds. Adorned in an off-white hue with soft Newport green trim, the cottage boasted front windows, and above the entrance, the words "THE OLIVER'S" was proudly displayed in prominent lettering. Gathering around the tables, they indulged in a feast consisting of turkey, venison steaks, and generous salads made from fresh vegetables harvested from the garden. Laughter permeated the air as they finally took a moment to breathe and unwind. No one watched the monitors, as they had faith that Jesus Christ would safeguard Maria and Greg during this transformative phase of their lives. Following the meal, Greg seized his cavaquinho while David grasped his guitar, and together they embarked on a night filled with singing praise and worship to Jesus Christ, the Lord of lords and King of kings.

Two days had passed in a blink of an eye, and Monday had arrived all too quickly. Brandon prepared himself for departure. The men carefully brought in the remaining snowmobile and placed it in the back cavern alongside Tim's dirt bike, aware they might require it. They couldn't leave it near the entrance of the Haven. Greg embraced Isaiah tightly and whispered, "I am grateful to Jesus for your visit. It was a true blessing. Do you think we will meet again in person?"

Isaiah replied, "We could be neighbors during the millennial reign of Christ. Only God knows these things Pastor Greg. God bless you. Maria is a wonderful woman, you two are perfect for each other!"

Brandon embraced each member of the group, expressing his affection and gratitude. Finally, he shared a heartfelt hug with Pastor Greg, and tears streamed down their faces. In a choked voice, Brandon uttered, "I love you, Pastor Greg!" To which Pastor Greg replied with equal sincerity, "I love you too, Brandon! I am filled with joy for you. May God bless you abundantly!"

The cave dwellers bid farewell, waving as Brandon and the other eleven rode away on snowmobiles. Returning to the Haven, the group walked inside, where Lisa looked at Greg with a smile and remarked, "Just another normal day, huh? Getting married to Maria with some of the 144,000 presents and witnessing the heavens opening up."

24

THE ANNIVERSARY OF
THE RAPTURE

Matthew 25:35-45

"35 for I was hungry and you gave Me food; I was thirsty and you gave Me drink; I was a stranger and you took Me in; 36 I was naked and you clothed Me; I was sick and you visited Me; I was in prison and you came to Me.' 37 "Then the righteous will answer Him, saying, 'Lord, when did we see You hungry and feed You, or thirsty and give You drink? 38 When did we see You a stranger and take You in, or naked and clothe You? 39 Or when did we see You sick, or in prison, and come to You?' 40 And the King will answer and say to them, 'Assuredly, I say to you, inasmuch as you did it to one of the least of these My brethren, you did it to Me.' 41 "Then He will also say to those on the left hand, 'Depart from Me, you cursed, into the everlasting fire prepared for the devil and his angels: 42 for I was hungry and you gave Me no food; I was thirsty and you gave Me no drink; 43 I was a stranger and you did not take Me in, naked and you did not clothe Me, sick and in prison and you did not visit Me.' 44 "Then they also will answer Him, saying, 'Lord, when did we see You hungry or thirsty or a stranger or naked or sick or in prison, and did not minister to You?' 45 Then He will answer them, saying, 'Assuredly, I say

to you, inasmuch as you did not do it to one of the least of these, you did not do it to Me.'"

On July 4th, Alex and Lisa were basking in the sun, its rays filtering through the trees and illuminating the front of the Haven's door. Jamie and Liz were also a couple, just like Alex and Lisa, and it wouldn't be long before Alex and Lisa tied the knot—they were engaged. As they lay there, they began reflecting on what had transpired a year ago on that very day: the sudden disappearance of their families, church members, young children, and babies. The world had changed in an instant.

For almost a year, they had found refuge in the Haven. Living in the cave wasn't easy, but it was undoubtedly a blessing. Greg had turned July 4th into more than Independence Day; it had become Rapture Day, which held profound significance for them. So much had transpired since that fateful event. The mandatory implementation of the mark of the beast referred to as the "Lifeline," had made life increasingly challenging. Without it, one's existence was severely compromised, and each passing day seemed to bring more difficulties to navigate.

The Christians' posts about the Bible were prohibited on social media platforms and in public spaces. Christians had to rely on their non-Christian friends to purchase food for them. Sadly, many of their friends were betraying and reporting them to the UN military. Some individuals had embraced Jesus Christ as their Savior following the rapture, but they were being captured and confined in various camps across the globe.

In the Middle East, the persecution and killing of Christians were, unfortunately, frequent occurrences. However, the hostility towards Christians and Jewish people by those who had embraced the mark of the beast had now reached alarming levels. The intensity of hatred and animosity towards these religious groups had significantly escalated.

Days ago, the cave dwellers had gathered in the living room area of the cave to watch Brandon and his eleven friends preaching in Washington, DC, right in front of the White House. They faced opposition and were shouted at because people were unwilling to listen to the message about the wrath of God. However, they were protected.

Dressed in white robes and sandals, their proclamation of God's Word in the streets was compelling. These words were not being shared on social media platforms. The dwellers were watching videos that World Watch had access to while World Watch itself was attempting to devise ways to eliminate these marked servants of God. The prevailing hatred towards God's Word was both prevalent and disheartening. Many neighborhoods were conducting bonfires, burning Bibles, and repeatedly chanting the antichrist's name.

It had not rained all spring, and now that July 4th still hadn't rained. The waterfall inside the cavern was still working, something from the Lord. It reminded the group of Revelation 22:1 "And he showed me a pure river of life, clear as crystal, proceeding from the throne of the Lamb."

They didn't think it was that, but something kept the waterfall going. Their bet was on Jesus.

Many more Christians had started dispersing worldwide, seeking refuge in hidden locations like the mountains. Maria and Alex used a hummingbird drone to monitor individuals who had constructed shelters amidst the rocky terrain. Additionally, they possessed two larger drones that were carefully concealed in the back cavern. These drones could swiftly travel to any destination worldwide. While they were unsure of the specific situations where these drones might prove helpful, being prepared for any circumstance was deemed essential.

The residents observed nearby campers within the Haven and deliberated whether they should invite them to join their community. Determining who among the campers were fellow Christians and who were rebellious proved challenging, especially when relying solely on the perspective of a hummingbird drone. However, a few individuals spotted reading Bibles, which served as a positive indication of their faith.

David and Jamie had built a hundred bunk beds in the third cavern, anticipating the arrival of more married couples and leaders needing accommodation. They also began constructing additional cottages. The cave dwellers couldn't help but wonder how all the materials were brought into the cave. They questioned whether non-Christian helpers were involved and whether they had taken the mark of the beast. In such uncertain times, faith in God and vigilance in identifying potential threats became paramount.

Maria emerged from the doorway and exclaimed, "We have a couple of people heading our way! The man is carrying a woman on his shoulder, and she appears to be injured!" The man and woman approached the cave dwellers cautiously. Keeping her gun pointed at them, Maria remained wary, knowing that it could be a ploy or deception.

Maria shouted, "Don't move an inch!"

The man held up two sticks and slowly made a cross. Doctor Sarah and Pastor Greg appeared from the Haven. The woman that the man was carrying had broken her ankle.

Sarah said calmly, "Please bring her in to the cave, I have a place that I can help her. Everything is going to be okay."

Sarah said, "I need the cot from the emergency room ASAP!"

The man struggled to catch his breath as he spoke, "My name is Thomas Moran, and this is my wife, Mimi. She tripped on a rock and broke her ankle. It may sound unbelievable, but God led us here and instructed us to erect a cross, just as I have done. We don't know what we're supposed to do, but we desperately need help. Please, can you assist us?"

Alex and Jamie ran through the three caverns and passed Ruth and Elijah in the garden; Elijah yelled, "What is happening out there!"

Jamie screamed out while running, "Two people just showed, and the lady has a broken ankle!" Within a flash, the two were back with a homemade ambulance cot! With a lovely voice, Sarah said, "Thomas, is it okay if I call you Tom?"

"Absolutely Doc, that's fine!"

"Tom, we need to gently place your wife on the cot."

That's what he did. Mimi let out a scream that echoed throughout the Haven; her ankle was practically hanging ajar!"

Pastor Greg spoke up quickly and said, "This is our calling, to help those who are our brothers and sisters in Christ. Doctor Sarah will have your wife doing better in no time."

David and Jamie gently but quickly carried the cot with Mimi to the Haven emergency room."

While walking way behind Mimi and her husband, Pastor Greg got close to Maria and jokingly whispered, "You can put the weapon away; everything's going to be okay. A lot more

Christians will be coming, so try not to kill anyone. Thou shalt not kill, remember."

He kissed Maria on her cheek as he walked by her side and said with a smile, "Maria, you're so dangerous."

He continued talking to his wife while walking towards the emergency room, "This is our calling. Not just to help hurt people but to feed and clothe them. Did you see the size of the box of military clothing out in the third cavern?

Maria looked at him with a smile and responded, "Yes, I saw the box with military clothing. After being stuck in this cave for this long, I think I've come across just about everything. And guess what? There are military shorts in that box, and they happen to be our favorite color... Camouflage."

Greg shook his head with a smile and said, "Camouflage, that's perfect! I could paint our house camouflage if you'd like?"

"Greg you're not even worried about Mimi!"

"Sarah was built for this stuff! Mimi will be playing ball in no time."

Maria said when they passed the garden, "Greg, we can't paint the cottage camouflage, silly. The others took so much time to make our place."

Dr. Sarah proceeded to attend to Mimi's ankle. The first step was to numb the area with Novocain before snapping the ankle back into place. Despite the numbing agent, Mimi couldn't help but let out a loud yell. Once the ankle was aligned, Dr. Sarah carefully applied a cast to provide support. She administered additional medication to help manage the pain and help Mimi relax.

Thomas looked at Greg while he was holding his wife's hand and looking at the cave and said in awe, "What exactly is this place?"

"I'm Pastor Greg, and we refer to this place as the Haven. It's like a fortress the Lord has provided for us to endure the tribulation. I assume both of you have accepted Jesus Christ as your Savior?" Mimi, barely able to speak, responded, "Yes, we did, right after witnessing the rapture. We initially stayed in our home, intending to remain there, but it quickly became unsafe. Then the Lord spoke to my husband in a dream, instructing us to head to the mountains in Maine. At first, I thought he was crazy! But now, I see why! I'm not feeling any pain, at all now!"

Sarah said, "Morphine will do that."

Mimi slurred her words, "Where was I? Oh, so here we are hiding in a cave with little houses in it—wow I want a house."

Tom said, "Honey, they don't even know us!"

Greg said, "We got a house for you, don't worry."

"Is my ankle going to be okay, am I going to be able to walk again?"

Dr. Sarah looked at Mimi and held her other hand, saying, "Sweetheart, you're going to be just fine. It will likely take around a month, maybe five weeks, but it should heal properly."

Greg said, "Have you guys eaten lately?"

Tom hastily said, "We haven't eaten in days, well we had some blueberries and some raspberries, but that's about it!"

"Maria said, "Then you guys must be starving! I'll go out into the kitchen and make you something."

25

THE MCGWIRE'S

Meanwhile, Director Joe Smith just got a phone call from Congressman Ed McGwire, "Joe, we need to meet."

"We can do that. Where would you like to meet?"

"Joe, do you know that diner at the end of your street?"

Joe looked at his watch and said, "Yeah, it's nearby. How 'bout we meet up in an hour?"

"Sounds good, see you there."

Smith arrived at Moody's Dinner with Congressman Ed McGuire sitting patiently with a cup of coffee in front of him, waiting for it to cool down a little before he took a sip "Cup of coffee?"

"Sure Ed."

"They have great pie here!"

"I know, I live right down the street."

"So... the mark is mandatory for everyone."

"The mark? It has been mandatory for quite some time now. Where have you been? Why haven't you received your mark yet? We need to be united in this. I won't tell anyone, but I can't believe you haven't obtained the Lifeline yet! How have you been getting your food?"

"Being a congressman has it's perks."

Joe leaned across the table, "You need the mark or they'll throw you into a camp, Ed. what are you thinking?"

"I've never liked needles."

Joe then held out his right hand and showed the mark that he had, "It didn't hurt a bit, honestly you of all people!"

He had an evil way about him that Joe never had before; he was constantly agitated!

"Like I said, I haven't got it yet, but you're right and I'm going to get it first thing tomorrow morning."

Joe said, "Well you better get it as soon as you can, we need to show an example for the rest of the people."

Then Joe angrily said, "Those Christians and Jews, they should kill them all, it's their fault the world is the way it is right now! It's just a tattoo Ed! Don't be like those idiots!"

Joe looked out the window and said, "The religious people are the reason the aliens had to come and rescue us! If they had just gone with the flow like the rest of the world, but no! So, they need to be eliminated. That's my opinion, and many others agree with me. We could have had this conversation on the phone, you know!"

Ed Maguire knew that Joe was getting agitated and said, "Oh, I wanted to catch up with you, old friend, and see how things are going. I was thinking about taking some time off with the wife. We could really use it, especially after I get the mark tomorrow morning."

"Yeah, get that over with. You could use the time off! I mean, you did put World Watch together! Go do something with your wife, take a ride or go fly somewhere, spend some time with Rose."

Joe's cell vibrated, and he received a text from Maria: "You know that's too much sugar. You're a diabetic, Joe. I'm looking out for your well-being, Joe. The director of World Watch needs to stay healthy."

Joe Smith glanced up at the camera behind Ed's dinner, which provided a convenient distraction for Ed. Joe still had a rogue agent on the loose.

The congressmen said, "You look upset Joe, is everything okay?"

"I have to confess that I have an agent on the loose. She accepted

Jesus Christ and defected from World Watch. She was my top agent, and she's been playing mind games with me. Every now and then, she sends me texts to let me know that she's watching me and how she's doing, as if we're still friends!"

Ed then turned the tables on Joe and said with his voice scratchy because he quit smoking, "Well what did she say?"

Joe, while shaking his head in disbelief and an annoyed smile, said, "You see the camera behind you? She's watching us right now!"

Ed was amazed! He thought that Joe was the best agent he ever had, and the idea that any other agent could do something like that to him was incredible! "What's this agent's name?"

Then Joe said, "Her name is Maria Silva, she used to be my top agent. But after getting involved with this Jesus stuff, she disappeared. She could be anywhere in the world, and now she's watching the director of World Watch. It's almost amusing. But mark my words, I will find her. It's not a matter of if, but when! She will pay dearly for betraying us!"

Ed smiled, "Big time!"

"Yeah, big time!"

"I have to go Joe. I'll talk to you when we get back. Stay safe and watch out for Maria!"

They stood up, and Ed waved at the camera. Immediately Joe's phone vibrated, "Tell.

Congressman Ed McGuire, I said hi."

"Man, I'm going to get her, she said hi."

"You need to get these loose ends fixed Joe."

The congressman left the diner and returned home to his wife, who had already packed their essential belongings. They were preparing to journey into the mountains of northern Maine as per Ed's dream, where God had revealed the GPS coordinates of their destination. Equipped with a handheld GPS for camping and riding an old Harley-Davidson, they had no clue their path would lead them directly to the Haven.

26

SAUL TO PAUL

Acts 9

"3 As he journeyed, he came near Damascus, and suddenly a light shone around him from heaven. 4 Then he fell to the ground and heard a voice saying, 'Saul, Saul, why are you persecuting Me?'

5 And he said, 'Who are You, Lord?'

Then the Lord said, 'I am Jesus, whom you are persecuting. It is hard for you to kick against the goads.'

6 So he, trembling and astonished, said, 'Lord, what do You want me to do?'

Then the Lord said to him, 'Arise and go into the city, and you will be told what you must do.'"

Congressman Ed McGwire stood around 5'8" with a receding hairline, showing signs of his sixty-one years. His years of smoking had left him with a persistent cough, but he had recently quit the habit. His wife, Rose, was almost ten years younger than him, a kind-hearted woman who maintained her physical fitness and had dyed blonde hair. Together, they had indulged in the luxuries of a wealthy politician's life, with extravagant houses, cars, and frequent dining experiences. Their passports held stamps from countless countries they had visited, yet they had never been blessed with children. The notion that Jesus could reach them was not difficult to accept, for when God desires someone, He will prevail.

Having recently experienced a spiritual rebirth, Ed felt compelled to assess Director Joe Smith's spiritual state. He received his answer during the encounter at the diner. That next morning, Ed and Rose embarked on a journey to the Haven, following a similar route Maria had taken. Leaving their home in Virginia, they headed towards the mountains of northern Maine. The trip lasted approximately eighteen hours, with only brief stops for meals and fuel. Upon reaching the mountain range, Ed emulated the actions of Pastor Greg, Maria, and Tim, discreetly concealing his large Harley-Davidson motorcycle amidst the forest foliage, camouflaging it with leaves and branches. However, their actions did not go unnoticed by Alex, who keenly observed them stashing the motorcycle before emerging with backpacks and a duffel bag. Their preparations seemed reminiscent of the Howells from Gilligan's Island, as they appeared to have packed more than necessary for the journey.

They ventured towards the Haven, maneuvering through the forest in a zigzag pattern. Ed, however, quickly realized his lack of physical fitness; climbing the stairs of his private jet had been the extent of his exercise routine. The irony was not lost on him, as he was the one who had initiated the establishment of World Watch. In a sense, he could relate to the transformation of Saul, where the hunter had now become the hunted.

They had a few weeks before World Watch would likely notice their absence. Making their way along the trail that led to the boulder, they were unaware that Alex's hummingbird drone was discreetly tracking their movements. Meanwhile, Maria sat on the couch alongside Greg, observing the unfolding scene. She couldn't believe her eyes when she recognized Congressman Ed McGuire and his wife. She had seen his face countless times before, especially since he had recently shared a coffee with Director Joe Smith.

Greg was mortified at the idea of a congressman headed towards the Haven and said, "Maria, this going to be a problem! I wonder if it's a trap?"

Maria looked at Greg and said, "Well, before he ever comes into this cave, we need to search him completely and ensure that that's not the case!"

Then Alex said, "If he holds the cross up than we'll know."

Many small cameras positioned around the mountain focused on the two newcomers, capturing their every move. The nine holographic monitors illuminated the control room, displaying various views of the couple. Greg and Maria observed Congressman Ed McGuire breaking off a branch and snapping it in two while his wife Rose did the same. Holding up their crosses, the couple proceeded up the trail.

Greg and Maria swiftly approached the trail, eager to meet the newcomers. However, they were cautious not to reveal the exact location of the entrance until they were confident of their intentions. They rendezvoused with Ed and Rose on the trail, ready to engage in conversation.

Maria spoke with her Latin American accent and a pistol sticking out of the back of her camouflage shorts, "Congressman Ed McGuire what are you doing out here in the sticks, out here in the middle of nowhere?"

Ed McGuire nervously said, "This is going to sound a little crazy, but God told us to come out here, to this location. I don't know why we're here. I just need to keep my wife safe!"

Pastor Greg then said, "So, I take it you two accepted Jesus Christ as your Lord and Savior, when exactly was that?"

Ed said, "We accepted Jesus Christ three days ago."

Maria said aloud, "Congressman Ed McGuire and Director Joe Smith had coffee together just a day ago, Pastor Greg, I watched them."

Ed surprisingly replied, smiling and laughing, "You're the Maria that was texting Joe! You're driving that man crazy!"

"My name is Pastor Greg Oliver, and this is my wife, Maria Silva Oliver," Pastor Greg introduced themselves. "Maria has been playing mind games with Joe to distract him from his job. It seems to be working to some extent. We're curious about the current state of affairs with the world leaders. I assume you have access to information that we don't."

Then Maria spoke abruptly and said, "I thought we were going to search them, Greg!"

"Honey, you can search them, but I find it highly unlikely that World Watch would send the guy that made World Watch to the Haven, and they held up a cross."

"I want to go through their bags inside the Haven."

"Absolutely, that's something that has to be done."

All the cave dwellers possessed a wealth of information, but having a congressman among them promised to bring a new level of insight. They assisted Ed and Rose with their bags, and as Greg pushed the boulder open, they all entered the hidden entrance. The metal bar sliding into the locked position echoed through the hallway, catching Ed and Rose off guard. With a sense of anticipation, they cautiously walked through the hallway, unaware of what awaited them. As Greg opened the second door, the cave dwellers revealed themselves standing inside the house.

"This cave is called the Haven, and these individuals are the cave dwellers. We have Lisa and her brother Tim, followed by Liz and Jamie, and then Elijah and Ruth. Those two over there are Alex and David. The lady sitting down is Mimi, and her husband standing next to her is Thomas. Lastly, the lady standing to the right is Doctor Sarah Green. I apologize for the inconvenience, but we will need to go through all of your belongings. It's a precaution I think you'd do if you were in my position."

Ed said, "Please go right ahead! You can checkout everything, we have nothing to hide."

Greg looked at Ed and said, "No cell phones or electronics that can be tracked... right?"

Rose babbled, "No, we destroyed everything in Virginia."

"That's very wise of you two. David and Tim, you guy's need to get Ed's Harley-Davidson into the cave. Tim, you think you can ride that bad boy up the trail?"

"I know that I can Pastor."

"Ed and I need to talk. I need Elijah and Ruth to give Rose a tour of the Haven."

Greg and Ed sat down on the couch together. Alex was keeping watch, sitting in the chair. Ed looked at the technology before them and said, "The technology you have looks like what World Watch has."

"Yeah, pretty much. Alex's mom and dad worked for NASA, and let's just say they knew a little bit about computers. Currently, we are untraceable. We actually watch World Watch."

Alex hit a few buttons on the keyboard, and World Watch appeared before their eyes and said, "I think we have better technology than World Watch."

Ed chuckled and said, "It's quite amusing, really. Joe Smith and the UN agents are all working together to establish this one world government. I believe they underestimated the time it would take to accomplish their goal."

Then Greg said, "That's Revelation twelve right there. It's amazing watching the God's word playing right out in front of us."

Greg then turned to Ed and said, "I don't know how familiar you are with the Bible, but let me tell you, the first three and a half years are just the beginning. The real chaos and tribulation come in the second half. The two witnesses have already made their impact in Jerusalem, and now we have the 144,000 preaching the truth all around the world."

Then Greg looked back at the monitors, thought for a second, and said, "Oh yeah, they're definitely working towards the new world order, have been for a long time!"

Ed looked at Greg and smiled at Director Joe Smith walking in the monitors, "Old Joe was really upset that I hadn't got the mark."

"Maria said I saw that."

"I needed to know where he stood with this whole thing."

"And?"

"He's marked and angry! I told him that I was going to get the mark and do a road trip with Rose."

"So you lied to him."

Ed laughed, "I did!"

"That's wise, he won't be looking for you for a while. So, what's going on with the demonic leaders?"

"They're completely on board with this guy."

"Lorenzo Calvo, the antichrist."

"Yep, they follow him around like little puppies."

"So evil! I've gotten to the point where I don't even want to watch. Alex and Maria seem to handle it better."

Then Pastor Greg said, "He made a peace agreement with these countries.

Israel being attacked from all sides like Zachariah twelve talked about."

Then Pastor Greg opened his Bible, showed Ed Zechariah twelve, pointed to the open page, and asked him to read one through five.

"Zechariah 12

1 The burden of the word of the Lord against Israel. Thus says the Lord, who stretches out the heavens, lays the foundation of the Earth, and forms the spirit of man within him: 2 "Behold, I will make Jerusalem a cup of drunkenness to all the surrounding peoples, when they lay siege against Judah and Jerusalem. 3 And it shall happen that day that I will make Jerusalem a burdensome stone for all peoples; all who would heave it away will surely be cut in pieces, though all nations of the Earth are gathered against it. 4 In that day," says the Lord, "I will strike every horse with confusion, and its rider with madness; I will open My eyes on the house of Judah, and will strike every horse of the peoples with blindness. 5 And the governors of Judah shall say in their heart, 'The inhabitants of Jerusalem are my strength in the Lord of hosts, their God."

Pastor Greg said, "You ever seen an angry drunk guy that wants to fight really bad, just utterly out of control?"

"We all have, haven't we? I think I've even been that drunk guy before back in my youth."

"It's played out right before our eyes, and then the rapture!"

Greg was contemplating out loud, sharing his thoughts with Ed, while Alex attentively listened. "I served in the Marines, and I've witnessed my fair share of intense battles, but nothing compares to the war of Gog and Magog. It's astonishing to see how Israel, a country the size of Rhode Island, was prevailing against formidable opponents like Russia, Turkey, and Iran. Truly, only God could orchestrate such a remarkable outcome."

Alex said, "We haven't even hardly mentioned the two witnesses. How intense was that?"

Greg took a deep breath and leaned back on the couch, continuing to speak or perhaps vent his frustrations. "And let's not forget about the famine. How can anyone not notice its devastating impact? It's becoming increasingly severe. The Global Elite have been orchestrating a worldwide famine for quite some time. They've bought up all the farmland, and the food processing factories conveniently burned down. The skyrocketing fuel prices have made transporting food incredibly difficult. It was all right there in plain sight, but anyone who dared to speak up was labeled a conspiracy theorist."

Alex was again putting up images of starvation around the planet, videos, and live satellite feeds.

Everything the two talked about Alex had on the screens.

Ed looked visibly upset as he watched the monitors and expressed his frustration. "Oh, I've noticed! The supermarket shelves are completely bare. We stocked up on food, and it only lasted us four months. That's when I started pondering more and more on what my Christian brother Bill had shared with me. Rose and I had discussions about it, and we came to the realization that Jesus had taken His church. Oh, how I wish I had accepted Jesus Christ a long time ago!"

"Tell me about it, and I was the youth pastor and didn't have a relationship with Jesus Christ as my Savior, didn't even believe He was God! Imagine how I felt!"

Then Greg, with a chuckle, said, "I find the whole alien phenomenon quite fascinating. It's a massive deception, if you ask me. I believe they've been planning this elaborate scheme since after World War II. That's when the reported sightings of aliens, or rather demonic entities, began to emerge, such as the famous incident in Roswell. They were abducting people and collecting their DNA. In my opinion, many of these world leaders are hybrids, a mixture of human and fallen angelic lineage. Fallen angels have been in existence since Satan's rebellion against God."

Alex turned around and said, "It would make sense considering Jesus said when he comes back it would be like the days of Noah. In Noah's days the people genome was completely corrupted by the fallen Angels. No doubt that the same thing has and is happening now."

Greg opened his Bible to Genesis, chapter six, verse four, and read it out loud,

Genesis 6:4-6

4 There were giants on the Earth in those days, and afterward, when the sons of God came into the daughters of men, they bore children to them. Those were the mighty men who were of old, men of renown.

5 Then the LORD saw that the wickedness of man was great in the Earth and that every intent of the thoughts of his heart was only evil continually. 6 And the LORD was sorry to Generate she had made man on the Earth, and He was grieved in His heart.

Greg continued with his hypothesis, "The sons of God mentioned in the Bible were fallen angels, and they intermingled their seed with humanity, resulting in the existence of hybrids, known as giants or Nephilim. I believe that there are still hybrids present on Earth today. There have been accounts from Marines who claim to have witnessed these Nephilim hiding in massive caverns, much larger than the one we're in right now. Lorenzo Calvo, in my opinion, appears to be a hybrid as well."

Alex said, "They don't have to be giants to be hybrids. The Bible tells us about various types of angels, such as Dominions, Cherubim, Seraphim, Principalities, Archangels, and battle angels like Michael. So, it wouldn't be inconceivable that these hybrids and fallen angels can take on various forms, some resembling humans and others looking completely different."

Ed said, "I saw Higgins and Calvo talking to each other in a language I had never heard before. It sounded so evil, I was there at the UN and I heard it!"

Pastor Greg replied, "Before, I could watch videos of people claiming to have been abducted and robbed of their seed all day long. That had been happening for so long. Before the Rapture, UFO sightings were becoming increasingly common. The sightings were on the rise, to the point where NASA had to release some information because they couldn't keep it hidden any longer. UFO sightings were frequently featured in the news. You know, Ed, what's interesting is that Christians were the only ones who weren't getting abducted, but that wasn't reported in the mainstream news. I believe that's why we've witnessed such rapid technological advancements. The car was invented in 1886, and now I have holographic computer screens. It really makes you think, doesn't it? The Book of Daniel even mentions that knowledge will increase in the last days."

Ed was already blown away with the Haven. He looked at the technology in front of him; he was speechless!

"Let me show you around the place."

He showed him the bathroom and the waterfall electrical room, and then they walked towards the garden part.

"Oh, there's Elijah and Ruth Davis in the garden, they are great gardeners!"

"I see that!"

Elijah and Ruth, while waving, yelled, "We'll talk soon, maybe some tomato juice at our place."

"At our place! What does that even mean?"

"You'll see brother. We have a place for you and your wife too."

"But this is a cave, how can we have places?"

"You already saw the house part. How's your health, congressman?"

"Please call me Ed. I'll never be a congressman again."

"And—how's your health, Ed?"

"I haven't had a cigarette or a drink in three days. I'm a post diabetic and out of shape, overweight old man."

They entered the final massive cavern, and Greg reassured Ed, "You're not alone, and as I mentioned earlier, we already have a place prepared for you. Look at your wife and Doctor Sarah!"

"This place is huge! We have a place to live? I never thought something like this could exist!"

"Hey Doc! Ed quite smoking three days ago! Do you have some of those nicotine patches?"

She walked out of their new place and grabbed Ed's hand like he was a child, "You're coming with me congressman."

"Oh, please call me Ed."

"Okay Ed, you young man need a check up. Let your wife get your new cottage ready, it's kind of a mess right now with the unpacking and all. You guy's packed a lot of stuff! Everyone gets a check up when they first get here."

27

YEAR TWO AND FOUR MONTHS

Matthew 10:33

"33 But whoever denies Me before men, him I will also deny before My Father who is in heaven."

Almost two and a half years into the Great Tribulation, seventy-seven Christians resided in the Haven. They all lived in cavern three, each with a bunk bed. Among them were twelve married couples, each having a small cottage similar to Ruth and Elijah's. Lisa, Alex, Liz, and Jamie were also married and had designated places near Maria and Pastor Greg. The front row of cottages was reserved for Pastor Greg and the other leaders who oversaw the Haven, all accountable to Pastor Greg Oliver. They firmly believed that God was in control, and Greg had a strong connection with the Holy Spirit. It was November in the second year, and the previous summer had been scorching hot, resulting in significant destruction across North America and Mexico, including a considerable portion of the United Nations. The three regions had merged into one, and the concept of sovereign countries no longer existed. The death toll surpassed two billion people, which did not even include the nearly one billion individuals who had been raptured.

Tim was out hunting, unaware that he was the one being hunted. Meanwhile, Alex needed to use the bathroom and requested one of the new individuals to keep an eye on Tim and the two other men on the opposite side of the mountain. Alex's absence lasted no more than ten minutes. When he returned, he noticed the wardens tracking Tim before he could even sit down and shouted, "LOOK AT THOSE! TWO WARDENS! TELL PASTOR GREG AND MARIA WHAT'S GOING ON! HURRY!"

He ran off to tell them. Meanwhile, Alex had the hummingbird following them, and he called Tim on his walkie-talkie, "Tim, you have company and they're not friendly."

Tim answered, "How far?"

"Close, twenty yards!"

"Twenty yards?!"

Pastor Greg and Maria rushed in and glanced at the monitors, immediately identifying Tim's location. They had become familiar with the terrain over time. Greg, a former Marine special operations forces leader, and Maria, an agent, swiftly wore camouflage attire and applied face paint, transitioning into military mode.

They carried homemade rifles that fired tranquilizer darts containing a potent sedative capable of inducing twelve hours of sleep in a grown man. Rushing out of the Haven, they made a beeline towards Tim, determined to assist. The Wardens had caught up to Tim, aiming their guns at him while one of them shouted, "DROP THE RIFLE AND RAISE YOUR HANDS IMMEDIATELY!"

Tim complied, immediately dropping the rifle and raising his hands. The wardens aggressively rushed toward Tim, tackling him with unnecessary force. One forcefully grabbed Tim's right hand and exclaimed, "Hey, look at this! He doesn't have the Lifeline on him!"

The other one said disgustingly, "You're one of those Christians, right?"

"Jesus Christ is my Lord and Savior! I am a child of the living God...Yahweh."

The two wardens quickly handcuffed Tim, and one turned to his partner, saying, "Hank, I say we kill him and dump him in the lake to the north of here. What do you think?"

Bo said, "We can just shoot him, no one cares anyway!"

"If we killed him, we'd be doing the world a favor!"

Hank wanted information, so he put a hunting knife to his neck and said, "I could kill him right now! You alone out here, or do you have some brothers and sisters?!"

"I'm never alone, Jesus is with me at all times for what is in me is greater than who is in the world—that would include you two."

Alex had all the monitors up, watching the unfolding situation in front of everyone in the cave through the hummingbird drone's feed. The residents of the Haven were gathered in the house, their eyes fixed on the scene playing out before them. They knew that Maria and Greg were concealed somewhere, but their exact whereabouts remained a mystery. Greg and Maria communicated silently, using hand signals to coordinate their actions. They were stealthily positioned, seemingly invisible. With their rifles loaded with tranquilizer darts, they patiently waited for the perfect moment when Hank would release the knife from Tim's neck, their sights locked on the critical crossroad.

That's precisely what happened. Hank removed the knife from Tim's neck, his gaze shifting to his partner, knowing their safety depended on each other. In the blink of an eye, there was a barely audible snap, and the tranquilizer darts, equipped with needles resembling IV needles, shot through the air and found their mark in the wardens' necks. The two men crumpled to the ground beside Tim, completely unconscious. Tim was oblivious to the stealthy approach of Maria and Pastor Greg, who emerged from the bushes mere feet away. The invisible couple materialized in front of the astonished crowd in the Haven, prompting a joyous cheer to erupt from their grateful onlookers.

Greg said, "You okay?"

"I'm okay, a lot better than these two! You didn't kill them Pastor Greg, did you?"

With a smile, Maria said, "Thou shalt not kill, but thou can put people to sleep."

"I guess so 'cause these two are out like a light!

Pastor Greg asked, " What will we do with these two?"

The walkie-talkie clicked. "PASTOR GREG! THOSE TWO NEW CAVE DWELLERS THAT SHOWED UP LAST

WEEK HAVE BEEN APPREHENDED BY THE WARDEN SERVICE ON THE OTHER-

SIDE OF THE MOUNTAIN!"

Pastor Greg shouted back, "THE NEW GUYS?"

"YEAH, RED AND JEREMY FROM ALABAMA! I CAN SEE THEM ON THE SATELLITE

FEED! I'M HEADED OVER THERE WITH THE HUMMING-BIRD!"

"Okay, okay, ROGER THAT!"

Pastor Greg looked at Maria and Tim and said, "Grab there wallets, and walkie-talkies...smash their phones. It looks like we're hot!"

Maria responded, "It seems like they were scouting the area. Alex mentioned that we're not the only ones hiding out here. He showed me four other small groups of people located a few miles apart from each other. Let's be honest, folks, there are people hiding all throughout these mountains."

Greg said, "I saw that, they're not Christians, just don't want to comply to the rules."

The walkie-talkie sounded off again, "PASTOR, I HAVE THE HUMMINGBIRD PERCHED.

ON A BRANCH RIGHT ABOVE THEM!"

"Alex, I need you to compose yourself and stop yelling."

"Yes, sir Pastor."

"I need to hear them, can you do that for me?"

"I can do that."

All the cave dwellers watched, standing behind the already occupied couches. Lisa stood next to Alex while Ruth and Elijah held hands. Red and Jeremy were new acquaintances but seemed nice guys eager to contribute and assist. The audio broadcasted through the speaker system in the Haven and via the walkie-talkies, creating a cinematic atmosphere. It became evident that there would never be enough time for Greg and Maria to reach the other side of the mountain, regardless of their speed. Alex didn't need to verbalize it; everyone in the room understood.

Their muffled voice sounded through the speakers and over the walkie-talkie. The first Warden

James asked Red and Jeremy, "What in the hell are you two doing here?"

Red answered with a thick southern accent, "We're just doing a little huntin, s'all."

The other Warden, Danny Ayres, pulled out his pistol, put it to Jeremy's head, and said, "Both of you show us your IDs!"

Jeremy replied, "We left our wallet back at home... sir."

"SHOW US THE BACK OF YOUR RIGHT HANDS!"

Red and Jeremy showed their hands without the mark of the beast.

Warden James stated, "You two don't have the Lifeline!"

Warden James took out his pistol, put it on Red's head, and asked, "You two Christians?"

Red answered, "Yes sir we are, Jesus is our Lord and He's coming back."

Jeremy replied, "Jesus is coming, and you two, because you took that mark of the beast are going to hell... sir."

The two Wardens exchanged glances and immediately killed Red and Jeremy on the spot. The sound of gunshots reverberated through the area, reaching the ears of the cave dwellers and Greg, Maria, and Tim, who were monitoring the situation through the walkie-talkies. The act was gruesome, clearly demonstrating the intense hatred that the followers of the antichrist harbored toward Christians.

Then Warden James called it into the UN military, "This is Warden Kevin James. We just stumbled upon two Christian dead men here in the mountains. I can send you their coordinates."

At the same time, Warden Bannock called the other two wardens, that were sleeping very soundly, "Hank, you out there? Bo, come in."

Pastor Greg, Maria, and Tim listened, "Come in Hank!"

Two people were thrashing through the woods toward the three of them. Greg signaled to Maria and Tim to back into the brush. It was two more Wardens! Maria signaled Tim to lay down, and he did."

The Wardens emerged from the underbrush and discovered Hank and Bo lying motionless. They appeared lifeless, resembling corpses. Reacting swiftly, the Wardens reached for their holstered guns. However, before they could react, Greg and Maria launched an attack. Within seconds, the Wardens were overpowered and forced onto their faces, restrained with their handcuffs. Greg and Maria were formidable adversaries, and their anger was palpable. The Wardens, now subdued, were warned about the consequences of their actions. Greg whispered menacingly into one of their ears, "Cross paths with me again, any of you, and you'll experience severe consequences. This is my territory, and I could be out here, anywhere, So, beware."

Then Greg and Maria swiftly rose and vanished into the surrounding foliage. Once they had distanced themselves enough to ensure the Wardens couldn't overhear their conversation, Greg spoke up, revealing their compromised situation. "We've been exposed! Tim, spread some of that fox pee around this area! You've been using it as a hunting to mask your sent, right?"

They were already running towards the Haven, and Tim said, "Yes, everywhere! I can't believe they killed Red and Jeremy!"

Greg said, "We can't worry about that now! We'll talk in the Haven! They hate us, Tim!"

"You two wrecked those guys!"

"We needed to give them something to think about!"

"Honey, I think you did that!"

"I wanted to kill them so bad! Jesus forgive me!"

The three of them ran like the wind, got to the boulder, and pushed it open! They shut the boulder and locked it! Then they briskly walked in through the big oak door! Lisa embarrassed her brother Tim with tears running down her face, "Promise me you won't go hunting anymore!"

Tim was visibly shaken, "I'm not going hunting for a while, I'll tell you that!"

The whole house part of the cave was complete, and the shocked people were chatting back and forth! Pastor Greg announced, "People, I need everyone to be quiet! Alex, where are the two Wardens that killed Red and Jeremy?"

"There getting in their truck and backing out. It's right there on monitor three and four."

Maria said, "They're going to the other Warden's truck."

Alex said, "Monitor one is the hummingbird drone. I'm following their truck!"

Tim asked, "How fast does that thing fly?"

Alex answered, "About fifty if there's no wind!"

Liz said, "What about Jeremy and Red's bodies Pastor Greg?"

Greg patted her shoulder and said, "Jeremy and Red are with Jesus with they're new bodies. We can't leave the Haven."

Then he said so all could hear, "We are on lockdown! No one goes in or out that door without talking with me!"

Alex said, "Look they're almost to the wardens!"

Pastor Greg said, "We need sound Alex!"

"Yes, Pastor Greg, let me land this thing right above them on a branch!"

"They're taking the cuffs off!"

Greg said, "Everyone listen."

"What happened?"

"It was a big guy and a woman dressed in camouflage, looked like they were military trained."

"A woman took you down!"

"Trust me, that was no ordinary woman!"

The other person stood up, his voice filled with trepidation. "I thought she was going to kill me! She was ten times stronger than she appeared! It's clear they had military training. I don't think we're safe anymore. They confiscated our firearms and walkie-talkies and destroyed my phone, and they have our wallets."

Warden James said, "I think we just killed two of their friends!"

The other Warden said, "You can come back here! I'm not coming back here. I'll look around a ways from this location."

Warden Danny laughed and said, "What are you two scared?"

"The two handcuffed individuals glanced at the two unconscious men and then turned their attention to James. Both of them nodded in agreement, "Yeah." The Wardens attempted to rouse the two individuals without success. Doctor Sarah intervened, saying, "It's no use. They'll be sleeping for at least ten hours. Eventually, they can be revived in a hospital setting. You could shake them all day, and they still wouldn't wake up."

"Pastor Greg, they're calling an ambulance. Look at World Watch!

"What are they doing?"

"They're sending drones here now and a hundred UN soldiers here tomorrow morning!"

Maria added, "Look at angry Joe. We definitely got his attention. If I know him, he'll be watching over this location for a while."

Pastor Greg looked preoccupied, and it wasn't about the people in the Haven, "Are there any Christians nearby that we can rescue tonight? Do those drones have FLIR sensors?"

Elijah said, "What is a FLIR sensor?"

Maria stated, "Most military drones are equipped with night vision and infrared cameras. They can detect human heat signatures from a considerable distance."

Alex said, "There are Christians on monitor seven. I've been watching them for two days."

Lisa, who was frequently beside Alex, remarked, "Look, there are three of them—two women and one man. The man appears to be in his late thirties, and the women seem to be around my age."

Standing beside Sarah, David said, "Can we save them?"

Greg and Maria exchanged smiles, knowing that Maria was about to share valuable information. She said, "We have these special jumpsuits that provide full-body coverage. They make us invisible to the FLIR system used for thermal imaging."

Alex said, "The ambulance is there and they're putting them on stretchers and wheeling them out."

Pastor Greg said, "Can you imagine how mad those guys are? Tim, Maria, and I will get the night vision goggles and grab three extra jump suits and get those brothers and sisters to Haven. We'll leave at midnight."

Alex said, "I've been watching World Watch and the UN Soldiers aren't just going into the northern Maine woods. This is a worldwide sweep. If there's a mountain range, they're going to hit it with drones and the military too."

Maria exclaimed, "I have the ability to shut down World Watch, causing a complete blackout in the military systems of the one-world order. I can also disable the drones, rendering them blind and causing them to crash worldwide. Additionally, I can disrupt the satellite network. I need my laptop. While the cameras and the hummingbird drone should still function, the satellite feed will be affected."

Alex leaned back in his chair and said, "I'm intrigued! You can do that?"

Pastor Greg wore a proud expression on his face, acknowledging that anything is possible with God's guidance and his wife's capabilities. He responded, "That's my blessing right there! However, we still need to exercise caution around the military. We can save those suits for another time."

Maria said, "I have to go play computer games in our cottage Honey."

Alex looked at Greg and said, "Can she really do that?"

28

THE RESCUE

Proverbs 20:1
"20 Wine is a mocker,
Strong drink is a brawler,
And whoever is led astray by it is not wise."

Director Joe Smith was at a convenience store, using the Lifeline mark on the back of his right hand to make a payment. Just as he was about to complete the transaction, he received a text message from Maria. It read, "Joe, you've been in to the sauce a lot. It's time to cut back."

Joe glanced at his cell phone and a camera above the store's entrance. Despite changing phones, he knew his actions were being monitored. Leaving the store, he settled into his SUV, only to feel his phone vibrate again, indicating another incoming text message.

"Joe the only way to quit drinking is cold turkey, you know that!"

At the same time as she was texting Joe, Maria swiftly went through his phone, searching for access to his computer back at the office. The mission to shut down the UN military was crucial, as it held the potential to be a miraculous intervention from God, ultimately saving thousands of Christians.

"Maria, your still alive and kicking?"

"I've never been better in my life. I got married to a wonderful man!"

"And I didn't even get an invite."

"I can send you some pictures later. You could drink water on ice instead."

"Why would you care about whether I drink or not? Stop watching me!"

"Thank you, Joe!"

"Thanks for what!? I didn't send you any gifts... lol."

There was no response to Maria's text. Joe continued drinking, consuming one swig of whiskey after another. The words "Thank you, Joe" from Maria's message haunted him throughout the night. As darkness fell, the lights went out, and Joe realized he couldn't access the internet on his phone. He repeatedly read his conversation with Maria, pondering the meaning behind her gratitude. In his drunken state, he couldn't help but laugh, suspecting Maria's involvement in the blackout. Despite his intoxication, his thoughts returned to Maria's voice with her charming Latina accent, saying those three words. Sleep eluded him, and he finished the entire bottle of whiskey. Little did he know that Maria's actions, starting with her access to his cell phone and World Watch, had set in motion a global virus and caused the blackout. Joe's reputation would suffer, and he found himself in a precarious position as his trusted agent went rogue. The Haven, too, would be without computer systems, relying solely on God's guidance. Meanwhile, Greg arrived at their bungalow to witness Maria's fingers flying across her specialized laptop, entering a command before shutting it down. She looked at Greg with a mischievous smile, giving him a passionate kiss and expressing her uncertainty about the outcome, hoping her plan would work, "I don't think I'll be able to do that again?"

"I kind of figured that might be a one-time thing. Will they be able to trace what you did to our coordinates?"

She surveyed her surroundings, contemplating the situation. "I don't think so, but they'll certainly make attempts," she mused. "As I mentioned, it's a one-time thing. Their technological advancements are impressive, approaching our own capabilities. However, their efforts to launch satellites are constantly hindered, with the satellites being taken out as quickly as they are deployed. In any case, let's proceed with our mission to rescue those people!"

The two of them, still clad in their camouflage attire, were joined by Tim as he emerged from his location. Equipped with two tranquilizer rifles and a compass, Tim confidently stated, "I know the precise location. It's approximately a twenty-minute walk, but if we pick up the pace, we might make it in fifteen minutes."

Pastor Greg said, "Will they trust us, that's the question?"

Tim laughingly said, "Maybe we need to bring my sister? She can talk anyone into anything."

Maria stopped and held the two back and said, "Go get Lisa, Tim! You're so right, she's a sweetheart!"

Minutes later, Lisa ran up dressed in camouflage and nervously started babbling, "I can't believe you guys picked me! I've never been on a mission trip like this before, and I told Tim not to go out again. Here we are, leaving the safety of the Haven... wow! I don't know if I can do this Pastor Greg. Maria, I'm totally stressed out!"

Maria calmly said, "Think of it as we're just going for a walk, at night."

Tim said, "A fast walk."

Maria glanced at Tim, "Yes, a fast walk at night. Don't think about soldiers. Remember, God is with us."

Greg agreed, saying, "She's right, as usual. It will be similar to our previous excursion to Elijah's and Ruth's place, just in darkness. But don't worry, you'll have night vision goggles with you."

She kept talking in a low voice, "I did watch two people get killed today y'know."

"Sis, everything is going to be okay."

The four exited the Haven, each equipped with night vision goggles. Tim took the lead, followed by Maria, Greg, and Lisa trailing behind. Lisa, who was using night vision goggles for the first time, was struggling to navigate the trail. She stumbled and asked, "How do you guys ever get used to these things?"

Pastor Greg chuckled softly and responded, "Once you've had them on for about five minutes or so, you'll completely adapt to them and forget they're even there. It brings back memories of our military missions. Maybe I should take the rear, and you can follow behind Maria?"

"I'm watching where your feet are landing so I can step in the same spots. Let's just keep things the way they are for now," Maria replied, understanding the need for caution.

Tim suggested they pause momentarily, realizing they were likely only ten minutes away. He advised against talking, as it might alert the others and make them nervous. Tim believed they had probably heard the soldiers, so they needed to be as quiet as possible. He turned to Lisa and advised her on what to do when they reached their destination.

"The first thing you should do, Lisa, is say 'Hi' and introduce yourself and us. Let them know what we're trying to do and the danger they're facing," Tim whispered.

Greg whispered, "You need to tell them that we're Christians, that should be the first words that come out of your mouth."

Lisa whispered, "You don't think they have guns, do you? I don't like guns."

Pastor Greg whispered, "I think Alex would've noticed if they were packing up. We need to move quickly. Lisa, you should approach their campsite alone with your arms raised. We'll be right behind you, hidden in the darkness."

In approximately ten minutes, the group reached the campsite. Lisa exchanged a fearful glance with Tim before bravely stepping forward. With night vision goggles on her head, dressed in camouflage attire, and her hair in a ponytail, she stood before three unfamiliar individuals. Lisa spoke rapidly, her voice betraying her nervousness.

"Hi, everyone. I'm Lisa, and I'm a Christian. I know this may seem strange, but I've been sent here to inform you all that there is a lot military nearby, and they will likely be coming to this location tomorrow morning... I apologize for the unfortunate news. It's certainly not the ideal way to meet, but these are truly challenging times we live in."

The man's voice carried a hint of surprise as he spoke a little too loudly, "How did you know we were here? I don't understand. What are you doing here alone?"

Lisa took a deep breath and replied, "As I mentioned before, my name is Lisa, and we're here with a mission to rescue and protect people like yourselves. I may have walked in alone, but, I'm not alone. I have a team with me."

Then she called into the woods, "Come on out, guys! This is my brother, Tim. The person with the rifle is Pastor Greg and his wife, Maria." They all emerged from their hiding places and stood together. Pastor Greg stepped forward and addressed the newcomers, "Hello, I understand this is an unusual situation, but we have a safe place where you can find shelter and food. Lisa mentioned that the UN military plans to search these woods tomorrow morning. Anyone found without the Lifeline mark will likely be executed on the spot. Take a look at our right hands. Do you three see any marks? I believe you can say the same. We all know that the Lifeline is not a true salvation but a path to destruction. You have about fifteen minutes to decide whether to come with us. Feel free to discuss this among yourselves and ask any questions. Keep in mind that if we know you're here, it's likely that the military knows too."

Right then, a drone flew directly over their heads and crashed into the woods about two hundred yards north, in the opposite direction of the Haven. The man named Bob was startled, and everyone instinctively dropped to the ground, except for Pastor Greg and Maria, who remained composed, and standing. Maria casually remarked, "Oops, that would be me! I shut off their internet!"

One of the girls, Hannah, about Tim's age and with blonde hair and blue eyes, said, "What do you mean you shut off the internet? How do you shut down the UN military's internet?"

That's when Pastor Greg stepped in to support his wife and added, "Yep, that's Maria for you. She has a knack for doing things like that. In fact, she managed to shut down the entire world's internet. It's a worldwide blackout! As I mentioned earlier, it's crucial for your safety that you come with us. We don't have fifteen minutes anymore. You need to gather your belongings and join us immediately. Our current location is not secure."

Uncle Bob, Hannah, and Ramona swiftly gathered their belongings, preparing to leave for their unknown destination. They lacked night goggles to navigate in the darkness. Suddenly, another drone, heading in the opposite direction towards the troop's camp, crashed nearby, engulfed in flames. Maria couldn't help but chuckle, remarking, "Those guys are going to be livid!"

Tim replied, "Angry? They're pissed! I can hear them yelling!"

Pastor Greg said, "We need to go as fast as we can!"

The twenty-minute journey was completed in half the time, and they arrived at the boulder door. Stepping through, they entered a dimly lit hallway, where the second door awaited them, already ajar. Beyond that door lay a cave-dwelling with a partially illuminated interior. The other cave occupants, except for Elijah, Alex, and Sarah, were fast asleep in their bunks.

"This is Elijah, Alex, and Dr. Sarah Green," introduced Lisa, gesturing towards each person. As she often did when new arrivals entered, Dr. Sarah took the initiative to address them. "Hello, I understand that you must have many questions, but first, I need all of you to take a deep breath and try to relax."

"Very good. How's everybody's health? Anything I should know about?"

Uncle Bob said, "Ramona has asthma, but she's been doing breathing exercises."

Right at that moment, the blackout came to an end. The holographic monitors displayed the return of the internet, and Alex excitedly rushed to the chair, exclaiming, "Maria, the world's power is back on!"

Maria said, "That quickly! Amazing! I thought that they wouldn't have it on until morning!"

Greg said, "It is morning, two thirty. Lisa, can you get these guys some clean clothing, show them their bunks and how to use the showers and stuff?"

Tim said, "I'll help!"

Elijah and Greg exchanged knowing glances, recognizing Tim's apparent interest in Hannah. It was no surprise, considering her youthful charm and Tim being the same age. Tim had transitioned from being a famous young man in high school to becoming a skilled hunter and provider for the Haven. It was a worthwhile transformation, as God significantly worked through him. He deserved to have a companion, a good woman by his side. They anticipated that as time passed, challenges would increase, but so would their collective strength.

Daybreak arrived all too quickly, and the military forces began their search through the woods. Meanwhile, the inhabitants of the cave watched the monitors anxiously. The military personnel passed by the cameras set up by Alex, which were so small that they were virtually invisible. Some soldiers were even walking along the path leading to the Haven, which made the cave dwellers extremely uneasy. Thankfully, by God's grace, they remained unseen, and the soldiers continued past the boulder without noticing anything. Inside the Haven, everyone remained silent, refraining from uttering a word. They were filled with worry, and many turned to prayer, although their lips moved soundlessly. They held each other's hands, seeking solace as they endured this challenging tribulation, yearning for the day Jesus would return.

Lisa looked at all the monitors and sadly said, "They're going to kill everyone that's hiding out here, aren't they, Pastor Greg?"

"Hopefully, they'll miss them. The soldiers all have the mark of the beast and they hate us Lisa, but you know that. Alex, check out the Jeep and the Prius, did they find it?"

"They walked right past there, sir. It looks like they completely missed it."

Greg sighed and said, "Good, thank God, we might need to use those someday, isn't that right, Maria?

"Oh yeah, every resource is important. A Jeep, we could use that in many ways in the future, and my soccer mom car—who knows."

Greg said, "God knows everything, He made them miss it on purpose. Someday we'll find out why, or maybe we'll need transportation after the tribulation is over."

Everyone said, "Amen!"

29

1278 DAYS INTO THE TRIBULATION

Revelation 13

"1 Then I stood on the sand of the sea. And I saw a beast rising up out of the sea, having seven heads and ten horns, and on his horns ten crowns, and on his heads a blasphemous name. 2Now the beast which I saw was like a leopard, his feet were like the feet of a bear, and his mouth like the mouth of a lion. The dragon gave him his power, his throne, and great authority. 3 And I saw one of his heads as if it had been mortally wounded, and his deadly wound was healed. And all the world marveled and followed the beast. 4 So they worshiped the dragon who gave authority to the beast; and they worshiped the beast, saying, 'Who is like the beast? Who is able to make war with him?'

5 And he was given a mouth speaking great things and blasphemies, and he was given authority to continue for forty-two months. 6 Then he opened his mouth in blasphemy against God, to blaspheme His name, His tabernacle, and those who dwell in heaven. 7 It was granted to him to make war with the saints and to overcome them. And authority was given him over every tribe, tongue, and nation. 8 All who dwell on the Earth will worship him, whose names have not been written in the Book of Life of the Lamb slain from the foundation of the world.

9 If anyone has an ear, let him hear. 10 He who leads into captivity shall go into captivity; he who kills with the sword must be killed with the sword. Here is the patience and the faith of the saints."

It was three and a half years into the Great Tribulation. The people in the Haven numbered one hundred and twelve. The third cavern resembled a small town. There would have been more people, but the UN military caught ten members last summer who were picking blueberries. Ed and his wife, Rose, almost got caught but headed home before the others. All ten tribulation saints were asked if they were Christians, to which they proudly confessed their faith but were shot down one after another. The cave dwellers watched the whole incident unfold on the monitors with the hummingbird drone. It was traumatizing, and the leaders took it the hardest. Liz was in the corner of the garden room, unable to stop crying. Jamie tried to console her, but it was futile. Elijah said, "Go talk to her, Lisa. She's your best friend."

Lisa put her hand on Jamie's shoulder and said, "Let me speak with her."

Jamie left the two alone. "What yah doing in the corner Elizabeth?"

"YOU KNOW WHAT I'M DOING IN A CORNER! I'M JUST NOT AS STRONG AS YOU

GUYS ARE! I DON'T KNOW WHY GOD CHOSE ME! I WISH THE MOB FOUND ME AT THE CHURCH!"

"You need a big hug. Someday, this will just be a memory, a story that people tell by a campfire. God chose you because you are sweet and caring. You're my best friend in the whole world, you know that?"

"Yeah... I know."

"I bet I can get Alex's laptop and we could watch a movie, maybe popcorn. We'll lay down in bed like when we were kids and watch anything you want."

Her nose ran, "But Alex doesn't let anyone use his computer."

"I bet I can make him do that. Just you and me, popcorn, and a movie. Let's escape from here for two hours and try to forget what happened. A timeout."

"I need a timeout."

"You got it sister. I'll meet you at my place."

"Okay."

Liz was due for a little breakdown and needed a timeout.

Joe Smith didn't get in trouble for the internet getting hacked. Maria could hide the tracks that led to the computer she had hacked. She couldn't let him lose his job. She knew his thought process, personality traits, and routine. She had known him for so long that she couldn't bring herself to do it, something she texted him the next day. On the bright side, Tim was now a pastor, and Tim and Heather were married; it was a beautiful wedding! Pastor Greg held a church service every night on the basketball court. The last three and a half years were tough, but many others had it much worse than the cave dwellers.

Lorenzo Calvo spoke in Israel, boasting about all his accomplishments. He discussed the peace agreement he established three and a half years ago. He spoke about how the UN military would search for the Jewish people who were in hiding. However, many of the Jewish people realized that the antichrist wasn't who he claimed to be, so they fled quickly. They sought refuge in the mountains, and by God's grace, they were kept safe. Unfortunately, not all Jewish people recognized Calvo as the antichrist, and thus, they accepted his mark.

Lorenzo Calvo gave his speech. He was constantly boasting that he was the true god.

"I am so happy to those have chosen to follow me. Anyone without the Lifeline will be hunted and either they take the Lifeline, or the consequences will be—"

At that moment, a shot rang out in the distance, fired from a high-powered sniper rifle. All cameras were focused on the beast's face as the bullet entered his forehead and exited through the back of his head, splattering blood onto the white curtain. He froze, and his body fell back, completely rigid. The cameras captured his face and various angles of his body during the fall. The cave dwellers watched in shock as Pastor Greg pointed at the monitors and exclaimed aloud,

"Revelation 13:3 'And I saw one of his heads as if it had been mortally

wounded, and his deadly wound was healed. And all the world marveled and followed the beast. We're watching it there! We're watching it live!"

They weren't the only ones watching it. Calvo's followers were also witnessing the assassination. The people who had access to the internet and were in hiding were also watching. The world watched as this ancient dragon executed the most demonic and deceptive trick ever. Director Joe Smith, too, was watching in complete shock and shouted, "NO!"

Then, every camera focused on Lorenzo Calvo's face captured something astonishing! The wound on his forehead began to heal, and his eyes opened wide! Defying gravity, his rigid body rose slowly until his face aligned with the spot where he was shot. He opened his eyes, revealing an eerie blackness. Standing tall and straight, he stood before the microphone.

Pastor Greg said, "Look at prophecy unfolding before our very eyes! You thought he was bad before, I imagine that we haven't seen anything yet!"

Director Joe Smith thought he had just witnessed a miracle, tears rolling down his face, and said aloud in his office alone, "Now that's god! I love this man!"

He was demeaning the name of Jesus so badly.

After everything had unfolded, Pastor Greg requested that the cave dwellers return to their bunks and cottages. He mentioned that only the leaders should remain, calling them out by name.

"Maria, Pastor Elijah, Ruth, Pastor Tim, Heather, Alex. Lisa, Liz, Jamie, Doctor Sarah, and David. Let's all sit on the couches together, we need to talk."

Everyone took their seats, and Pastor Greg proceeded, "The good news is we have made it this far— praise Jesus! The bad news is that we still have three and a half years of hell on Earth to endure. I would like to hold a special service tonight. David and Elijah, could you two make the necessary arrangements?"

Elijah spoke to the group of leaders and Pastor Greg excitingly, "Yes, we can make that happen, can't we, everyone?"

They all answered at the same time with a yes. Pastor Greg continued, "Ruth, I heard you singing a beautiful song yesterday, can you sing it tonight?"

Ruth smiled cause' she knew the exact song he was talking about, and with her sweet voice, she said, "Anything you want, Pastor Greg. I love that hymn as well."

Elijah laughed and said, "If we love it, can you imagine how much Jesus loves it?"

They all chuckled. Pastor Greg gazed at each of their faces one by one, a loving smile on his lips while a tear streamed down his cheek. "I love all of you so deeply. We have endured so much together. Each one of you has shown tremendous dedication. All I can say is, keep being true to yourselves, and with Jesus guiding us, we will persevere until the day we witness His glorious return. Pastor Tim, would you please lead us in prayer?"

"It would be my pleasure. 'Father, we are grateful for this fortress that You have bestowed upon us. We thank You for Your limitless love and grace. We pray for the other people in the Haven, Lord, that You would extend Your protection to them as You have done for us. Surround this place with Your angels. We also pray that many more people will find their way here, guided by Your divine hand... in Jesus' name, Amen.'"

30

THE SERMON

Hebrews 4:12

"12 For the word of God is living and powerful, and sharper than any two-edged sword, piercing even to the division of soul and spirit, and of joints and marrow, and is a discerner of the thoughts and intents of the heart."

The third cavern had been prepared for Pastor Greg's sermon. The basketball court had been transformed into a church sanctuary, as it had been on numerous occasions before, and was half full of cave dwellers. The plastic chairs were neatly arranged, and David had crafted a few additional benches for the garden, which were temporarily placed on the basketball court when not in use. Furthermore, before Brandon departed to preach to the nations, he fashioned a large cross from a pine tree. The bark, which had begun to peel, was intentionally left intact, symbolizing the old, rugged cross. It remained untouched as everyone recognized the profound significance of Christ's accomplishments for them and us.

The lights were on the verge of dimming, a routine that had occurred since Tim and Lisa first arrived in the Haven nearly three and a half years ago. They would gradually shut down around 7 p.m.; by 9 p.m., complete darkness would envelop the cavern. As you may recall, this has been the established schedule. David and Greg led the gathering in singing a few praise and worship songs, with David skillfully strumming his guitar and Pastor Greg playing his Cavaquinho. David possessed a beautiful voice, smooth as butter, and it resonated magnificently within the cavern due to its excellent acoustics.

Then Pastor Elijah stood behind the pulpit and prayed with his deep, beloved voice. He appeared more emotional than usual as he spoke, "Oh Father, we thank You for Your providence throughout these years. I feel a deep sense of humility as I offer this prayer to You on this significant night. Your love is truly remarkable, granting salvation to someone as unworthy as myself, a wretched sinner, through Your Son Jesus, who endured unimaginable suffering on the cross and triumphantly rose from the dead three days later. I pray, dear God, that You would grant Pastor Greg the words to speak. In the name of Jesus, amen."

Pastor Greg walked up to the pulpit with a giant old bible with thick pages. Pastor

Greg held up the old Bible and said, "This is my old pastor's Bible—Pastor Frank. Pastor Frank was obedient to the Holy Spirit, he and others participated in putting the Haven together. His faith was, intense as you can imagine. I look around this place and it still boggles my mind. We are so blessed!"

Pastor Greg's voice grew louder as he began to preach, "This Bible dates back to 1809! Can you even comprehend how many people have come to Jesus Christ through this ancient scripture? It consists of sixty-six books, seamlessly joined together, and reads as one unified message! It contains approximately 450 prophecies solely concerning Jesus' ministry here on Earth, including His crucifixion and resurrection!"

Then Pastor Greg's voice softened as a hundred pairs of eyes remained fixed on the seasoned and anointed pastor. "I often find myself wishing that I could go back in time and accept Jesus before the rapture occurred. Don't we all?" Pastor Greg's voice grew louder as he lifted the old Bible. "Honestly, if given the chance to go back and redo it all! If we had a TIME MACHINE, WOULDN'T WE GO BACK?! Of course, we would—all of us. But God, yes, but God... He has placed us here for a purpose! It wasn't His doing, but rather our own stubbornness and, quite frankly, our attachment to this fallen world. It reminds me of Romans 8:28, which reassures us that all things work together for good for those who love God and are called according to His purpose."

Pastor Greg moved towards the church members and released a shout that reverberated, catching a few by surprise. "FOR HIS PURPOSE, NOT FOR PASTOR GREG'S PURPOSE, NOT FOR YOUR PURPOSE! God had a plan for us to be here as tribulation saints and His love and grace never wavered!"

Pastor Greg made his way back to the pulpit and laid down the old Bible and said this in such a compassionate way, and by memory, he spoke again, "John 3:16-17 for God so loved the world that he gave his only begotten son, that whoever believes in him should not perish but have everlasting life. For God did not send his son into the world to condemn the world, but the world through him might be saved."

Most people don't want to talk about John 3:18. Listen to this, 'he who believes in Him is not condemned, but he who does not believe is condemned already; because he has not believed in the name of the only begotten son of God!'"

There was a pause, and Pastor Greg continued, "Acts 2-21, and it shall come to pass that whoever calls on the name of the Lord shall be saved. Romans 10:10 For with the heart One Believes unto righteousness, and with the mouth, confession is made unto salvation."

The challenge lies in that God's moral values far surpass those of human beings. If it were up to me, everyone would be granted entry into heaven except those who have committed murder, or something like that. However, my moral values fall short of God's standards! I understand that now, but before the rapture, I didn't!"

Pastor Greg's emotions were shaken. He stepped back in anguish and admitted, "I don't understand why I'm delivering a salvation message when we are all saved here. However, I wholeheartedly believe that this message is intended for anyone with ears to hear what the Spirit has to say."

Pastor Greg found himself doubting whether he had preached the right message. He glanced toward the dimming lights and the expanse of the massive cave before lowering his gaze to the floor. As the lights dimmed further, Rose suddenly stood up, her voice trembling as she cried out, "THIS MESSAGE IS FOR ME!" With tears streaming down her face, she, too, directed her gaze toward the cave ceiling and continued, "I didn't know! I didn't understand! But now I do!" Rose then walked up to the Cross and humbly knelt in prayer.

Rose's response completely took aback Pastor Greg. "Rose, do you desire to accept Jesus Christ as your Savior?" he asked. "If so, please repeat after me. 'I am deeply sorry for the sins I have committed in my life. Cleanse me, Jesus. I repent and express my gratitude for sacrificing Yourself on my behalf. You took my place. I commit to following You for the remainder of my days. You are my God, and I am Your servant. In the Name that is above all names, Jesus Christ.'"

Rose repeated those words, and tears filled the eyes of everyone in the Haven. Sitting next to the pulpit, David began stringing his guitar in a way he had never played before. As darkness descended, a spotlight illuminated him, followed by another light shining on Ruth as she commenced singing. Her voice resonated with incredible power, captivating everyone's hearts. Soon, other members joined in, creating a harmonious chorus. At that moment, Pastor Greg experienced a glimpse of the heavenly realm, witnessing angels dancing just as Isaiah had described and as he had seen on his wedding day. The vision illuminated the massive cavern, captivating the attention of everyone present—angels, cave dwellers, and choir members alike.

"On a hill far away stood an old rugged cross
The emblem of suffering and shame
And I love that old cross where the dearest and best
For a world of lost sinners was slain
So I'll cherish the old rugged cross (rugged cross)
Till my trophies at last I lay down I will cling to the old rugged cross
And exchange it some day for a crown
To the old rugged cross I will ever be true
It's shame and reproach gladly bear
Then he'll call me some day to my home far away

Where his glory forever I'll share
And I'll cherish the old rugged cross (rugged cross)
Till my trophies at last I lay down
And I will cling to the old rugged cross
And exchange it some day for a crown I will cling to the old
rugged cross
And exchange it some day for a crown."
Then the lights in the Haven went out.

31

COFFEE BEANS

1 Chronicle 16:11

"Seek the LORD and His strength; Seek His face evermore!"

Two years had passed, and significant events had unfolded. Lisa and Alex celebrated the birth of their son, Joseph, who was approaching his first birthday. His birth during the tribulation, within the confines of a cave, had raised concerns about potential complications. The cave, which had once housed 150 souls, now held around 130 individuals. Twenty members had chosen to leave the safety and refuge Jesus provided. Unable to endure the confinement of the cave, they ventured out into the fallen world, hoping to survive on their own. Tragically, their journey was cut short by a devastating solar flare emitted by the sun, a flare that had been occurring with increasing intensity for some time. The temperature swiftly rose from a comfortable 65 degrees Fahrenheit to a scorching 300 degrees, instantly incinerating the twenty cave dwellers. The severity of these solar flares was not limited to their immediate vicinity; they were wreaking havoc across the globe, affecting the entire universe. Although solar storms have been a recurring phenomenon, their current intensity is unprecedented.

At times, these solar flares were powerful enough to engulf an area the size of Kentucky, reducing it to ashes. On other occasions, the flares were more minor in scale, devastating neighborhoods and reducing houses, people, and all living things to nothing more than charred remains. The impact of the flares left behind a trail of ashes capable of melting bridges as if they were made of plastic. Any vehicles—automobiles, trucks, motorcycles—within the range of the flares would instantly explode and disintegrate into almost dust. Additionally, meteorites were once again hurtling toward the Earth, wreaking havoc on buildings, houses, and human lives. These fiery rocks were igniting forest fires of unprecedented scale, surpassing any previous records. It was as if the sky was raining supersonic projectiles, engulfing everything in a destructive inferno.

The woods and mountains of northern Maine weren't out of danger from this. There were fires everywhere! The Haven was insulated with dirt and rocks, but it was still scary! The leaders were doing fine; their faith was at an all-time high! The others, well, they were scared!

The mountain would shake at times! To the leaders, that meant they needed to sweep the floor again—no biggie.

The deer, moose, bears, wolves, and mountain lions hid in the lakes and ponds, trying to make it through that horrible time! There were also people hiding in those bodies of water, but most weren't Christians. Millions upon millions of people were killed! Jesus was slow to anger, but He was angry is to be feared! How many babies were murdered by mothers supposed to care for their children? Only God knew because the numbers were so overwhelming! They could have found homes for those children; anything would have been better than killing them. It makes sense what Jesus meant in *Matthew 19:14 "Let the little children come to me, and do not forbid them; for of such is the kingdom of heaven."*

Jesus knew that an uncountable number of children would be appearing in heaven at an alarming rate, especially in the last days! It seemed that before the rapture, abortion had become widespread, similar to when children were sacrificed to the god of Baal. People were celebrating their right to terminate unborn children! The blood of Jesus Christ forgave many mothers who had abortions, and their children met them in heaven on the day of the rapture. It was indeed a remarkable sight!

As Greg said, God's moral values are much higher than ours, so Moses wrote the ten commands through the Lord. God gave those rules for humanity to follow, but all people had failed. That's why Jesus Christ died for us and was resurrected for the sins of anyone who wanted forgiveness through a relationship as a born-again Christian with Christ.

California was devastated by the big earthquake that everyone had predicted. Unfortunately, the state experienced significant damage, and portions ended up in the Pacific Ocean. The pornography industry associated with the state had reached alarming levels, resembling the immorality of Sodom and Gomorrah. Hollywood, known for producing countless horror movies, was submerged under a hundred feet of water, ending their production. The film industry had been increasingly antagonistic towards Christianity, blaspheming and mocking Jesus, but He ultimately intervened to halt such actions.

The peace and security covenant had vanished! People were filled with anger, violence, and a demonic spirit. Small-scale wars erupted, with individuals killing each other over necessities like a bag of rice. The situation was truly horrific! Although the prayers of the tribulation saints continued, they were happening on a smaller scale. The cave dwellers prayed constantly and held Bible studies in small groups throughout the Haven. Greg, Elijah, and Tim preached passionately every night! They were determined not to hinder Jesus' fulfillment of prophecy; no one could.

God will always have the final say, and just as in the days of Noah, His wrath was being unleashed. Jesus was fulfilling prophecies that the unbelieving people once mocked before the rapture. Only those in the Haven and other faithful Christians understood the significance and were not laughing. Pastor Greg often reminded them, "With Jesus, we can weather any storm that comes our way." Life was becoming more challenging within the Haven. Although the garden thrived, the meat supply had to be rationed into smaller portions. Interestingly, Greg, of all people, may have struggled the most with this change since he enjoyed a good steak!

Elijah invited Greg and Maria to his place early before breakfast. He had a small bag of instant coffee stashed away and felt that Greg, of all people, deserved it the most. With the tremendous responsibility of running the Haven, it was only fitting. In many ways, Haven resembled a large church, and running a church was no easy task. Almost everyone slept in bunk beds, and the constant lack of privacy could take a toll on anyone.

They walked into Elijah's and Ruth's abode. Elijah spoke a bit quieter than usual, "Pastor Greg, Maria, I have a surprise!"

Greg and Maria smelled the coffee before they ever saw it! Maria said a little too loudly, "You have coffee!"

"Yes, yes, please keep it down to a whisper. We only have this small bag!"

Ruth said, "We've been saving it since we got here dear."

They all gathered around the table, with Elijah and Ruth perched on the edge of the bed, taking a sip of coffee simultaneously. Greg jokingly remarked, "Ah, so you've been enjoying coffee and keeping it a secret from your fellow brothers and sisters in Christ? Hmmm."

Elijah took another sip and swallowed, "Well now that you put it that way, yeah I guess I have!"

Ed poked his head through the window, "Do you have coffee?"

Ruth said, "Why yes we do, would you like some Ed? And how about your wife?"

"She doesn't drink the stuff and she's probably in the kitchen by now."

Maria laughed, "That's horrible that she doesn't drink coffee, can I get her portion Ruth?"

"Yes dear, you can have Rose's coffee."

Then Tim came around the corner; his wife Hannah was still sleeping. He looked in through the door, "I know that smell, you guys have coffee!"

At that moment, Lisa, with her baby in her arms, pushed Tim

out of the doorway, jumped into the cottage with a crazed look, and demanded, "I need coffee!"

Greg laughed and said, "There's going to be a stampede of people coming! We need to drink the evidence ASAP! I need a refill!"

They all drank the coffee while that wonderful smell poured out of that little cottage in a cave on a mountain in northern Maine.

After another sip, Elijah said, "It's the little things in life that we took for granted before that is so enchanting these days. I don't know about you guys, but my hair is standing on end!"

Lisa said, "Do you think we'll have coffee after the tribulation?"

With his eyes wide open, Tim said, "We haven't had caffeine in years!"

Elijah said, "And this is really strong coffee!"

"I don't know dear. That's a great question for Pastor Greg."

Pastor Greg replied, "I'm ready to go build a garage or something! My heart is going a hundred miles per hour!"

Elijah and Ruth were overcome with joy, their eyes welling up with tears. Elijah exclaimed, "We could really use a small garage next to the garden. The shed is currently packed with garden tools and, of course, your and Maria's 'weapons of mass destruction'!"

Ruth noticed Doctor Sarah and David, who had just gotten married two weeks earlier, approaching them. She quickly poured the last two cups of coffee and handed them out of the window, almost like a drive-thru. "The last two cups are for you, Doctor Sarah and David! God bless you both!" she exclaimed.

Lisa was getting annoyed and again asked, "Pastor Greg, do you think we'll have coffee after the tribulation?"

Greg looked at her, then looked at David and asked, "We have enough wood to build a small garage, right Dave?"

"We still have more wood than we could ever use, Pastor Greg. Would you like Jamie and I to start building you a garage?"

"Pastor Greg, you still haven't answered me about my coffee question!"

"I want to help! I'm thinking we could start building it now!"

Lisa asked Ruth, "How much coffee did you give him anyway?"

Pastor Greg turned with his eyes like dinner plates and snapped, "Not enough! Are you sure that you only stashed a bag Elijah?"

Congressman Ed McGwire said, "We might have coffee after the tribulation? I hope so!"

Lisa called out to Pastor Greg as he and Dave approached the lumber pile, "Pastor Greg, you should do a sermon on coffee and the millennial reign of Christ! Or how about a Bible study!" The comment sparked laughter throughout Elijah and Ruth's cottage, with some even shedding tears of joy. Elijah warmly patted Lisa's back and remarked, "You are such a blessing in this place!" Lisa then handed little Joseph to Maria, gave Elijah a big hug, and playfully added, "Delight yourself in the Lord, and He will give you the desires of your heart, like coffee... right?"

"Ruth, show her the picture or our baby."

"Are you sure dear?"

"Yes, she never got an answer to her question when we met her."

Ruth reached into an old purse and pulled out a picture, "This was Noah."

"Oh, he was so beautiful!

"Yes, he was, Ruth and I loved him so much."

"Dear Noah had Necrotizing Enterocolitis and we spent exactly fourteen days with him before he passed."

"I can't wait to see my son at the end of this."

"I'm so sorry. I didn't know."

"How could you dear."

"Well anytime you want to borrow Joseph, he's yours!"

"On behalf of my wife and I, we accept."

"Great! Here ya go Elijah! I'm going to have some breakfast in peace and quiet!"

32

BURNT TOAST

Proverbs 15

31 Whoever heeds life-giving correction will be at home among the wise.

Five and a half years into the great tribulation, the Haven housed a hundred and fifty inhabitants. Earthquakes occurred nearly daily, and tornadoes wreaked havoc across the world. Straight-line winds, hurricanes, and various other severe weather phenomena were commonplace. The violent weather often rendered it impossible for anyone to venture outside the Haven. However, this did not faze the leaders, who calmly sat on the couches, enjoying their breakfast. They had grown accustomed to these challenges and had developed a profound closeness to Jesus over the years, remaining unfazed by the storms. Their bond with one another had also grown incredibly strong. They were all best friends and envisioned living near Elijah's and Ruth's cottage, next to each other, after the tribulation, provided the cottage remained standing. Their love for one another was genuine, and their conversations, especially in the mornings, were filled with unique depth. Meanwhile, the other cave dwellers in the Haven felt a sense of melancholy as if weighed down by an invisible heaviness.

Pastor Greg, like, every day, started the conversation.

"Alex, what's going on in the world today?"

"I think that we might be on the precipice of a geomagnetic pole reversal. A lot of chatter about in the UN and World Watch!"

Maria said, "Isn't that where the north pole and south pole change places?"

Elijah answered, "That's exactly what he's talking about!"

Sarah replied, "Well, that sounds like a ride, can we even live through that? Also, Ed gets seasick. I think we know everything about everyone in here."

Ruth said, "Dear, I think that getting seasick would be the least of his worries."

Pastor Greg pondered aloud, "I wonder if that's what Revelation 6:14 meant? 'Then the sky receded as a scroll when it is rolled up, and every mountain and island was moved out of its place.' It certainly seems like it. We're in the mountains, and it feels like we're being moved."

Lisa said, "Elijah grab Joseph again, would ya? No one tell the other cave dwellers, those people need some good news!"

Sarah said, "Why aren't we more worried about news like that? It's like nothing bothers us, must be a Holy Spirit thing."

Ruth said, "Jesus has seen us through so much!"

Liz said, "I'm worried about the others, someone needs to talk to the other cave dwellers and see how there doing?"

Elijah said, "Lisa, little Joseph went poo again."

"Let me know how that goes Grandpa Elijah."

Ruth said, "Dear give him to me, I'll change him."

Liz said, "Thank you Ruth. Maybe Pastor Greg should go see how the others are all doing?"

Alex said, "I believe a pole shift has been occurring gradually over time. However, with the accelerated melting of ice at the poles causing the world to wobble, it's possible that a pole shift could happen much more rapidly."

Sarah looked at Greg, expressing concern, "I'm not sure if you should talk to them. You're different, somewhat distant, when you're around them. I value our friendship and needed to be honest with you. By the way, I might have a solution for seasickness."

Ruth said, "Dear, you've stiff when you're around them. Is it possible you're traumatized? We did lose some of the cave dwellers, but it wasn't your fault. Please don't carry that burden. Perhaps this upcoming pole shift will feel like a thrilling ride at the fair. I absolutely adore the fair!"

Elijah said, "My wife is right Pastor Greg, something's are out of our control."

Pastor Greg said, "I'm not stiff, maybe a little quiet. Alex the last time a pole shift happened was seven thousand years ago. We know that's a lie. I wonder how long ago the last pole shift really was, maybe it happened in the days of Noah?"

Lisa said, "My life resolves around washing cloth diapers. Your really stiff around them Pastor Greg, kinda like a burnt piece of toast."

Maria said, "I was thinking that he's more like a dead fish that has been dried out. I remember studying about a pole shift, it's really interesting. I bet it happens quick!"

Elijah said, "Are you talking about salted fish dried in the sun? I've had that and it's really good, especially on a cracker!"

"We used to eat it in Mexico when I was a child, it's delicious!"

"Wait a minute. I'm not like a piece of burnt toast, or dried-out fish!"

Alex said, "It could happen in a month, maybe less. It could happen in a day. I love my toast a little burnt Pastor Greg, you're good."

Sarah said, "When you preach your very warm, but after, not so much. I would kill for a cracker right now!"

"I'm always warm and a cracker would be awesome right now! A month, that's a fast pole shift! I wonder what that would do to the world?"

"Maybe my Burnt Toast husband should go and talk to them and see how they're doing?"

"Oh, come on Maria, I wasn't calling you names!"

Honey, "I was just expressing my concern. Alex now you've got me thinking. What would actually happen if the Earth flipped over in a day?"

Elijah chuckled and interjected, "Pastor Greg, you're their shepherd.

You should go over there and see how they're doing. Trust me, I have a surprise waiting for you if you do."

"What's the surprise?"

"I've had two boxes of coffee, and a box of dark chocolate back at our old cottage! Maybe we could do a special mission? I didn't want to endanger anyone, so we didn't say anything."

Lisa leaned over, slapped Elijah's shoulder, and said, "No way, you have coffee! Alex, is Elijah's and Ruth's house still in one piece?"

Elijah said, "Alex was showing me yesterday and it sure is, not even a mark on the cottage, hasn't been burned up—it's a miracle from Jesus!"

Sarah said, "Pastor Greg if I were you, I wouldn't run for president anytime soon."

Tim said, "I could zip over there on my bike and comeback in probably three hours considering the road is all beat up."

Lisa said, "I love your voice Elijah, you should've been on the radio."

Maria said, "President Greg Oliver, that's not happening anytime soon."

Tim yelled to the kitchen, "Hannah, I'm going to take my dirt bike for a ride!"

"Okay, just be home for dinner!"

"I have permission."

Greg looked at Maria and said sarcastically, "We don't have a president anymore, we're in the midst of the great tribulation—remember."

Ruth excitingly said, "Oh dear, he was a DJ for years weren't you honey. Joseph is getting so big Lisa!"

Maria replied, "Maybe if you took Lisa with you the dead fish stiffness would be less noticeable!"

Lisa said, "I would've been a good DJ. Do you think that we'll have a radio station in Millennial reign of Christ—Pastor Greg?"

"I'm actually very loose Maria! I don't know Lisa, maybe we'll have a radio station, it is a thousand years."

Alex said, "The Earth spins at about a thousand miles per hour. I'll do some calculations later today. Pastor Greg take Lisa with you, she has a gift from God, it's like a superpower with people or something."

Lisa hugged Alex and said, "That is so sweet honey! Pastor Greg I have a superpower!"

Pastor Greg and Lisa silently rose from their seats and walked toward the cave dwellers seated at the back of the bus. With his eyes fixed ahead, Greg turned to Lisa and confessed, "I'm not sure what to say to them. I feel at ease and confident preaching God's word to you all, but with them, it's different. Are my sermons good, right?"

"I truly believe you deliver excellent sermons," Lisa reassured Greg. "They strike the right balance - not too hard, not too soft - and you consistently uplift and encourage everyone at the end. You truly are a remarkable preacher!"

"What should I say to them?"

"Say good morning. I want to know how everyone is doing. We're here to help you guys anyway we can!"

"They look like they're wary of me or something?"

"Maybe it's the special forces thing, Pastor Greg? They've been arguing a lot too, like a lot!"

"I need your superpower."

It felt like a long journey as Greg walked across the basketball court toward the back of the cave. The cave dwellers suddenly sprang out of their bunks, almost as if they were expecting trouble. Whispers circulated among them as they speculated about the reason for Pastor Greg's presence.

"Umm, good morning everyone. How are you all doing?"

The crowd all replied, "We're fine. everything is good. Couldn't be better Pastor Greg."

Lisa looked at the much taller Pastor Greg and whispered, "Are they telling the truth?"

"No, they're not and I can read body language."

Lisa smiled and said, "That's what Maria said you thought. Do you want me to say something, Pastor?"

"Please!"

"Hi everyone, I'm Lisa, everyone remember me?"

They all started to smile a little bit and together said, "Yes."

"We couldn't help but notice that you all seem a bit down, and it's completely understandable given that we're in the midst of the great tribulation, confined to this cave," Pastor Greg addressed the cave dwellers. "Just look at you all, packed together like sardines. It must get tiresome after a while!"

A few individuals stepped forward, expressing their grievances. One person complained, "Many of us can't sleep due to the snoring." Another voiced their desire, saying, "We want to stay informed about what's happening in the world. We only receive fragments of information, but it would be helpful if someone could provide us with daily updates, like a real news source." A third person lamented, "Just look at my height! I can't fit comfortably in the bunk, and it's making my back hurt."

Pastor Greg could not address the situation, but Lisa stepped in confidently. She glanced at the individuals who had spoken up and declared, "I have a solution for this. If you're someone who snores, please take two steps forward. I know it might be embarrassing, but let's address it openly. And for those who don't snore, please point them out. I'm determined to fix this issue."

A group of approximately fifty individuals stepped forward, and Lisa addressed them again, wearing a wide smile. "Don't worry, I'm not kicking you out!" she exclaimed jokingly. "But we do need to make some changes with the bunk beds. We'll need some bunk switching, or at least for a lot of people. Those who snore can move to the far right side, where there will be enough bunks to provide some space in-between. Oh, and I have a great idea! I'll ask David and Jamie to put up a wall between the snorers and the non-snorers!"

She continued, "We're all aware that the living quarters of the cave are becoming too cramped for this many people. Even in this huge cave, space is getting tight, we're trying to build houses as fast as we can. So, here's what we'll do: Each day, one person should go and sit next to Alex. He will provide you with the day's news. Today, we were discussing the possibility of a geometrical pole reversal. But don't worry, Jesus over and over has shown that He's taking care of us. After receiving the news, bring it back and share it with the others. We can call it 'Haven

News'! We can set it up on the basketball court. Oh, and you, the tall guy, I'll talk to David and have him create a custom bed for you. It'll be all pimped out. How does that sound?"

One person began to clap, and soon others joined in until the entire group applauded. Lisa had a unique aura about her, an anointing that everyone recognized. Pastor Greg addressed them, "From this moment on, Lisa is officially the ambassador of the Haven! Allow me to present to you, Ambassador Lisa!"

Lisa blushed slightly but maintained her composure. "Thank you, Pastor Greg, for entrusting me with this position. I consider it a great blessing. Also, I believe we need a leader specifically for this section of the Cavern. I have known Uncle Bob for a long time, and he's a great, honest guy. With that said, I choose you, Bob Heald, to be the leader for all of us here. If that's agreeable to everyone?"

All the people liked Bob and agreed. Uncle Bob was asked if he would take the job, and he said yes.

33

SIX YEARS IN

Revelation 9

1 Then the fifth angel sounded: And I saw a star fallen from heaven to the Earth. To him was given the key to the bottomless pit. 2 And he opened the bottomless pit, and smoke arose out of the pit like the smoke of a great furnace.

One year remained, and it was a beautiful July day. Last spring, there had been several bouts of rain, resulting in lush foliage, green grass, and blooming flowers. However, the leaders of the Haven had a vital discussion planned for that morning. David had constructed a lightweight wooden box and attached it to the back of Tim's dirt bike. While the box wasn't aesthetically pleasing, its purpose was clear—to retrieve coffee and chocolate from Davis's house.

The morale within the Haven had reached an all-time low, and it wasn't solely due to the lack of coffee and chocolate. Six months ago, their meat supply had run out, but venturing out for hunting had become extremely risky. The organization known as Smith and World Watch relentlessly hunted down Christians daily, utilizing drones that patrolled the world. Their goal seemed to please the antichrist, but their motives went far beyond that. Anyone caught without the mark was typically shot on sight, while others were flown to Jerusalem for Calvo.

The dragon had taken its place in Jerusalem, at the temple, presenting a blasphemous and horrifying spectacle. It had turned against everyone except the witness and its military forces. The dragon's actions resulted in an alarming escalation of killings, far surpassing the hysteria of the French Revolution. The streets of Jerusalem were now filled with numerous guillotines, serving as instruments of death. The dragon's motive for these mass executions stemmed from its deep-rooted hatred towards humanity, simply because God had created mankind. The beast had always harbored envy toward humanity, and now it seized the opportunity to unleash its wrath and claim as many lives as possible. Shockingly, the crowds of people reveled in these horrific acts, with the events being broadcasted live on various media platforms and social networks.

Pastor Greg often referred to Matthew 24:12, which states, "And because lawlessness will abound, the love of many will grow cold." However, this verse failed to capture the true magnitude of what was transpiring among the remaining survivors. The cruelty and depravity witnessed were far beyond what could be conveyed by words alone.

Pastor Gregg spoke as usual but was in military mode: "Give me the news about the bull moose at the lake."

Alex had all nine monitors with the image of the big male moose knee-deep in the water eating, and he said, "He's still right there."

Elijah said, "What a stunning animal!"

Maria said, "And tasty!"

"Here's the plan: tomorrow morning, before sunrise, Tim will ride his dirt bike to the Davis's place and retrieve the goods. Have you familiarized yourself with the necessary information? Elijah has provided you with all the details you need, correct?"

"Yes sir, he did, everything is set."

"David, Jamie and I will take down that moose and get the meat back to the Haven as quickly as possible."

Maria said, "I'm going too! After you I'm the best one for the job, and you know that!"

"I also know that angry Joe wants you dead!"

Maria looked visibly upset, "Greg, I'm going!"

"Okay, so David, Jamie, Maria and I will put the stunning moose down."

Elijah, always wise, said, "Why don't we get some of the other cave dwellers to go with you guys?"

Pastor Greg had reservations about the idea, but he acknowledged its validity. "We have acquired additional thermal suits, which should help conceal us among the trees. We also have two compound bows and arrows at our disposal. Lisa, can you suggest two or three capable and strong guys who could accompany us on this mission?"

"Definitely Uncle Bob, he's a bull, really strong. We also have his friend Luke; both spend half the day working out. The tall guy is strong, but I don't think he'd fit in the suit."

"Well tell Bob we need three."

"Honestly that would make the other cave dwellers feel like they're helping more. I'll have them praying starting tonight until you guys get back safe and sound tomorrow."

They all held hands, and Pastor Greg led them in prayer, "Lord, you knew that we were going to do this before the beginning of time. We would ask that you keep us safe like you have been for the last six years. We are Your servants, and You are our Father, watch over us, in the name of Jesus... amen."

The plan was set in motion, and the tension among the Haven's inhabitants was palpable. Nervousness filled the air, causing many to forgo sleep that night. Although there was no church service, the entire community engaged in fervent prayer. Some may have questioned whether the coffee and chocolate were worth the risk, but Tim had received a divine directive to retrieve them. Jesus intended to reward the cave dwellers for their endurance thus far.

It was early morning, and the darkness still enveloped the surroundings as the group set out together. Tim revved the engine of his dirt bike and quickly sped down the road toward Davis's place. Meanwhile, Greg, Maria, Jamie, Luke, Uncle Bob, and two others rushed toward the location of the moose. Maintaining utmost stealth, Greg and Maria skillfully aimed their compound bows and arrows, delivering precise heart shots that instantly killed the moose. The animal fell near the water's edge, just a short distance from the land. However, they found themselves positioned between the lake and a field, not strictly at the exact location as the moose had been the day before.

The drones had flown over their position throughout the morning. There was no way to stop what they started. Not everyone in the Haven is a vegetarian. The meat was neatly washed and bagged. They had some poles and hung the carcass in the middle, and the guys were running back and forth to the Haven! Greg and Maria were cutting up the meat.

It was eight thirty when Director Joe Smith, filled with demonic influence, entered World Watch. The organization had detected the cave dwellers' presence through drone surveillance, and Jimmy and the others had observed them while they were dismembering the moose. Although the thermal suits provided effective camouflage, the cave dwellers were exposed and lacked any significant cover in the open. Joe instructed, "Bring the drone down to a lower altitude, Jimmy so that we can get a clearer view. People, do we have any troops in proximity to their location?"

Kelly said, "We have a military helicopter with ten troops near their location."

"Good they can land in that field and do away with those traitors!"

Jimmy yelled, "IT'S MARIA SILVA, DIRECTOR! SHE LOOKED UP AT THE DRONE!

CHECK OUT HER PHOTO!"

Director Joe Smith was filled with malicious delight, relishing his long-awaited revenge. She had incessantly messaged him countless times, inundating him with updates about her marriage and even sending him pictures of plates filled with Mexican food she had prepared.

"I WANT HER ALIVE IN WORLD WATCH CUFFED!"

Maria and Greg were almost done with the remaining meat when Alex's urgent call came through, "World Watch has spotted your location, and they're dispatching a helicopter towards you!"

At that moment, the low-flying helicopter appeared with rifles pointed at the two! The rest were in the house part of the Haven, packed with everyone watching!

They were forced to raise their hands as the soldiers quickly approached them. With guns pointed at them, the soldiers ordered them to stay down and warned that anyone who resisted would be killed. Among the chaos, a man placed a pistol against Greg's head. In a moment of courage, Greg turned to Maria and declared with unwavering love, "I love you so much!"

"I love you too!"

One of the soldiers yelled at her and said, "Are you Maria Ana Silva?"

She yelled back, "I AM A CHILD OF GOD! JESUS IS COMING AND YOU'RE ALL

GOING TO HELL!"

One of the soldiers showed a picture of her in army uniform on a tablet, "It's her sir!"

"World Watch wants you, Silva! Kill the other one!"

At that very moment, smoke poured into the air from the middle of the Earth, and the sky darkened worldwide! Joe yelled, "What the hell is going on out there!"

Out of the forest emerged a horde of hundreds of menacing, black demonic creatures adorned with large teeth, stingers on their tails, and wings. The soldiers, in panic, opened fire on the advancing creatures, but their efforts proved futile as the creatures only accelerated their charge. The soldiers restraining Greg and Maria became the primary targets of the demonic onslaught. Surprisingly, the demonic beings ignored the two cave dwellers, recognizing them as children of God and thus untouchable. Within moments, the relentless onslaught overpowered and subdued all the troops.

The cave dwellers were all watching this unfold on the holographic monitors!

The troops ran and jumped into the military helicopter in horrific pain, but they weren't alone! The helicopter took off and made it across the lake, only to crash in the distance. A frightening explosion occurred, and flames shot into the air. The director ordered the drone to make a suicide run at the two. They both drew their pistols and started shooting as the drone headed straight for them. Director Joe Smith and the World Watch team last saw the drone being shot down. The two ducked and watched the drone smash into the field behind them. The demonic creatures were everywhere, but God would not allow them to harm any Christians worldwide!

The people in Haven celebrated while those at World Watched yelled profanities! Greg and Maria embraced and shared a passionate kiss. The cave dwellers continued to watch, cheering loudly. They were thrilled to see Greg and Maria safe. Jesus supported the two leaders!

After the kiss, Maria said in confusion, "Thou shalt not kill—right!"

"But you can shoot down a drone; after all, there wasn't anyone in it! I think they now have a good idea of your location. However, with these creatures roaming around for the next five months, the Earth will be in darkness, and everyone will be safe! Thank you, Jesus!"

Maria said, "Lets grab the rest of this moose meat and head home! Jesus is so good! That was a close one!"

The demonic creatures were running by them, and Greg said, "That wasn't that close, did I ever tell you about a mission we did in Colombia?"

Right then, Alex called again, "Pastor Greg, there's another bull moose at the beaver pond, what should we do?"

"We should hunt that moose as soon as possible. It's already getting dark, and it's not even noon yet. Let's have Tim, David, Jamie, and a few others go and retrieve it before the opportunity to leave the cave closes for months. Maria and I will freshen up and head to the cottage. We need some relaxation after today."

"Pastor Greg, they don't need the thermal suits, right?"

"Nope, everyone will be safe!"

The cave dwellers went to the beaver pond and obtained the other moose! More people were able to help because they weren't under constant surveillance. They stored nearly two thousand pounds of meat in the freezers, a tremendous blessing. Everyone felt exhausted after such a day.

The demonic creatures spread across the planet, inflicting painful stings upon everyone marked by the beast. The sting was worse than that of a scorpion. The people in Haven decided to throw a party the next day, finding solace in the place Jesus had prepared for them. With only a year remaining, the final year of the tribulation proved to be the most severe yet.

34

LET'S PARTY

Philippians 4
4 Rejoice in the Lord always. Again I will say, rejoice!
5 Let your gentleness be known to all men. The Lord is at hand.
6 Be anxious for nothing, but in everything by prayer and supplication,
with thanksgiving, let your requests be made known to God; 7 and the peace
of God, which surpasses all understanding, will guard your hearts and minds
through Christ Jesus.

After the successful moose hunt, everyone slept soundly. The following day, there was an air of excitement in Haven, and everyone was
joyful. The presence of meat in the freezer and coffee and chocolate
brought immense happiness. Could it get any better than that? A party
was planned in the third Cavern at the basketball court. The tables were
set up with chairs arranged everywhere. The people had come close to
losing their beloved Pastor and his wife, which gave rise to a newfound
appreciation for Greg and Maria. The party celebrated God's blessings
upon this beautiful couple, and Ambassador Lisa of Haven was en-
trusted with organizing the festivities. She took her role very seriously.
Mexican food was being prepared, following Maria's grandma's recipe,
with Maria unable to assist due to the ambassador's insistence.

Additionally, they were making Brazilian food for Pastor Greg, courtesy of Ramona. Ramona, who hailed from Brazil, was currently spending time with her Uncle Bob and Hannah, who had married Tim. Ramona and Hannah had become the best of friends.

Ramona could sing Brazilian hymns very well; she had an incredible voice. Pastor Greg and

Ramona and Hannah were the only two Brazilians in Haven, actually Hannah was half Brazilian like Greg, and Lisa persuaded a hesitant Ramona to sing a few songs at the party. It's important to note that the party was dedicated to Jesus, utilizing His servants and their obedience to His calling. Jesus saved them just in the nick of time!

The love between Greg and Maria had grown even stronger after they narrowly escaped danger. Greg almost faced a gunshot to the head, while Maria narrowly avoided being abducted by Smith's team. Seeking relaxation, the couple lounged in their bungalow. Maria had a mischievous expression and suggested, "Let's send Joe a text and see how he's doing, shall we?" It wasn't a question, and Greg understood her intentions. Knowing she was aware of the risks, Greg glanced at her. Joe was hiding at home in his basement, though he would never admit it. He was terrified of the creatures that were attacking everyone.

"Joe how are you doing, is everything okay? I just wanted to check in, make sure that you're okay."

"Maria, we have a location or at least an idea were you and I'm guessing that was your husband, thought you should know that!"

"Well, it doesn't take a rocket doctor to know that, Joe. Are those creatures in Virginia?

Have you been stung by any yet? You know they don't sting born again and believe in Jesus Christ. You knew that, Joe, didn't you?"

"They're stinging everyone Maria, don't be foolish, and that's a rocket scientist."

"You need to watch the video again, Joe, because my husband and I weren't stung. I have to go now, as we're having a party tonight. I'll talk to you soon. Say hello to the team for me. Oh, I know you're not a rocket scientist, Joe. I was just kidding. You really need to lighten up, you know? If you weren't working for the devil, we would invite you to the party. It would be much better than hiding in the basement."

The world had plunged into darkness, with demonic creatures scurrying and flying. Joe opened his computer and replayed the video once more. He observed as the helicopter landed and soldiers equipped with video cameras disembarked. With the aid of satellites, Joe had a clear view from multiple angles. He watched in awe as the creatures emerged; their incredible speed shocked him. Not only were they running, but they were also capable of flying. Every individual they encountered became attached and stung, except for Greg and Maria, who seemed to pass through unharmed. Joe couldn't believe his eyes and exclaimed aloud, "That's impossible! They didn't get stung!"

Another text from Maria, "Joe?"

"Maria, I thought that you have a party to go to traitor!"

"You watched the video, didn't you?"

"LEAVE ME IN PEACE MARIA!"

"Okay, Joe, but I suggest finding a better hiding place than your basement. They might find you there. Perhaps under the bed would be a safer option. That's what I did as a little girl in Mexico when my big brother told me there were monsters after me. Of course, that was just pretend. But in your case, it's not a game. Oh, and Joe, it's only five months."

"WHAT IS ONLY FIVE MONTHS!"

"It's only five months until these demonic creatures disappear, and then the sky will clear. You can try to come and find me then! It's almost like a game of hide and seek. In Mexico, I used to love playing that as a little girl, and I was the best at it! No one ever found me! Oh, and Joe, all this talk about demonic animals is actually in the Bible. Check out Revelation 9! Alright, maybe I'll send you some pictures of the food, Joe! Bye!"

"STOP WITH THE INNOCENT LITTLE GIRL FROM MEXICO THING! I KNOW

WHO YOU REALLY ARE!"

"My husband Greg said, 'See yah, wouldn't want to be yah.'"

"I didn't say that you're lying to that man."

"Chill, you've said it before, we all have!"

Greg laughed and said, "You're driving that man crazy!"

"Greg, he's responsible for killing our brothers and sisters every day. He nearly killed my husband yesterday. Don't feel sorry for him; he chose his path when he embraced the dragon as his savior."

The residential area of Haven was bustling with people cooking, and the temperature was scorching hot due to the mouthwatering aromas wafting through all three parts of the Cavern. Greg and Maria remained in bed, holding each other tightly, grateful for being alive. Ambassador Lisa was busily pacing back and forth, entirely dedicated to her role. She would wave at little Joseph as she passed by the Davis family.

The tables began filling with food, and Elijah gave Greg and Maria four Snickers chocolate bars to satisfy them. However, Lisa had instructed everyone not to touch them. Elijah strolled past Oliver's shack and tossed the chocolate bars through the window. Since none of the cottages had glass windows, it was easy.

Tim also acquired several large plastic containers of powdered Kool-Aid from the Davis' place. It would be a refreshing addition to the coffee and assortment of chocolates. It seemed like Elijah had quite the sweet tooth! At last, the table was set, and Lisa banged a wooden spoon against a pan, exclaiming, "LET'S PARTY!"

The party began with an emotional Pastor Greg leading a prayer, saying, "Lord, we want to thank You for this food and for our brothers and sisters who are gathered here to fellowship with us." As Pastor Greg continued his prayer, he choked up, saying, "Father, we want to thank You in the name of Jesus for keeping us all safe, for protecting my wife and me."

That's when tears streamed down his wife's and many other cave dwellers' faces. Pastor Greg asked if Elijah would finish the prayer with a desperate look towards his direction, and Elijah continued without missing a beat, "Yes, Lord, we thank you for Your grace and mercy! We love you, Jesus! We are Yours Jesus! Thank you for chocolate Jesus! In Your holy name we pray, and everyone said—amen!"

The third Cavern was a lively party, with everyone enjoying the food and sharing stories. Inside the refuge, the atmosphere was delightful. However, outside the Haven, not only in Maine but worldwide, God's wrath was being unleashed upon the enemies of the people who had turned against Jesus and His chosen Christians. Even Jerusalem was facing its challenges. The antichrist was furious, as his wicked mission had been significantly hindered.

The Davis couple were talking to Greg and Maria, and that's when Lisa grabbed Greg's and Maria's hands and said, "I need both of you to mingle with people you two don't know well!"

She guided them to the rear of the Haven, introducing each person by name and sharing their personal histories one by one. She had a personal connection with each individual and shouted over the music and conversations, "Pastor Greg and Maria, this is Will Jackson! His wife Elizabeth was raptured along with the rest of his family!"

Pastor Greg, for once, felt a sense of belonging and responded, "It's a pleasure to meet you, Will! I had a close friend in the military named Will, and I always thought that you bear a striking resemblance to him!"

"God picked the perfect guy for this job Pastor Greg. We watched when you had a gun to your head! We heard what you said, it was heroic!"

With a smile Greg said, "I wasn't heroic Will; I was scared to death!"

Then Maria conversed with Will while Lisa grabbed Greg's hand and led him to another person. "This is Dakota," she said, "she witnessed her entire family vanish during the Fourth of July parade, just like Tim and I did at the cookout!"

"It's a pleasure to meet you Dakota, obviously I'm Pastor Greg, if you don't mind me asking; how old are you?"

"I'm twenty-three years old, so I was seventeen when the rapture happened."

"How did God direct you to the here?"

"That's an excellent question with an even better story! I was all by myself, having just accepted Jesus as my Savior, and immediately He began guiding me on my journey. God instructed me to go to the flagpole at my old high school, where they used to gather for prayer. When I arrived, I met Julie."

Dakota grabbed Julie's arm and pulled her over, laughing, "This is Julie!"

"So, you two met at the flagpole at your high school—wow!"

Julie grabbed Emilio's hand and pulled him over, "This is Emilio. He showed up at the flagpole too."

"Emilio, you must be Latin American?"

Maria overheard the name Emilio and realized that she hadn't spoken to him yet. Before Greg knew it, Maria and Emilio conversed in Spanish, and Maria looked incredibly happy to speak her native language. Julie and Dakota, who had been trying to learn Spanish, attempted to keep up with the conversation. Meanwhile, Greg glanced towards the front of the Cavern and saw Elijah, Ruth, Ed, and Rose laughing so hard that tears were streaming down their faces. He then turned his attention to Tim, holding Hannah and conversing with Sarah and David, all wearing broad smiles. As he observed Liz chasing after little Joseph around the basketball court with Jamie laughing, he wondered where Brandon might be. While Maria and Emilio continued their lively conversation, Lisa grabbed Greg's hand and asked if he knew other cave dwellers. He spent some time conversing with the other residents, realizing that this would become a remarkable story to share during the millennial reign of Christ. At that moment, Greg felt an overwhelming sense of love, and he reciprocated that love toward everyone there. He felt that he was genuinely embodying the role of a pastor, and he knew that God loved that.

After everyone had finished eating, coffee was served at the table along with the chocolate. Lisa had carefully calculated the exact amounts each person could have. When Ambassador Lisa spoke, people listened attentively except for Elijah, who had secretly stashed away his supply of chocolate and coffee in their cabin.

Pastor Greg, David, and Ramona made their way to the improvised stage and began to play. They started with a Brazilian hymn, and Ramona beautifully sang it in Portuguese. To everyone's surprise, except for Greg, Maria sang an old hymn in Spanish from her child-hood, a song her mother used to sing. Pastor Greg followed with a song dedicated to the Lord, "Celebrate," a Brazilian tune. Dave joined in singing in English, and soon everyone in the Haven was singing and dancing in the Holy Spirit. At that moment, as Pastor Greg played and sang, Jesus again gave him and everyone else a glimpse into the heavenly realm. They saw angels dancing and singing, catching sight of a majestic throne, though they couldn't directly behold the Father of Glory.

Seeing the heavenly realm was an experience that had the power to elevate their faith to new heights. And that's precisely what happened to the cave dwellers—they felt their faith increase exponentially again. With this newfound faith, they knew that they would persevere no matter what challenges lay ahead, even death itself. Fear no longer had a hold on them.

35

GEOMAGNETIC POLE REVERSAL

Revelation 16:20

"20 Then every island fled away, and the mountains were not found."

Only seven months remained until the arrival of Jesus and the body of Christ, who would destroy the antichrist and his followers. The world now featured robotic soldiers that resembled dogs, with guns and cameras in place of their faces. The level of technology in robotics has reached unprecedented heights. The UN military possessed various types of robotics, but the four-legged models were particularly effective in locating and eliminating individuals hidden in forests or mountains. Since the smoke and demonic creatures disappeared, these robotic dogs have been deployed alarmingly. Director Joe Smith saw this as his opportunity to capture Maria. A team of twenty robotic dogs was dispersed throughout the mountains of northern Maine. Some of them were dropped off at the same field where Maria and Greg were previously caught but managed to escape. The leaders observed the entire operation unfolding on their screens. These robotic dogs possessed remarkable speed, agility, and climbing abilities. Equipped with thermal imaging, they could detect fingerprints and swiftly identify individuals.

Director Smith closely monitored these developments. His deep-seated hatred for Christians, in general, had intensified, and he harbored a personal vendetta against Maria and her husband, Greg.

All one hundred and fifty cave dwellers had either married or were engaged. Pastor Greg would occasionally officiate the weddings of three or four couples at once. It was evident that God's plan was unfolding in every aspect, even in bringing together individuals who would get along so well that they would choose to marry. Our God is a God of details! Meanwhile, the leader's breakfast took place, and the concerns over the robotic dogs paled compared to what lay ahead. They were all aware that they stood on the threshold of a geomagnetic pole shift.

Pastor Greg, as always, started the conversation at breakfast, "How long do you think we have, Alex?"

"Pastor Greg, if it doesn't start in the next couple of hours I'd be surprised."

"David did you put rope seat belts in each of the bunks? The couches have a rope. I guess we have makeshift seat belts."

"Yes, I did. I also secured the legs of the couches. Ed and Rose will be staying in their place, so they're all set. Ed has a bucket if he needs it."

Doctor Sarah said, "I gave Ed some seasick pills, he should be fine."

Ruth added, "I'm glad Congressman Ed is in his cottage. Seeing people throw up always makes me sick to my stomach. How bad is this going to get, Alex?"

"No one really knows. I can only guess that it's going to be a ride we'll never forget!"

Elijah said, "We'll be fine, Ruth, and you always loved roller coasters!"

Greg said, "I think that it's going to be like no roller-coaster ride any of us have ever been on! How long will this last Alex?"

Maria said, "I had a dream last night and Jesus said it would be fast!"

Pastor Greg replied, knowing the Lord was speaking to them in dreams and visions, "You had a dream from God last night. Did He say anything else?"

"He said to hold on and watch His power!"

Lisa said, "I had a dream last-night that a young woman was coming here to the Haven."

Pastor Greg thought briefly, saying, "That would be difficult with those robotic killer dogs running around!"

Alex said, "Check out monitor five, did the woman in your dream look like her Lisa!"

"No way! That's her, that's the young woman that I dreamed about!"

Elijah said, "She has the same skin color as I do. Are you seeing this Ruth?"

"Dear, how could I miss it, and she is stunning! Aren't those dog things going to kill her, Pastor Greg?"

"They might, she's in the field near the lake. Maria, we might have to go down there and save her!"

At that moment, the robotic dogs surrounded her, resembling a pack of wolves. The leaders of the Haven felt deep concern, knowing they wouldn't reach her in time. World Watch was monitoring the situation on their computer screens. Smith, who had fallen ill, was home in bed, too sick to care about anything. Jimmy was now in charge of World Watch, the notorious organization responsible for unjustly killing innocent people.

Alex had the hummingbird trailing behind the young woman. The woman was dressed in loose, soft white pants that reached three-quarter length, paired with a white t-shirt. Tied tightly around her waist was a light blue sweatshirt. Her hair, dark and curly, cascaded down her shoulders. Carrying a pink backpack, she also wore a pair of sandals, and used a walking stick. Her appearance conveyed innocence and vulnerability.

The search-and-kill dogs spotted her and quickly made their way toward her. However, she remained unfazed, looking directly at the metal dogs and even smiling at the cameras Jimmy and his team used to monitor her. Her loose clothing seemed to float in the breeze as she walked, adding to her ethereal appearance. Both World Watch and the leaders of the Haven couldn't help but notice her fearlessness, a quality that caught their attention simultaneously. In frustration, Jimmy exclaimed, "She doesn't have a Lifeline on her hand, eliminate her!"

Maria, worried, said, "Jimmy just gave the order to have her killed!"

All twenty robotic dogs that had surrounded her suddenly experienced a simultaneous malfunction. Their legs folded, and smoke began to emanate from their bodies. The last image that Jimmy and his crew witnessed was her smiling at them. In frustration, Jimmy threw his pen and exclaimed, "What just happened, people?"

Kelly answered, "All of the dogs malfunctioned, maybe it's because of the polar shift that's about to hit sir?"

"Yeah, I think you're right. We need to hunker down during this polar shift. If anyone wants to go home, I'll understand. Just make sure you're back in the morning. The UN said things might get a little bumpy, but we'll be okay," Jimmy said.

Greg asked, "Did you just give the dogs a virus or something Alex?"

"I didn't do anything!"

Elijah said, "God has intervened, surely she's been sent by Jesus!"

David asked, "Are you and Maria going to let her in Pastor Greg?"

Greg replied, "Most definitely we're going to let her in!"

Maria reminded everyone, "If she doesn't make a cross than it could be a trap."

Liz said, "I bet you a trillion dollars that she makes a cross. There's a lot of fantastic walking to the Haven, and I want to meet her!

Lisa handed Joseph to Alex and said, "I want to meet her too, like right now! Remember Pastor Greg, you made me the ambassador!"

Greg smiled, "How could I forget Lisa. Let's all go meet her!"

The ten of them made their way to the boulder and opened it. They all piled out while the mysterious young lady appeared with her walking stick and a branch, making a cross. She joyfully said, "Shalom, my name is Abigail Kogan! Peace be with you all in the name of Jesus Christ, our Lord and Savior!"

Lisa walked up to her, forgot her title, and said, "You are so cool with the dog thing you did over there! Oh, I'm Lisa!"

Abigail smiled as if she knew Lisa and said, "It's a blessing to meet you, Lisa. That was God who did the dog thing over there. The Lord is really cool!"

Liz looked at her and said, "You are gorgeous! My name is Liz!"

"Hi Liz and thank you! It is a pleasure to meet you!"

One by one, they introduced themselves. Then they quickly went into the Haven and shut the boulder door behind them.

Maria said, "Abigail, you can sit on the couch next to me. All the other cave dwellers are tied up at the moment."

Pastor Greg asked, "Abigail do you know what a geomagnetic pole shift is?"

Abigail answered calmly, "No, I do not, Pastor Greg."

While manipulating the holographic monitors, Alex said, "Check out monitor one. That's the Earth, and watch it flip. Now the South Pole is where the North Pole was, and vice versa."

Sarah said, "I hope no one will get hurt here!"

Abigail giggled slightly and said, "I assure you that no one in this cave, which you call the Haven, will be harmed. The Lord watches over us. The waterfall provides us with electricity. We have a garden with vegetables. This cave in the mountains is our place of safety, and it symbolizes the refuge and strength we find in Jesus."

Pastor Greg asked, "How do you know about the waterfall?"

"I know many things, Pastor Greg. I know that you have a small town within this large cave. I also know that Elijah has more chocolate and coffee hidden in his cottage."

Lisa almost yelled out, "She's like a prophet or something! How much coffee does he have!"

Tim said, "I'm more interested in the chocolate."

Liz asked, "Is he hiding any kool-aid?"

Elijah interrupted with a clearing of his throat and a smile, saying, "This woman seems delirious; she's likely dehydrated. Doctor Sarah, you should check on her before it's too late!"

With a laugh, Doctor Sarah said, "I think she's fine, and you need to be checked out!"

"Dear, I've been saying that since we got married Doctor Sarah."

Maria butted in, "Actually since he has coffee and chocolate, you, Ruth, are an accomplice to his crime."

Everyone started laughing, knowing that Elijah had more coffee and chocolate stashed away. The pole shift began, and the world was shaking and quaking! It felt like being on a roller-coaster, ascending the first hill, knowing that something big was about to happen. The Haven echoed with creaking sounds. Greg shouted, "Make sure the ropes are securely tied! David, show everyone the proper knot to ensure they're secure!"

Alex yelled, "HERE WE GO!"

Earth began to undergo a rapid and unprecedented transformation, flipping end over end. Everyone in the Haven started yelling as they witnessed the house section twisting and swaying. They looked at the holographic monitors, which displayed various camera angles world-wide. The first thing they saw was the collapse of the building where World Watch was located, with Jimmy, Kelly, and over half of the crew inside. As they continued to watch, numerous buildings across the globe collapsed, creating a horrifying spectacle. The seas were in turmoil, with tsunamis beginning to form. One tsunami struck the east coast of the United States, towering at a hundred feet in height. Mountains crumbled, and even the Grand Canyon swayed back and forth. Roads that remained intact were being destroyed worldwide. Alex, acting wisely, landed the two bigger drones in separate fields to keep them safe for future use. Out of the nine monitors, two stopped functioning. Alex shouted, "Many satellites are being destroyed! I'm rerouting to others! The world is spinning out of control!"

Hannah yelled, "I'M SCARED!"

Tim hugged her, "WE'RE GOING TO BE OKAY! GOD WILL KEEP US SAFE!"

Lisa hugged Jamie, "I'M SCARED TOO!"

Pastor Greg yelled over the noises of the Earth ripping apart, "I DON'T THINK THE

EARTH CAN HANDLE MUCH MORE OF THIS!"

Alex screamed out, "WE JUST PASSED WHERE THE EQUATOR WAS!"

Ruth laughed, "THIS RIDE IS WAY WORSE THAN A ROLLER-COASTER RIDE

AT LONG ISLAND!"

Elijah yelled, "I CAN'T BELIEVE THAT JOSEPH IS SLEEPING THROUGH THIS!"

Lisa yelled back, "HE'S ALWAYS BEEN A SOUND SLEEPER! ALEX ARE WE

ALMOST DONE BECAUSE I HAVE TO PEE!"

Alex yelled back, "LOOK AT THE VOLCANOS GOING OFF IN THE MONITORS!

MILLIONS OF PEOPLE ARE BEING KILLED! YOU NEED TO HOLD IT!"

Abigail smiled and confidently said, "GOD WILL HAVE THE LAST WORD! WE'RE ALMOST THERE! YOU CAN HOLD IT LISA!"

The leaders rocked back and forth like they were in an airplane crash, "HOW DO YOU KNOW ABIGAIL?"

"THE LORD SPEAKS TO ME SOMETIMES, HE SAID THAT WE'LL GOING TO

MAKE IT!"

"I WAS TALKING ABOUT ME HOLDING IT!"

Pastor Greg yelled, "I THINK WE MUST ALMOST BE DONE!"

Right then, the world returned to an average speed, albeit upside-down. Lisa quickly handed Joseph to Ruth and rushed to the bathroom, shouting, "Thank God!"

Elijah asked, "Alex, where's the United States?"

"I don't know yet? We could be where Russia was, or we could be where Argentina was? I just don't know yet."

Maria said, "I hope it's Argentina because I don't speak Russian."

Pastor Greg said, "Abigail, you must forgive us and our joking. We do that when we're nervous."

Tim laughingly replied, "We do that when we're nervous! We are constantly joking around! My sister might be the worst!"

Lisa coming out of the bathroom, said, "I wasn't joking, I really had to pee. The water in the toilet spins the other way now!"

Alex replied, "That's because we're at the southern hemisphere. The water, and weather systems spin in the opposite direction."

Alex had the drones flying around, capturing the scenes of destruction. Abigail spoke urgently, "Jesus has had enough and is coming soon! He is angry! We must stay out of His way and pray for the new Christians, the Jewish people who have accepted Jesus and are hidden in the mountains! The lawless one wants them all dead!"

Elijah smiled at Abigail, "We've made it this far, surly Jesus will keep us safe! Ruth, I imagine that the garden is a mess, anyone want to help?"

Pastor Greg took charge, as was expected of him. "Jamie and David, you guys help the Davis's out. Lisa, let's go see how the other cave dwellers fared, and we'll get a clean-up crew started. Do we have a bunk available for Abigail?"

"Yes, she can take the tall guy's bunk. Abigail, do you snore?"

"Excuse me?"

"I have the snorers and the non snorers split up."

"Oh, I'm a non snorer."

Greg thought aloud, as he often did, "We have seventy-five men and seventy-five women, all married or on the way to getting married. I'm sure God has a plan for you, Abigail. You're number seventy-six. I'll ask David and Jamie to create a small space for you, so you can have some privacy. I believe Jesus will send you a husband. Liz, could you show Abigail around? I'm sure she would appreciate a shower. Also, please provide her with some military clothing to match everyone else. Abigail, do you like the color camouflage?"

Liz said, "Pastor Greg, camouflage isn't a color!"

"Maria, did you hear what Liz said?"

"No, what did she say?"

"Camouflage isn't a color!"

"She's young Greg, she doesn't understand."

Liz went off in another direction and asked, "Pastor Greg, I've asked this before, so forgive me. Why does Jesus want us and other Tribulation Christians to survive until the end of the tribulation?"

"Okay, pay attention Liz. We have flesh and bones; we missed the rapture, and that's a big bummer. After Jesus and probably billions of Christians come down from the sky and defeat the antichrist and his followers, we'll be able to interact with spiritual beings who can freely travel between different realms with just a thought. Your mom and dad could instantly appear in front of you and give you a hug, see how you're doing. Essentially, during the thousand-year period, there will be people with glorified bodies and people with flesh bodies coexisting on Earth. Remember how God hid many Jewish people in the mountains from the antichrist once they realized who he truly was? Those Jewish people will also be part of this new era."

Then Pastor Greg looked up at the ceiling and then back at Liz, recognizing that she had been struggling to understand the concept of the millennial reign of Christ. "The Bible doesn't provide extensive details about these thousand years, so this is my interpretation, but time will reveal the truth. During that period, there will be people like us, and we will have children, who will in turn have their own children, and this will continue for a thousand years. I believe that we won't experience sickness like we did before the rapture. So maybe some of us could potentially live until the end of the thousand years, but since we will still be human, it's theoretically possible for us to die. Towards the end, God will release the devil for a short period, and even with Jesus, the angels, and those with resurrected bodies present, some people will still choose to follow the devil. Then, according to Revelation 20, the devil will be ultimately defeated and those who sided with him will be sent to hell. It truly reveals the rebellious nature of humanity against Jesus. We will discover more in due time. So much we don't know about the Millennial reign of Christ. I'm sure that it won't be boring.

36

TWO DAYS UNTIL JESUS
COMES BACK!

Matthew 10:22

22 And ye shall be hated of all men for my name's sake: but he that endureth to the end shall be saved.

"Maria, I know your location. I know where the boulder is that you use as a door! We're coming this morning! I have a hundred soldiers and abundant firepower! You will feel my wrath!"

"Good morning Joe! We're running low on coffee, can you get me some on the way?"

"Lol Maria, but we're almost there, and the jokes are coming to an end! I told you that I would find you and put you in a small prison for the rest of your life, and anyone else will be killed on sight!"

"Joe, tomorrow the return of Jesus Christ and His followers happens! Many of those followers you've killed, and they're not happy with you. The seven-year Great Tribulation is coming to an end. Calvo and all his followers will be killed, just like you, Joe. You have so much blood on your hands! You really should've listened to me when I told you about the rapture, Joe. I won't have a chance to say this before Jesus comes, but I TOLD YOU SO!"

"I CAN SEE THE MOUNTAIN! YOU TERRORISTS TRAITOR! YOU'RE MINE! THIS
CAT AND MOUSE GAME IS COMING TO AN END!"

"My money is on Jesus. I read the book and we win."

A convoy of military equipment and soldiers had arrived at the mountain, and Joe was in the front seat of the first military Humvee. The Maine mountains and forest landscape were burned up, along with the rest of the world! It looked like a nuclear bomb had gone off. They had a clear view of the boulder door. A rocket launcher would most likely blow the boulder to smithereens! Greg and the other leaders watched the whole thing unfold on the monitors. Abigail was with them; she seemed to understand things in the spiritual realm better than anyone else in the Haven and needed to consult with the leaders. Her unique connection with Jesus was repeatedly proven during the last seven months. However, she would only give the leaders limited information. It was evident that she was holding back, and when confronted, she would say, "God only told me to say what I said, no more, no less."

How could someone argue with that? Lisa called her the Mystery Woman when she wouldn't give her the details she wanted.

So, after breakfast at the Haven, Greg, while looking at the monitors, stated, "Well that stinks! That's a lot of weaponry!"

"It's only angry Joe, he's harmless."

Alex said, "Maybe he's harmless but the UN military is definitely not!"

Tim said, "They're all getting out of their trucks and boy are they armed to the teeth!"

Lisa looked perplexed and said, "That's a strange idiom! 'Armed to the teeth,' what exactly does that mean anyways? Is that from the olden days or something, Elijah?"

"It actually just means that they have a lot of weapons, it's not a saying from anything specific, and I'm not that old."

"Well, you're not that young, Grandpa Coffee. Where is Joseph?"

Abigail smiled and said, "They are definitely armed to the teeth, but we do not wrestle against flesh and blood, but against principalities, against powers, against the rulers of the darkness of this age, against spiritual hosts of wickedness in the heavenly places. This battle is not ours to fight."

Greg said, "That's Ephesians six twelve. I love that verse and it explains everything that's been going on not just right now, but our whole lives."

Elijah said, "God will fight this battle for us because, as Abigail said, we are ill-equipped to do anything against them. Look at them, they are getting ready to attack this fortress that Jesus has placed us in! Ruth, take Joseph to safety please."

"That's a good idea dear. Let's go play in the house little guy."

Lisa said, "Who is the guy walking with kind of like the clothes that Abigail was wearing when she got here? He's definitely walking towards the military. Even Abigail wouldn't do that! Would you?"

"If Jesus told me to I would."

"I definitely need to step up my game!"

Liz said, "I don't know if I could do it."

Lisa looked at Liz and then Abigail, "I might, if they had a breakfast sandwich with eggs, ham and cheese!"

Tim looked at his vegetables and a tiny piece of moose meat and said, "Sis, stop with the breakfast sandwich stuff."

Not paying attention, Alex said, "Let me buzz the hummingbird over to him to get a better look!"

Once in plan view, Liz yelled, "IT'S BRANDON, AND THEY HAVEN'T SEEN HIM YET!"

Tim spit a piece of food out, "BRANDON!"

Ruth and Joseph came back in, because she over heard them, and she tried to hand Joseph to Lisa, but she was jumping, "IT'S BRANDON! WHAT'S HE DOING HERE ALONE? WHAT HAPPENED TO ISAIAH?"

Then Lisa looked at Abigail, "It's you Mystery Woman! You two have the same skin tone! You have a Jewish name! He is Jewish! Do you know Brandon?"

Abigail said, "Ruth, I'll take Joseph! I don't know him. I was told by God to come here. My purpose is to be here with all of you. I don't know a Brandon."

Lisa said, "You two are perfect for each other! He's like a walking bible, knows every verse. He's one of the 144,000!"

Liz said, "That's not the skinny Brandon I remember, he's way more handsome than before!"

Hannah grabbed Tim's hand and said, "They see him, they're going to kill him, aren't they?"

Maria laughed, "He can't be killed, he's one of the 144,000! Can he be killed? We need good sound Alex!"

"MY NAME IS SARGEANT LAWD JAE! STOP WHERE YOU ARE! PUT YOUR

HANDS ON YOU HEAD AND GO DOWN TO YOUR KNEES OR YOU WILL BE SHOT!"

"I AM A SERVANT OF JESUS CHRIST WHOM YOU ARE PER-SECUTING! YOU

WILL BE HELD ACCOUNTABLE FOR THE KILLINGS OF GOD'S CHILDREN! THE

WRATH OF CHRIST WILL BE UPON YOU, HE IS SLOW TO ANGER... BUT HE IS

FURIOUS WITH YOU ALL!"

Director Smith looked at Sergeant Jae and said, "End his suffering. This is a waste of time. He's not even armed. We're here to capture Maria Silva!"

"YOU TOO DIRECTOR JOE SMITH WILL BE HELD RESPON-SIBLE AND THERE'S

A SPECIAL PLACE IN HELL FOR YOU!"

Right then, two soldiers started shooting machine guns at Brandon! However, the bullets stopped about seven feet before him and landed on the ground around Brandon. Brandon kept speaking, but the noise was too loud, and the troops couldn't hear him until the gunfire stopped. Joe was wondering how Brandon knew his name.

"AS GOD BE MY WITNESS YOU'VE ALL ACCEPTED THE MARK OF THE BEAST

AND YOUR DNA HAS BEEN MADE UNACCEPTABLE TO JESUS CHRIST FOR

JUST LIKE IN THE DAYS OF NOAH—FALLEN ANGELS HAVE CORRUPTED YOU!"

Now they had everyone with a gun shooting at him, and again the bullets wouldn't penetrate! They shot at him for minutes, but nothing happened except Brandon continued preaching about the wrath of God!

"EVERY TONGUE WILL CONFESS THAT JESUS IS LORD! THE DAY OF THE

LORD IS ALMOST AT HAND—THE MESSIAH IS COMING!"

Brandon kept speaking while all the cave dwellers eased their way into the house! They could barely fit, but this had to be watched by all of them!

Lisa yelled, "THAT'S OUR FRIEND BRANDON! HE'S ONE OF THE 144,000! I GUESS HE WAS PASSING BY, PROBABLY WILL VISIT US! JESUS FIGHTS FOR US!"

"YOU ALL WILL BE IN THE LAKE OF FIRE WHERE YOU WILL PAY FOR YOUR

SINS IN TORMENTED DAY AND NIGHT! YOUR BODIES WILL TURN BACK TO

DUST! YOUR SOULS ARE GOING TO BE IN HELL! JESUS IS COMING SOON!"

It was time for the rocket launchers! Brandon didn't even pay attention and started to walk past them. Some soldiers made the mistake of trying to tackle him, but they could not touch him. They bounced off him and flew onto the road! The rocket launcher had absolutely no effect on him. The fire from the explosion surrounded him, and for a second, he became visible, only to disappear again with the next explosion. Brandon was completely unharmed and unaffected by the attack. He was so used to being shot at that he could have quickly napped while being protected by the Lord. Brandon's mission was almost over, and God had directed him back to the Haven!

Pastor Greg went to the boulder door, and amidst the flying bullets,

Brandon was allowed in. On the other side, hand grenades landed, but Greg swiftly closed and locked the massive rock. The hand grenades rested against the boulder, and when they exploded, nothing happened. There was no damage whatsoever, not even a scratch. The military personnel looked at the event in confusion, scratching their heads. Joe, who had witnessed similar events on World Watch before its destruction due to the geomagnetic pole reversal, had never seen anything like this in person.

Back at the Haven, Brandon embraced Greg, who looked at him and noticed that YHWH was written on his forehead. With a tear running down his face, Greg exclaimed, "You look so different! You're a man now! I have so many questions!"

Brandon was emotional, and to break the tension, he jokingly said, "Wow, look at all the people! I didn't know you had company! I can come by later if you'd like?"

Lisa, Liz, Sarah, Maria, Alex, Elijah, and Ruth made their way through the crowd and enveloped him in hugs. There was a lot of crying during those embraces as their friend had been gone for years. They had witnessed him preaching in all four corners of the Earth. His presence in the Haven was deeply cherished, and they were grateful that God had chosen him to fulfill His will. The leaders had no concerns about the military attack because they had faith that Jesus would protect them, and with Brandon's presence, they felt even more reassured.

Uncle Bob yelled, "Guys—they're pointing every gun and rocket launcher at us and are going to shoot!"

Brandon said, "Those demons have no chance! Jesus sent a thousand battle angels with me like my friend here! They've surrounded this mountain!"

A colossal battle angel adorned in the attire of an ancient Roman soldier materialized behind Brandon. Resembling the angels who anointed the leaders with oil, he wielded a majestic golden staff in his right hand.

Lisa looked at the golden staff while everyone stepped back, "I don't think that I've ever seen a golden staff before; that must be heavy?"

Brandon laughed, "No one here could pick it up, I guarantee that! A staff is the symbol of power, and the gold is a symbol of knowledge, wisdom and faith!"

Greg announced to the cave dwellers, his voice resonating through the Haven, "The angel has been sent to us by Jesus Christ, and he is accompanied by a thousand more warriors fighting on our behalf! As we have an abundance of cave dwellers in the main area of the Haven, let us establish a system where one person at a time can come here to receive the latest news and then rotate with others. This way, everyone will stay informed. Lunch and dinner will continue at their regular times. Tomorrow, when Jesus Christ returns, we will gather here in the main area, or perhaps even outside. May you find rest in the unparalleled peace that only Jesus Christ can provide!"

Brandon loudly said, "There's nothing to worry about, God's got this!"

They all made their way to the third Cavern, assured that they were safe no matter what unfolded. God's watchful eye was upon them, guarding and protecting them. They understood that one day this tumultuous journey would become a memory, a tale to be shared and retold.

Lisa grabbed Brandon's hand and yanked him to Abigail, "I'd like to introduce Abigail Kogan! Abigail, this is Brandon Stewart!"

Brandon looked at her and said, "Shalom, it's a pleasure to meet you."

"It's a pleasure to meet you too Brandon."

Brandon looked at Liz and said, "I'm starving; got any breakfast for me?" He sat down, checked out the monitors, and was handed food by his long-time friends.

Lisa pulled Greg over near the door and whispered, "That didn't work out like I thought it would."

"What didn't work like you thought it would?"

Pastor Greg—Abigail and Brandon! He hardly looked at her!"

Greg smiled at her and said, "What did you think would happen?"

"I don't know. A hug maybe? A where have you been all my life? God told me that you'd be here! A love at first sight kind of thing!"

"Lisa, he's still doing his mission until Jesus comes back tomorrow."

"So, in another words, he's still on the clock, hasn't punched out yet?"

"Yeah, something like that. Go over there before he notices that you're over here talking about him."

"Roger on that Pastor Greg."

Greg smiled while he looked at all the people he loved so much and asked, "Alex, what's going on out there?"

"Pastor Greg they're talking about backing off and using ballistic missiles if they can't get through the boulder."

Brandon, his mouth full of food, burst into laughter and exclaimed, "Like that's going to work!" Elijah, keeping a close eye on the situation, reported, "It appears that twenty soldiers are approaching the Haven boulder armed with explosives, a jackhammer, and a few sledgehammers."

Maria laughed when she spotted Joe with them, "That little man is fill of hatred right to the end—unbelievable!"

Ruth asked Maria, "Who is that dear?"

"That's Director Joe Smith coming to my front door!"

Brandon, with his mouth filled with food, spoke, "They're wasting their time! They can't see the angels, but the angels see them. We don't worship the angels; we worship

Jesus, something that people got wrong for thousands of years, but they're important."

Abigail smiled and said, "They're so filled with hate, they have no idea who they're up against."

Lisa looked at Abigail and said so Brandon would hear more of her wisdom, "When will they know Abigail?"

Pastor Greg saw right through what Lisa was doing and said with a bible in his hand, "They'll find out tomorrow when Jesus is in the clouds—remember these verses?

Revelation 19:11-21

11 Now I saw heaven opened, and behold a white horse. And He who sat on him was called Faithful and True, and in righteousness He judges and makes war. 12 His eyes were like a flame of fire, and on His head were many crowns. He [a]had a name written that no one knew except Himself. 13 He was clothed with a robe dipped in blood, and His name is called The Word of God. 14 And the armies in heaven, clothed in [b]fine linen, white and clean, followed Him on white horses. 15 Now out of His mouth goes a [c]sharp sword, that with it He should strike the nations. And He Himself will rule them with a rod of iron. He Himself treads the winepress of the fierceness and wrath of Almighty God. 16 And He has on His robe and on His thigh a name written: KING OF KINGS AND LORD OF LORDS.

Throughout the day and night, the military relentlessly fired at the mountain housing the Haven, attempting to collapse the massive caverns. Consumed by demonic rage and fueled by pride and vengeance, Joe Smith stayed awake all night, devising plans to infiltrate the Haven. The military even resorted to launching ballistic missiles at the mountain, but their efforts proved futile, further enraging Jesus. Eventually, they withdrew their forces, perplexed and uncertain of their next move. The following morning arrived, and within the Haven, everyone had enjoyed a peaceful night's sleep. The leaders gathered on the couches, observing the baffled enemy while enjoying their breakfast. All the cave dwellers united in anticipation, joined them in the house, watching and waiting.

Lisa said, "Hey, they're drinking coffee!"

The angel pounded the Haven floor with his golden staff and opened the big wooden door.

Brandon and Abigail both said simultaneously, "Jesus is coming now!"

The cave dwellers had a calm way about them; they fearlessly followed the angel. They stood, gazing at the sky. The military was meaningless to them! The soldiers also looked up at the sky, along with Director Joe Smith.

The heavens opened up, and trumpets went off! Jesus Christ, seated upon an enormous white horse, came into view for the entire world to see. Pastor Greg screamed, "JESUS OUR LORD AND SAVIOR HAS COME! HE'S FAITHFUL AND TRUE AND IN RIGHTEOUSNESS HE MAKES WAR AGAINST HIS ENEMIES!"

Everyone yelled while crying, some falling to their knees, "HALLE-LUJAH!"

His eyes were like flames, and on his head were many crowns. His clothes were a robe dripped in blood, and His name was called the Word of God! The armies in heaven, clothed in fine linen that was white and clean, followed him on white horses. There were billions of believers behind Jesus, many of whom were killed because of their faith. They, too, were furious at the dragon, the witness, and their followers. Out of his mouth came a sharp sword, which was the word of God. Jesus gave a great shout that echoed worldwide, saying, "ENOUGH!"

Director Joe Smith couldn't believe his eyes, and at that moment, he realized that what Maria had said was true. With one scream from Jesus's mouth, everyone who had the mark of the beast died instantly, including Joe. The instant Jesus said, "Enough," everything stopped.

The cave dwellers looked behind them as they heard a massive flock of crows flying toward the dead soldiers. They quickly devoured the bodies of the fallen. The Antichrist and the witness were condemned to hell even before the devil! The cave dwellers surveyed the land, now in ruins. In less than a second, the world was transformed—a new landscape emerged, with lush grass, vibrant trees, majestic forests, and towering mountains more beautiful than ever. The animals, birds, and creatures thrived abundantly. Jesus had renewed the planet, restoring it to its former glory. He reverted the Earth to its original state, returning the northern Maine mountains to their rightful place. The sky adorned a beautiful blue hue, birds joyfully chirped, and frogs in the beaver pond sang melodic tunes. The military and their trucks, weapons of war, vanished, along with the remains of the fallen soldiers. Ugly cities, trash, and pollution were no more—the world had become perfect!

Maria, crying, hugged Greg and said, "We made it, praise Jesus, we made it!"

"I know, we made it! I love you, Maria Silva!"

"I love you!"

A different angelic messenger instructed everyone, except the leaders, to walk east for five miles, as Jesus had a surprise in store for them.

Abigail began to join the others, but the angel said, "You must stay." Lisa cast a triumphant glance at Pastor Greg, silently conveying an "I told you so" message. The cave dwellers followed the trail that led them to a pristine, brand-new road made of an unprecedented pavement built to endure for a thousand years. Once they arrived, the angels guided them and provided information about their destination.

37

JESUS IS LORD!

Colossians 2:9-10

"For in him the whole fullness of deity dwells bodily. and in Christ you have been brought to fullness. He is the head over every power and authority."

Greg, Maria, Tim, Hannah, Lisa, Alex, Liz, Jamie, Sarah, David, Elijah, Ruth, Brandon, and Abigail stood before the Haven. The angel vanished into thin air! They gazed down the path they had walked countless times, and suddenly, Jesus materialized and approached them, wearing a tender smile. The cave dwellers all dropped to their knees in reverence. Jesus was indescribably beautiful; words could not capture the magnificence that radiated from Him. It's no wonder the disciples initially failed to recognize Him!

He spoke with a beautiful, captivating voice, "Please, everyone get up, I want to speak to you all."

They all stood up, wiping the tears off their faces, eagerly waiting to hear what He was about to say. "Congratulations, all of you have made it!" Jesus declared. "You, along with the other survivors around the world, are the foundation of My people who can bear children. Indeed, I have magnificent plans for the cave dwellers!"

Jesus embraced Greg as He had done with all the leaders and spoke affectionately, "Oh Greg, your unwavering faith fills me with pride!

You have truly stepped up and become the leader I intended you to be. I love you dearly and have significant plans in store for you. There's a surprise awaiting you. I need you to write a book about the events that unfolded here. Future generations will yearn to know about them."

He embraced Maria and expressed, "Your faith, Maria, was unstoppable! I knew Greg needed a strong woman by his side, and I specifically chose you. I have delighted in observing you, a true warrior for Me. You have grown remarkably! I love you dearly!"

He approached Tim and acknowledged, "Tim, your faith from the very beginning has been remarkable! I observed you and Lisa being among the first to reach the Haven. Your diligent efforts in providing food have been commendable. You are a good-hearted man, filled with love, faith, and justice. I love you dearly!"

"Hannah, my faithful little prayer warrior! So humble, loving, quiet and a hard working! I heard all your prayers at night when people were sleeping! You have the gift of intercession, and it's priceless! I love you so much!"

He stepped up to Lisa, and she hugged Jesus before He had a chance to hug her, "Lisa, you have grown so much in your faith! Your glorious sense of humor and your encouragement was so enjoyable to watch! I laughed at your jokes so many times! I need you to oversee the Haven, make it into a museum. I love you so much!"

"Alex, the eyes and ears of the Haven! Faithful and always watching to keep the people you love safe! Your intelligence, wisdom, and faith! I love you so much!"

Liz cried, "My faith was weak, I'm so sorry, Jesus."

"Liz, you never stopped believing in Me, knowing I was coming. Your faith has been extraordinary! You tirelessly fed everyone and worked diligently every day. Your presence inspires others, and your smile has the power to brighten up the darkest room. I love you deeply!"

"Jamie, faithful and true, there were moments when you felt alone, but you were never alone—I was always with you! You worked diligently with David, and the cottages you built are a testament to your dedication. I cherish you dearly!"

"Sarah, the caretaker! A faithful woman! Your bedside manor was so much more than that, it was authentic, because of your loving nature! You too have worked so hard! I love you so much!"

"David, the fisherman. I love fish! You too showed great faith! Your building the Haven was so refreshing to watch! You have the ability to do anything you set you mind to! I love you so much!"

"Elijah, you are a man of great faith! Your knowledge of My word and wisdom is impressive. The way you have encouraged everyone during these difficult years is truly remarkable. You are like a skilled gardener, nurturing growth and positivity. I love you so much!"

"Faithful Ruth, you're so sweet and inviting to everyone! Your love that pours out of you! Your gardens are incredible! Feeding everyone, both you and Elijah are such a great team! I love you so much!"

"Brandon, my son, you have impressed me greatly! You have preached my message throughout the world and have remained pure in your endeavors. Your mission of the 144,000 has come to an end. I want to personally introduce Abigail to you. Look into her eyes, Brandon. What do you see?"

"I see love in her eyes."

She is your blessing, and he is yours, Abigail. You shall marry her, for she is of your tribe! I love you so much!"

"Abigail, what do you see in Brandon's eyes?"

"I see a wonderful love."

"You've walked the falling Earth and your faith never wavered! I watched over you and prepared you for Brandon and he for you! I love you so much!"

Jesus said, "Everyone, please, show me the Haven! I need to let you know that I've been doing a little work in there. I think you'll all like it."

"Joseph ran in first, and the rest followed. The Haven, a familiar house, awaited them. Figures of the leaders were seen laughing on the couches. In a split second, they found themselves clinging on for dear life as the geomagnetic pole reversal occurred. Meanwhile, Brandon was eating breakfast and watching the military's unsuccessful attempts to attack the Haven. The holographic monitors displayed the events to the entire world."

"Ambassador Lisa, I took the liberty of making sure everyone in the future sees what I saw. Greg what do you think?"

"I love it and I never want to forget it."

"You should see what I did with the garden room, Elijah. There's your wife beside you, both of you keeping that beautiful garden thriving! The plants won't grow anymore or die; I halted the garden just like that. Pretty cool, right, Ruth?"

"Cool doesn't even express how wonderful this is Jesus!"

Lisa said, "Awesome might be a good word!"

"I like awesome! Love the garage, Greg! Oh, look at you and Maria getting married. Elijah, you did a great Job!"

"I was so nervous, only Ruth knew how nervous I was!"

Greg said, "You think you were nervous? I was completely stressed out! The idea of getting married in a cave during the tribulation with twelve of the 144,000 watching!"

Maria said, "We were all stressed!"

Jesus said, "I was preparing you for things that would come in the future."

Lisa started to talk really loudly saying, "You were there weren't you!" and Tim said, "Lisa, please let Jesus talk."

"I bet you never thought those words would come out of you mouth, Tim!"

Jesus smiled and said, "It's okay, she's naturally inquisitive. I love that about her, and all of you. She asked what you were all thinking. I enjoyed watching the wedding; I stood in the back observing! Let me show you what I did in the third cavern."

Tim said, "How'd you get a Jeep and Prius in a cave with a boulder for a door?"

Elijah lightly slapped him on his head and said, "He's Jesus, and He has no limitations! I see that you have us in my place for the coffee morning, that was funny! The images of us are perfect!"

"Tim, I created universe, surely I can get a couple of vehicles in a cave."

"Check out in the back with Greg and Lisa talking to the other cave dwellers. He made you into an ambassador Lisa. Ambassador of the Haven—perfect!"

Greg said, "I don't know why I was having such a hard time relating with them?"

"It was because of your military training, but you grew Greg and overcame."

"At the moose party I had a breakthrough of sort, thanks to Lisa."

Lisa jokingly said, "That's Ambassador Lisa Pastor Greg!"

Jesus looked at Lisa, smiled, then turned to the leaders of the Haven and finally glanced around the cavern. He said, "I wanted to demonstrate my grace in the midst of a storm because these next thousand years will begin on a positive note and then... you'll see. You all are the beginning, and each of you possesses a wondrous faith in Me. Have you ever considered how your great-great-great-great-grandchildren will be? And have you ever wondered why I will release the devil for a brief period at the end of the thousand years?"

No one had an answer, and Jesus said, "I have more surprises! You're all going to love this, especially since you've been in a cave all these years!"

In the blink of an eye, they found themselves on a grassy hill overlooking a small town. Jesus said, "Welcome to Haven Town! As a skilled carpenter, I was able to construct it swiftly for all of you. There are seventy-six customized houses, each designed for a couple and equipped with multiple bedrooms. I want all of you to have many children during the next thousand years, and they will continue to have children until the end of the thousand-year reign. Since you missed the rapture, you didn't receive resurrected bodies, but you all shall live a long long time."

"Greg, you have two questions, why you, and obviously the people in church of God didn't build the Haven?"

Jesus paused and then said, "I wanted to give everyone a second chance, but after the rapture, very few embraced it. I called it the Great

Falling Away. It's one thing to know it's coming, even to have seen it before the beginning of time, but it still hurt. I had my angels construct the Haven for all of you before the rapture. I will also be speaking to all the other cave dwellers. I'm great at multitasking."

Maria said, "I can understand that. The people in the world were falling away so fast!"

"Greg and Maria, do you see the camouflage barn and the massive log cabin next to it? That's your place. I know each of you better than you know yourselves, and I assure you that all of your houses will exceed your wildest dreams."

Jesus put His hand on Lisa's shoulder and said, "Everyone gets an SUV that holds ten people—hint hint."

"I'm going to be a baby factory, aren't I?"

"How would eight children be? But if you desire to have more, I have designed a vehicle that can accommodate all of them. Additionally, I have created pick-up trucks for each of you. All the automobiles are powered by a chip about the size of a dime, ensuring their longevity. I built things to last, and that includes the cars."

Maria looked at Greg and said, "Jesus built us two trucks and a house."

Elijah said, "I bet you never thought you'd say that!"

"Good point!"

Tim said, "Did you build me a new dirt bike?"

"You'll see Tim, remember Psalm 37: 'Delight yourself also in the LORD and He shall give you the desires of your heart. Well all of you did that! So all of you get the desires of your heart.'"

Jesus looked incredibly happy and said, "I have constructed a massive church for you to preach in! Pastor Greg, you are the leader of this town. Brandon, you and Abigail will be married in two days. It will be a simple wedding, Greg, but the reception will be the highlight! It will take place in the church, followed by a cookout in the front yard. Does that sound familiar, Lisa and Tim?"

"Is my dad and mom going to be there?"

"You'll see later Lisa. I must go! I'll have my team set up everything! I have a party in New Jerusalem to go to!"

38

〰

GLORIFIED BODIES!

John 21:1-14

After these things, Jesus showed Himself again to the disciples at the Sea of Tiberias, and in this way, He showed Himself: 2 Simon Peter, Thomas called the Twin, Nathanael of Cana in

Galilee, the sons of Zebedee, and two others of His disciples were together. 3 Simon Peter said to them, "I am going fishing."

They said to him, "We are going with you also." They went out and immediately got into the boat, and that night they caught nothing. 4 But when the morning had now come, Jesus stood on the shore; yet the disciples did not know that it was Jesus. 5 Then Jesus said to them, "Children, have you any food?"

They answered Him, "No."

6 And He said to them, "Cast the net on the right side of the boat, and you will find some." So they cast, and now they were not able to draw it in because of the multitude of fish.

7 Therefore, that disciple whom Jesus loved said to Peter, "It is the Lord!" Now when Simon Peter heard that it was the Lord, he put on his outer garment (for he had removed it) and plunged into the sea. 8 But the other disciples came in the little boat (for they were not far from land, but about two hundred cubits), dragging the net with fish. 9 Then, as soon as they had come to land, they saw a fire of coals there, and fish laid on it, and bread. 10 Jesus said to them, "Bring some of the fish which you have just caught."

11 Simon Peter went up and dragged the net to land, full of large fish, one hundred and fifty-three, and although there were so many, the net was not broken. 12 Jesus said to them, "Come and eat breakfast." Yet none of the disciples dared ask Him, "Who are You?"— knowing that it was the Lord. 13 Jesus then came and took the bread and gave it to them, and likewise the fish.

14 This is now the third time Jesus showed Himself to His disciples after He was raised from the dead.

There were 153 people in a church that could easily accommodate 12,000. The wedding was scheduled to begin promptly at noon. It was 11:50, and no one had shown up yet except the cave dwellers, and worst of all, Jesus wasn't there. Brandon stood next to Greg, dressed up and looking good in his suit and tie. Greg asked, "Are you nervous?"

"I've never been more stressed out in my life!"

"I've married quite a few people in the last few years, but never with Jesus in person there."

"So, you're nervous to pastor?"

"Never more nervous in my life!"

"You're not helping."

"I wanted to be honest."

"Thanks, I think."

A humongous, loud organ blared with an angel playing it in a way that had never been heard on Earth before! One by one, people with their resurrected bodies appeared out of thin air and took their seats. "Brandon, have you ever seen anything like that before on your mission?"

"Definitely not pastor!"

Behind them, two hundred angel choir members appeared and started singing in a different language. It was noon when the door opened, and Abigail entered, looking stunning. Jesus accompanied her, walking behind her to give her away to Brandon. It was incredibly emotional, and Greg and Brandon tried to compose themselves. Everyone in the enormous church stood up and turned to Abigail and Jesus as they walked down the aisle. Jesus handed her to Brandon, kissed him on both cheeks and congratulated him. Jesus then looked at Greg and whispered, "You've got this."

The music stopped, and sobs could be heard in the distance. Greg cleared his throat and started.

"Dearly Beloved, we are gathered here together to join this man and this woman in Holy Matrimony, to be united as one body, just as Jesus and the church are united. We have a representation of that unity here in this house of God. We all understand the significance of the body of believers and what it means to follow Jesus, so I won't delve into that further. Jesus has instructed me to keep this ceremony brief and heartfelt."

Jesus looked at Greg and gave him a nod and a smile.

Pastor Greg spoke with such authority,

"Do you, Brandon Moses Hoffman, take Abigail Schwartz Kogin to be your wife, to have and to hold from this day forward, for better or for worse, for richer or for poorer, in sickness and in health, to love and to cherish, from this day forward until death do you part?"

Brandon looked into Abigail's stunning eyes and said, "I do."

"Do you, Abigail, take Brandon to be your husband, to have and to hold from this day forward, for better or for worse, for richer or for poorer, in sickness and in health, to love and to cherish, from this day forward until death do you part?"

Abigail looked at Brandon's eyes and said, "I do."

"The exchange of rings please. Please Brandon, place the ring on Abigail's finger."

Brandon slid the ring onto Abigail's finger as tears rolled down his face.

"Wonderful, and you Abigail, place the ring on Brandon's finger... thank you."

Pastor Greg looked at Brandon and Abigail. He glanced at the packed church filled with Jesus and his followers in their resurrected bodies. He also noticed the multitude of angels preparing to sing and play various musical instruments beyond imagination. The cave dwellers watched in complete awe!

Pastor Greg said, "I've had the privilege of officiating many weddings in the Haven, and I've caught glimpses of the heavenly realm on a few occasions, but this is simply amazing! The heavenly realm is present in this house of God. Perhaps it has always been here, and I couldn't see it. Nevertheless, it is my honor to declare, by the power vested in me by Jesus Christ, that Brandon Mosses Stewart and Abigail Schwartz Kogin are now husband and wife. Brandon, you may now kiss the bride!"

They kissed, and everyone stood up and cheered! The church pews slowly sank into the floor, making way for a massive throne that appeared behind where the pulpit once stood. The celebration, accompanied by vibrant music, continued as everyone started dancing on the now-open floor. Thousands of people danced joyfully, reminiscent of King David's exuberant dance when the Tabernacle arrived in Jerusalem with the presence of the Lord, as described in 2nd Samuel 6:14. However, unlike David, they were all fully dressed, not wearing only a linen ephod. Many had held back their praise and worship before the rapture, concerned about what others might think, but that was now a thing of the past. They no longer cared about anyone's opinions; even the cave dwellers were filled with the Holy Spirit!

Lisa began a train with Maria's hands on her shoulders, followed by Greg, Liz, Alex, Elijah, Brandon, Ruth, and Abigail behind them! They all chanted "Jesus" and kicked their legs to the side. Jesus sat on his throne, smiling as Joseph ran up and jumped on his lap. Jesus was overjoyed to be with his bride! The happiness in the church was unbounded by human limitations and driven by God, with worship that was pure and pleasing to the Lord. The heavenly realm manifested itself in the house of God in Northern Maine, a new town built by Jesus and his angels called Haven Town. The celebration was not just for Brandon and Abigail but also Jesus himself. The cave dwellers may not have known whom they were dancing with, but they knew whom they were dancing for. The people with resurrected bodies were unrecognizable to the inhabitants of the Haven.

It was two o'clock when the front doors swung open, and people poured out of the church, laughing and filled with joy. Multiple barbecue grills were set up on the church's front lawn. Lisa scanned the crowd, and her eyes landed on her dad, wearing an apron and tending to one of the grills. Overwhelmed with emotion, she sprinted towards him and embraced him tightly, tears streaming down her face like a baby.

"You made it through the tribulation! I'm so very proud of you!"

"I missed you so much daddy!"

"I missed you too sweetheart!"

Their mom greeted Tim and said, "Tim, it's me!"

"Mom!"

"Yes!"

The two hugged each other while Jesus watched! Pastor Frank approached Greg and said,

"Great job on taking care of the teens!"

"Pastor Frank?"

"I'd say in the flesh, but I got this new body and all! I heard all about how you guys made it! The tribulation saints, pretty heroic!"

"I don't know why Jesus picked me. I do feel extremely blessed! I have that old Bible of yours if you'd like it...."

"You keep that, Pastor Greg!"

Elijah and Ruth came out and heard, "Dad—Mom, it's me Noah!"

Elijah said, "You're a full-grown man!"

Ruth, speechless, hugged the child she had lost long ago. Elijah embraced them both, and it felt like a beautiful family reunion. All the cave dwellers were meeting Christians from their past, some from generations ago. It was a remarkable cookout filled with cheeseburgers, hot dogs, steaks and salads. It was an unforgettable experience for the tribulation saints, etched into their memories forever.

The End

Printed in the USA
CPSIA information can be obtained
at www.ICGtesting.com
LVHW041233091123
763265LV00076B/2776